Fire in the Head

by Les Wilson

Vagabond Voices
Sulaisiadar 'san Rudha

First published in September 2010 by
Vagabond Voices Publishing Ltd.
3 Sulaisiadar
An Rubha
Eilean Leòdhais / Isle of Lewis
Alba / Scotland HS2 0PU

ISBN 978-0-9560560-7-8

Printed and bound by Thomson Litho, East Kilbride

The publisher acknowledges subsidy towards this publication from Creative Scotland

For further information on Vagabond Voices, see the website, www.vagabondvoices.co.uk

For Jenni

I went out to the hazel wood,
Because a fire was in my head
...
W.B. Yeats

Café Sarti (1)

His end must have been agonising and terrible. I struggled to take in the story from the newspaper spread out in front of me on the café table. He was an old man of over eighty, and I had always assumed that Campbell Aaronson's eventual demise would be caused by one of those doleful trials of old age, death by creeping inevitability. I had not expected his sudden death by fire, and certainly not death by self-immolation, suicide or sacrifice.

The report was tucked away at the foot of an inside page, just a tight paragraph or two that told the tale of an old man somewhere in the West Highlands who'd got himself killed in a freakish manner. It made it sound like a stupid accident. It said he'd been famous once.

I had been lucky to spot the article. I'd been away a lot and somewhat preoccupied with just-keeping-going. I don't always read *The Herald*, and it's been two years since I worked there. That's more than six hundred issues that have been produced without me, without my by-line, without my informed and insightful comments on the cultural life of our nation – a nation that doesn't seem to have missed me much.

Tracking down Aaronson changed my life. Did I like him? I'm not sure I could ever like a man who had done that terrible work in the desert. But he was an impressive man and – ultimately – an honest man. Now he was horribly dead.

After the first shock had passed, I phoned Harry, an old colleague and still my friend. He'd seen the story and promised me that *The Herald* would publish an obituary. On page sixteen the following morning, there it was. At the top of the double-column article was a photograph, taken at a Campaign for Nuclear Disarmament demonstration in the early sixties. Aaronson stood, tall and imposing, in the centre of frame. He was strikingly handsome back then, but clearly recognisable as the person who would grow into the old man whose secret, or at least forgotten past, I would expose in print. I read the text and was immediately struck by the familiarity of phrases, and even whole sentences. It was a sloppy piece of work, obviously not one of those obits that are kept on file for years and regularly brought up to date until their ageing subjects are called to their maker, or oblivion. It wasn't like the obituary of the Queen Mother that, dutifully once a year, some hapless graduate-trainee was told to update with the latest news of a Cheltenham Gold Cup winner or swallowed fish bone. No, Aaronson's obituary was a hasty cut-and-paste job, something cobbled together from the cuttings library. It was a careless last-minute production, a list of dates and facts, lacking in depth or insight. And, of course, it did not contain the confession I wrung from Aaronson in the hazel wood of Calltain.

It mentioned Aaronson's once notorious environmental protest composition, *Cantus for Complete Cunts*, but not his beautiful *Gaia Symphony*, or *Black Dog Bacchanal*, his visceral sonic account of his struggles with the hellish twins, the Castor and Pollux of depression and drink. There was no mention of his moral force, nor of the artists and activists he inspired and nurtured. But at the core of the dull prose I sensed the shade of a yellow and crumbling feature I'd written more than two years before – a profile of an eccentric avant-garde composer who lived in a so-called hippy community, but turned out to have been one of the architects of the A-Bomb that devastated Hiroshima. It had been, in its day, "a good story" and a rare "exclusive" for an Arts and Culture correspondent, and of course it was the assignment that threw my life into a convulsion from which it will never recover.

I tend to think of all my old articles as yellow and crumbling newsprint, but they're probably now on some computerised data base – my mistakes and limitations scanned and digitally preserved for as long as anyone is around to read them. The obituary that had been cribbed from my old article may have been a glib and shoddy piece of journalism, but at least I took some satisfaction from (Dougald) Campbell Aaronson getting more column inches than (John) Joshua Argo.

The Herald, 21st March 2003
(Dougald) Campbell Aaronson – composer and atomic physicist (1920 - 2003)

Campbell Aaronson, one of the founders of the art of electronic music, has died at the age of 83 on the Calltain peninsula in the West Highlands. Although the wider public has largely neglected his work, many modern musicians, including "ambient" pioneer Brian Eno, have cited Aaronson as a formative influence.

Although associated with CND and the environmental movement for much of his life, as a young man Aaronson had been a brilliant nuclear physicist, and played a significant role in developing the atomic bombs that destroyed Hiroshima and Nagasaki.

Aaronson was born in London in 1920, the son of H. K. Aaronson, a German Jewish immigrant, and Margaret Campbell, the strong-willed daughter of the chemical magnate Sir Hector Campbell, who had made his fortune during World War I. Sir Hector strongly disapproved of his daughter's relationship with the penniless – and politically radical – Aaronson, and did not attend their wedding. He did however provide Margaret with an allowance that allowed her to cultivate a bohemian salon that revolved around the young couple's Chelsea home, and gave her and her husband the freedom to pursue radical and utopian causes. Margaret and her friend Naomi Mitchison were among the founders of the North Kensington Birth Control Clinic, while her husband was an active anarchist and pacifist.

Campbell Aaronson, an only child, was brought up amidst a progressive and intellectual set that included H. G. Wells and Aldous Huxley, and Aaronson could recall a party in his parents' house to celebrate the publication of W. H. Auden's *Poems* in 1930. Educated mostly by his mother at home, the precocious Aaronson went to Oxford at the age of 16 having become obsessed with recent developments in experimental physics. On graduating in 1939, he accepted a research post at the University of Chicago. His decision not to return to England at the outbreak of war was proudly boasted of by his pacifist parents, who were unaware that their son's work had caught the eye of theoretical physicist J. Robert Oppenheimer. In January 1943, when Oppenheimer was assembling the team that would build the atom bombs that would bring Japan to its knees, the young Aaronson was one of the first to be called to his Los Alamos laboratory in New Mexico. Reclusive and reticent in later years, Aaronson rarely spoke of his work on the Manhattan project.

When interviewed by *The Herald* in 2000 he maintained that the science that built the atom bombs was neither good nor evil. “It is just people, not science, that have the capacity for good or evil,” he said.

As soon as World War II ended he returned to England to teach quantum mechanics at his old university, but became disillusioned with the role of science in society and spent much of his time in Paris, where he became a friend of Samuel Beckett. In 1952 he began frequenting the Musique Concrète Studio, where he met Karlheinz Stockhausen and Pierre Boulez. The following year he resigned his Oxford teaching post and moved to Cologne where Herbert Eimert had opened an electronic music studio. Both a bohemian and a scientist who had a deep understanding of sonics and electronics, Aaronson quickly established a cult following as a composer in progressive music circles. 1958 saw the release of a recording of his first widely known work, *E = H. G. Wells²*.

Although his Dumfries-born mother had instilled in him the notion that he was Scottish, Aaronson had never visited the homeland of his arms-manufacturing grandfather. Then, in 1964, artist and cultural activist Richard Demarco lured him to the Edinburgh Festival for the first live UK performance of his work. In *Bomb Bast* four musicians, picked at random from other groups or orchestras, and who had never previously met, improvised to a taped electronic recording that Aaronson had created. Aaronson and Demarco toured the Hebrides and Orkney Isles together the following spring, visiting Neolithic sites. The effect on Aaronson was so profound that he changed musical direction and began incorporating into his compositions sounds from nature and the music of primitive – often Celtic, African and Native American –instruments. In many ways this new work prefigured the rise of “world music”. *The Edinburgh Military Hullabaloo*, a percussion work composed entirely of the ringing sound of rocks on the Calltain peninsula struck by Aaronson with an iron bar, was dedicated to Demarco. His 1967 composition *Titania's Hurdies* – for Celtic harp and slapping sounds – was re-discovered in the mid nineties and remixed with a pounding beat for the dance club scene. Thanks to John Peel's patronage,

Aaronson's three-minute *Muttering*, a work comprised of the looped sounds of his own bodily functions, became a cult bed-sit soundtrack of the early seventies. *Muttering* was dedicated to Dadaist Marcel Duchamp who had signed his seminal 1917 work *Fountain* – a porcelain urinal – "R. Mutt". It was followed by *Genes and Recollections*, a work inspired by the writings of Darwin and Jung that made it into the lower reaches of album charts in Germany.

Margaret Campbell-Aaronson had been reconciled with her father shortly before his death and inherited the bulk of his fortune, much of which she poured into radical causes including the ANC and CND. On her death in 1972 she still left sufficient money for her son to realise his dream of rebuilding the semi-derelict croft house at Calltain where he had begun to spend his summers.

From then on, Aaronson became steadily more reclusive, rarely venturing to Edinburgh despite Demarco's repeated pleas. The composer's early visits to Calltain had coincided with the arrival of the first members of the "alternative" community that established itself on the former crofting peninsula. Aaronson's presence at Calltain drew more musicians and artists there, and he became affectionately known by many of the residents as "the tribal elder". Although he rarely spoke publicly, Anderson's later years were much concerned with the peace movement and environmental issues. In the 1980s he was quick to see the possibilities of digital sampling and installed a state-of-the-art electronic sound studio in his house, with which he created music for documentaries produced by Greenpeace and other pressure groups. In 1992 he contributed *Cantus for Complete C***s*, a five-minute work, consisting entirely of spliced together and rhythmically arranged insults, obscenities and curses in 15 different languages, to a CD by Scottish rock musicians released to raise funds to fight international whaling. The track was banned from virtually all radio and TV stations in the world, but nevertheless won the CD notoriety and significant sales. "I got angry," Aaronson explained tersely to a tabloid newspaper that had condemned him for obscenity. "Whales are fellow musicians." In recent months he was active in the campaign to prevent Argo Aggregates from turning the Calltain peninsula into a giant super-quarry.

Campbell Aaronson never married.

The obituary contained every single mistake in my original article, and a few more. When my story about him was published, back in 2000, Aaronson snipped it out, ringed and corrected my errors with his fountain pen, and posted the cutting back to me. Perhaps the newspaper was damp when he did this, because the ink had run and blotched. The accompanying letter thanked me for my efforts, but expressed surprise that the newspaper treated the fact that he had worked on the Manhattan Project as a revelation.

"As you know, Armour," he wrote, "I have never concealed my work with Oppie. How could I? The experience is the foundation on which I have built my subsequent life as an artist." He went on point out that his work *E = H. G. Wells*[2] was released in 1957; that it was 1963, the year of the notorious "happening" with the naked model in the wheelbarrow, that Demarco first brought him to Edinburgh; and that it was the alternative Fringe, not the city's official International Festival, that hosted the first UK performance of *Bomb Bast.* I still have, somewhere among a shelf of box files, his letter and the blotched cutting.

I carefully read the obituary a second time before signalling to the waiter for more of the strong coffee and sweet Italian brandy that punctuate my midmornings. Before me, like an accusation, lay my mistakes of more than two years ago, reincarnated in that day's newspaper.

"We know nothing about anyone," I heard myself murmur out loud. Only now do I realise that from the fortress of our selves we can never really understand another human being, no matter how close they are to us. It is, I admit, a strange opinion for someone like me to hold – someone whose job it was to write revealing profiles of people for a national newspaper.

The shallowness of the obituary annoyed me, and I was particularly angered by the curt final sentence, "He never married." Of course, as far as I know, Aaronson never did, but the blunt assertion – with its implications of homosexuality, physical incapacity, misanthropy, or the inability to give or inspire love – served only to conceal his character, not reveal it. Campbell Aaronson loved, and was loved by, women. The obituary writer missed a few tabloid tricks there! Although he was in his 40s during the "Swinging Sixties", Aaronson had preserved his lean good looks and was famously described in his Edinburgh years as "more horny than the Monarch of the Glen". Numerous women fell for him, and perhaps he was loved too by the brilliant, reckless, Grizzel Gillespie.

The waiter glanced at me with curiosity as he placed the coffee and brandy on the spread-out *Herald*. Ordering a second round was a break in the routine I have built for myself since I left the paper. I have, after all, my liver and dwindling redundancy payment to consider. He is, with other customers, as charming and loquacious as his broken English – now tinged with the cadence of Glasgow – allows. But he knows me, and my solitary routine, well enough, and we rub along with monosyllabic politeness.

"Thanks," I said. He nodded and murmured something I didn't understand. He's serving at another table now as I write, any sense of curiosity he once might have had about me, and what I write in my A4 notebook, now blunted by the familiarity of the scene. What can he know of Grizzel, the woman with the witch name and my lost muse?

THE SHAMAN – by Jonathon Armour

He pressed the fleshy part of his thumb onto the flint to test the sharpness of the point. The oil from his skin made the arrowhead shiny so that it glistened in the light of the tallow lamp. The wooden haft was true, not warped, and the feathers were as firm as they had been when he first plucked them from the wing of a great hunting bird. He slid the stone-tipped arrow into the quiver along with six iron-pointed ones. He had no plans to use these, but there was no reason to miss the chance of taking small game, and there was always the risk that he'd meet a party of whites. Even in the deepest desert there was danger from that unpredictable tribe. While some of the white men at the Mission spoke of their Jesus and of peace between their peoples, others killed, carried off horses and women and burned villages. He kept the iron arrowheads sharp.

Outside he breathed deeply, holding the morning air in his lungs and wincing at the stab of old familiar pain as he faced the eastern sky. Already the unfailing miracle had begun to colour the horizon blood red. Although the village was barely stirring, it was time to begin the journey. Soon the sun would drum down relentlessly on the desert and any who travelled there. He shouldered the tree-bark quiver and a sagging leather pouch, grasped his bow, and set off at a steady lope towards the west.

The path that wound out of the valley up onto the plain was steep, and at the rim he paused to rest, looking back down at the green and fertile land that the serpent of running water nourished. He could see the whole village now, revealed in the early morning light. Smoke rose from the first fires. Digging deeply into his pouch he took out a river pebble to suck against the dryness of the desert, tugged at the lacings of his moccasins, and began the slow, steady run that would take him to the edge of the hunting ground before the sun climbed to its cruellest height. There was a rock out there that had shielded him for fifty-two pilgrimages. The Sheltering Boulder stood high and alone in the flat desert, a day-and-a-half's journey on foot from the sacred Black Mountain. He had first travelled there long ago with his father's brother when the old Shaman had deemed him strong enough in body and grave enough in demeanour to accomplish the ritual. The great erratic rock concealed the mouth of a small cave from the eye of the sun. It was the gateway to the Otherworld where lay his prey, waiting to play its part.

By the time the Sheltering Boulder rose out of the shimmering place where desert met sky, the sun was at its full height and weighed down heavily on the red earth. His body craved rest and nourishment. Once he would have been there already, taking a mouthful of bitter water from the skin bag and resting until the fire in the sky began its descent. He was old now, living in his sixty-fourth cycle of seasons, too old to be making the journey without a disciple. There had been one. When his only son had seen ten summers the Shaman had begun to teach the child the lore of plants and animals, and the dances and chants of his tribe and caste. At twelve summers the boy had first come on the pilgrimage, and had fulfilled his role like a man. At thirteen the youth had joined in the hunt for two girls who had been taken while gathering berries. The tracks of iron-hoofed horses were discovered and a band of twelve warriors rode out to hunt down the white men who had taken the women. None of them, warriors or women, had returned.

The memory made his left side ache. Many years before, when he was no older than his son had been when the boy had joined the war party, he had fought the whites at the great bend in the river. One of their bullets was still inside him. It had smashed a rib that had never healed. He'd learned mostly to conquer the pain, but when memories returned to stalk him so too did the lead and the shattered bone inside him. He focused on the horizon, and strode on. Not even a lizard or a snake moved in the desert waste.

At last he crawled into the welcoming darkness of the Sheltering Boulder and lay there, unable even to drink from the water skin until the oppressive heat was lifted from his body and the blood stopped pounding in his chest. He knew he was not alone in the cave. Every heartbeat, every breath he took blended with those of the spirit of the place. Free from the glare of the sun, the tiny black dots of his irises began to swell into great orbs. The gateway began to reveal itself. Before him lay a landscape. He could reach out and touch flowers, insects, reptiles, deer, bison, a cougar. Gradually the Great Piping Spirit came into view. The spirit had been the first creation of the most ancient of all the Gods, the ancestor of all things. The world began because the Sky God had wished to dance and created the spirit to make the first music. As the God danced, the spirit had piped the world into existence. With each note it created mountains, rivers and deserts and all the plants, animals and peoples of the earth. He leaned forward, touching the cool rock face and tracing the carving with his fingers. When the world was new-made the first Shaman had etched this image of the spirit in gratitude for his creation, and countless generations of his kin and kind had since come to this place to seek the spirit's guidance in the dangerous journey to the Otherworld.

He took a carved stone bowl from his pouch, filled it from the water skin and laid it before the ancient image. When the water stilled he began the low chant. It echoed eerily within the rock cavity. The Shamans gathered. Others of his kind, long dead, had returned to take part in the ritual and were chanting with him. He touched the carving once more with the two fingers that would pull the bowstring and then began to trace the shape of all the living things he could remember on the surface of the water. The cougar, the deer, the bison, the fire ants, the rattlesnakes, the fish in the river, the white men, his own people and all the plants of the valley and the desert. His knowledge of his world was immense, and the shadows were long when he crawled from under the Sheltering Boulder. He shrugged himself free of the muscle-ache and cramp of the tiny cavity, and notched the flint-headed arrow to his bowstring.

In the west, a column of smoke or dust rose from the sacred Black Mountain where the Sky God had first begun to dance. The sight of it disturbed him, and he had to struggle to subdue the speculations that flitted through his mind. He had never seen such a thing before and could not explain it – none of the people of the plain would camp or cook so close to a sacred place. He sensed that it was an omen, and it unnerved him. He knew that if his heart were not pure now, if his mind was not serene, his prey would hide in the earth from him. He struggled to drive out dark thoughts from his mind.

At last he turned to face the low sun and began to chant, asking the Piping Spirit to guide him to his prey as he had guided the first Shaman on the first day. In a little while he began to move forward in the crouching, stalking gait of the hunter. His footfalls were silent, yet his chanting rose and fell. All around was silence.

His shadow lengthened and his voice became deep and cracked with thirst and fatigue. The sun was close to slipping behind the distant mountain when the spirit rewarded him with prey. He approached with stealth, the rhythm of the chant quickening. Two fingers, the notched arrow between them, drew back the bowstring. He dismissed from his mind the ache of prolonged tension in his arms. His heart was full of love for the Piping Spirit, and the notes of the music with which it had created the peyote plant were on his lips.

His heart. His voice. His eye. His fingers. He was at one with his prey. The arrow drove itself forward, its hard flint head striking deep into the heart of the cactus. The Dancing God was bountiful.

Calltain: The First Visit

It was, as Aaronson had promised, only a minute and a half's brisk walk from where Jonathon Armour stepped off the train to the crumbling concrete and timber pier that jutted out into the harbour.

"Ninety seconds, but Allegro, Armour, Allegro, for Tyler our boatman does not tarry!" The old man had been quite precise on the telephone.

Armour was at the end of the line – the single-track railway line built a century or more ago beside an ancient road that wound its eccentric way up the rugged coast to Vallaig. It was the heavy hooves of Highland black cattle being driven to medieval markets in the south that had first pounded out the route. In time, the cattle track became a narrow road. Even today it remains a slow and bone-shaking ribbon of pitted tar. When energetic early Victorians first recognised the commercial fishing potential of Loch Vallaig they followed the cattle drovers' road, and blasted and hacked a railway line alongside it to feed Billingsgate's great appetite for haddock and cod, mackerel and herring, fresh from the sea. The port of Vallaig was built, grew, flourished, and then declined when the sea could give no more and the silver shoals and profits vanished. The town grew poor and disheartened. Today, a few boats still routinely dredge for prawns and meagre profit. Barely enough to keep the railway line open.

Armour mused. The description "end of the line" was both literal and figurative for shabby Vallaig. There was no steel track or tarmac road beyond here, no reason to arrive with a one-way ticket. To the north of the harbour wall, a mile across a deep sea-loch, lay the dark whaleback mass of land that was Calltain. You could walk there, for Calltain was a peninsula not an island – but the track was rough and waterlogged, a fifteen-mile plod to the scattering of houses that made up the village. Hikers, attracted by some famous Neolithic remains, or perhaps by the New Age reputation of the place, sometimes tramped there in the spring and summer to camp or doss in the bunkhouse, but the people who lived on Calltain always travelled on Matt Tyler's boat.

About twenty-five feet long, the *Ran* had a tiny three-sided cabin where a passenger or two could huddle beside the skipper on a blustery day. Most travellers perched on the stern transom or sat on their luggage, martyrs to the elements and the boat's Spartan facilities, for when Tyler's *Ran* was not a ferry it was a working lobster boat or a platform from which Tyler dived for scallops. On the deck from which mackerel-baited creels were plunged into the sea, or the wet-suited Tyler himself would plunge, the Calltain community's supplies were piled up on the thrice-weekly journeys across the sea-loch. A pile of cardboard boxes now lay on deck under a salt-caked and faded green tarpaulin.

Tyler the boatman was on the pier, standing beside the moored *Ran*. He was easy to recognise, as there was no one else around. Tyler wasn't a small man, but somehow had a head that seemed too big for the wiry body that supported it. His hair was copper red and would have been shoulder-length if not tied back in a ponytail with a red rubber band. He had just slipped a battered Golden Virginia tin into the top pocket of the blue overalls that are the national dress of the West Highlands, and stood waiting by his boat, deftly rolling a cigarette between thumb and forefinger. He lit the roll-up with a cheap plastic lighter, inhaled deeply, and spoke, breathing smoke with his words.

"Uh-huh, you'll be the Armour guy, from *The Herald*." His accent wasn't West Highland, but growly, long-vowelled Glaswegian. His tone was matter of fact, as if he was simply making an observation to himself.

"That's me!" Armour spoke heartily, hiding the surprise of being expected.

"Headin' for Campbell's place and daein an interview." It was not a question. Armour was caught off guard by Tyler's bluntness and felt compelled to blurt out an explanation.

"That's right, I'm a journalist writing a feature article for the paper. Have you been waiting for me?"

Tyler took a drag from the roll-up, regarded it for a second with seeming distaste, nipped the burning tip off, and put the skinny dowt behind his ear.

"Nae chance," he jerked his head. "A'm waiting for him."

Armour turned to look back along the pier. Behind him came a man in a railway uniform carrying a small clutch of letters.

"Just the usual, Trooper," the man shouted, quickening his pace.

"Aye, thanks man."

"You've a passenger then?"

Armour now recognised the uniformed man as the one who had perfunctorily checked his ticket on the train.

"So it seems." Tyler seemed reluctant to talk further and thrust the letters into a pocket. "We'd best get you over Mr Armour. Campbell's expecting you. Oh aye ... welcome aboard."

The tide was evidently high, for it was but a short clamber down onto the deck. Tyler started *Ran's* engine as the railwayman cast off her bow and stern lines from the pier's black iron bollards. The boatman was brisk and efficient as he gathered and coiled the ropes, but taciturn to the point of rudeness. After a couple of conversational gambits failed to engage the man, Armour left him to his work, laid his expensive leather shoulder bag on a damp wooden bench at the stern and settled down beside it. The *Ran* cleared the harbour entrance accompanied by a chevron of gulls, and Tyler pointed her towards the dark headland that lay to the north. On maps, the sea loch they now crossed was like a stumpy crooked finger that curled itself around the Calltain coast, but from where the *Ran's* sole passenger was sitting his destination looked like an island. The grey water of the open loch was choppier than the harbour, and Armour took several astringent slaps of salt spray across his face. When it became clear that the *Ran* wasn't fishing, the gulls lost interest and turned back to their perches on the harbour wall. Armour could make out a scattering of houses now, some strung along the coast as if they had been washed up on a high tide, a few others clinging to the hillside above. Even at a distance he could see that they were brightly painted, and that many of them sat among patches of cultivated garden. He made a mental note of the scene rather than risking a sea-soaked notebook. As they chugged closer, a little jetty came into view, and behind it a short row of cottages. Clearly, this was downtown Calltain.

Calltain had once been a traditional Highland crofting area where families lived off the produce of tiny plots of which they were tenants not owners. After the Second World War economics had discouraged such small-scale farming and the crofts had dwindled away until, in the mid 1960s, the last native Gaelic-speaking family moved to what their kind had always called "the mainland". And then the hippies moved in. That's what the people of Vallaig called them. In everything Armour had read or heard about Calltain the same express-ions had kept coming up – hippies, dreamers and dropouts, idealists, refugees from the rat race, potters, poets and artists, vegans and pagans. His editor had said of Calltain that when the sheep-shaggers moved out, the tree-huggers moved in, but from the boat Armour could see very few trees to hug.

Somehow, over more than three decades, the free spirits that had settled on Calltain had coalesced into some sort of community that had survived and grown. It had built a reputation for self-sufficiency and as an arts and crafts centre. Now at least a dozen of the old crofts had been reoccupied, and as many new homes had been built. The estate that owned the Calltain peninsula was glad of the small rents and had taken a tolerant line with the settlers. The hard-pressed shopkeepers and tradesmen of Vallaig had welcomed the extra custom. Armour had heard there was even a primary school with two full-time teachers now, and sure enough there was a little gang of half a dozen children waiting on the jetty. Tyler threw them a line and they scrambled noisily for the privilege of tying up the boat. Armour swung his bag onto his shoulder and clambered warily from the bobbing *Ran* up three or four rusty rungs onto the jetty. He stood back to observe. Children and a few adults traded cheerful greetings with Tyler in exchange for boxes of groceries, cases of beer, or letters. With them, Armour noted, the boatman behaved like a normal human being. A few inhabitants cast curious looks at the stranger as they left with their goods. Tyler's sole passenger was overdressed among the local thick sweaters and worn jeans. Under a Barbour jacket that had seen more wine-bars than grouse moors he wore a fashionable black suit and a white linen shirt, without a tie but buttoned to the neck.

"Campbell Aaronson's house ... can you direct me?"

Tyler took the nipped dog-end from behind his ear and used it to point.

"Nae need to. Here's Grizzel come to fetch you." He put the stub to his lips and lit it, inhaling sharply.

When the journalist saw her coming along the jetty he thought he might have noticed her earlier as the boat came in, a slight figure standing on the shore, keeping a short distance from the others. She strode the length of the jetty now, her long, waxed, stockman's coat open, its tails slapping in her wake. The young woman's long dark ringlets were tugged and teased by the wind. She wore jeans and tan calf-length boots, and Armour thought she looked like the heroine of a Western movie. The name the boatman had used – Grizzel! Was it real? The wacky legacy of hippy parents? Perhaps it was just something they called her behind her back? A witch name! But everyone seemed to know her and she had words or smiles for each of them as they passed her on the pier.

"Hi Matt. You've brought the visitor."

"Aye, and three days' papers." He took a bundle from the little cabin and tossed it up to her. Armour thought he caught the flicker of a smile on the man's thin mouth.

"Campbell's expecting him, see you later." She turned to Armour for the first time, regarding him for a few seconds before speaking. Her eyes were too deep-set and her face too long to be conventionally pretty, but Armour was forever haunted by the way she looked then.

"You better come," she said simply.

With a curt backwards "Thanks!" to the boatman, he followed her.

They turned left at the end of the jetty, passing a terraced row of white single-storey cottages facing the sea, each with a window on either side of a brightly painted door. She walked him briskly for a hundred yards or more along an old, worn-out single-track road until they came to a modern timber building that had the upturned aluminium hull of a boat for a roof. By the door was a painted sign: a white-on-black swirl that looked like cream new-poured onto recently stirred coffee. Below this logo were the words: "Calltain Publishing Unlimited. Quality Thought on Quality Paper." Armour wanted to ask about it, but the woman with the witch name was clearly in no mood for conversation.

Beyond the hull-roofed house a faint footpath continued along the shore, but the main track turned sharply inland and uphill and looked, from this point on, only fit for tractors and Land Rovers. They followed this steep incline in silence, but not a comfortable one. She seemed distracted, ill at ease.

"I'm Jonathon Armour, I write for *The Herald,*" he ventured. "I'm here to interview Campbell Aaronson."

"Yes, I know. Campbell sent me to get you, although I'm sure as a journalist you would have found him yourself." Her tone was brusque and he sensed that, for some reason, she did not want the interview with the old composer to take place.

So, he thought, the lady with the witch name is protective of Aaronson. It didn't surprise Armour. This was, after all, what journalists lazily like to call "a tightly knit community" and Aaronson, the atomic bomb builder who had become a peacenik, was its most remarkable citizen. References to Aaronson's work on the Manhattan project did not appear in any of the composer's writings about his music, on the covers of his recordings, or on the programmes of his performed work. While not actually airbrushed, it seemed to the journalist that Aaronson's brilliant first career had been removed from the public domain. Armour had stumbled across it by accident. A combination of the journalistic magpie mind and a haphazard insomniac reading habit had led him to the connection. His discovery that a reclusive but internationally acclaimed composer, now living in an alternative eco-community, had been one of the architects of the atomic bombs that destroyed Hiroshima and Nagasaki was undoubtedly a journalistic coup. The woman was edgy, and if she was close to Aaronson who could blame her? Armour found himself wanting to reassure her. He told her that he had only recently become aware of Aaronson's music, but was really impressed. He mentioned the CDs he'd bought – they weren't at all easy to find. He said that he was amazed that Aaronson wasn't better known.

"I don't think Campbell gives a damn," she said. They walked on without speaking after that.

The track rose steadily, but the woman never slackened her pace. Armour, who was nearly fifty, plodded in silence, determined to keep up and not appear short of breath, while all the time hoping that Aaronson's cottage was the low whitewashed one beside the circular construction halfway up the hill, before the track began to zigzag up the even steeper gradient towards the summit.

"That's it," she said with a nod in the general direction, as if reading his mind. "Not far for you now."

"Great," he said. Patronising bitch, he thought.

Armour knew that Aaronson had converted an old cottage back in the seventies, but the house they now approached was bigger and stranger than he had imagined. One end of it was, as he expected, a low single-storey structure with thick dry-stone walls, tiny windows and an ox-blood red corrugated iron roof. It was a traditional single-storey Highland croft house of the nineteenth century that had been carefully restored instead of being allowed to crumble. But the other end of Aaronson's home was an extraordinary modern drum-shaped timber and glass building. Armour had seen the stubby tower as they had climbed the hill and thought it was some sort of agricultural silo or water tank. Round and on two floors, it had a pointed roof like a coolie hat. The upper floor had a wide arc of windows, and the walls and roof were clad with wooden shingles that had turned almost white in the sun and salt air. The only door appeared to be on the upper floor and was reached by a wooden ramp like a ship's gangway. The whole structure sat amid a garden where patches of vegetables and soft fruits were tucked among plots of small saplings that had been carefully staked against the wind. Bamboo wind chimes played fortissimo in the breeze. The spinning blades of a wind-powered generator etched a blurred halo in the sky.

"It's quite a house."

"I suppose it is. People are ... like ... pretty original here. You get used to it."

She led the way up the steep gangway and into the tower. He half-expected it to be pulled up behind them like a castle drawbridge.

The best photograph Armour had seen of Dougald Campbell Aaronson had been taken a quarter of a century previously at a CND demonstration outside the Faslane Nuclear Submarine base. The picture had been shot from behind the lines of massed police. Aaronson, almost a head taller than the demonstrators around him, was caught frozen in time with his right arm outstretched, palm open, as if commanding the police to halt. It was a stunning photograph. At the centre of the busy frame, and apparently staring into the lens, the man dominated the image. He looked, Armour thought, a bit like Charlton Heston as Moses, or perhaps Herbert von Karajan conducting the Berlin Philharmonic. Now, in more or less the centre of the large round room, an old man was sitting crouched over a trestle table, cutting something out of a newspaper with a pair of scissors. Armour recognised him at once. His forehead was large, and though his hair was receding it was thick and long and white. The old man looked up to peer over a pair of half-rim glasses.

"My love! You've brought the newspapers. I've not even finished snipping the old ones."

"And a man from the newspapers. This is Mr Armour."

A low whistle came from the far end of the room, as if announcing the journalist's arrival in the manner of an admiral boarding his battleship. Steam was blowing from a kettle that juddered atop a black iron stove with a glass face and a fiery heart.

"He's expected. I saw you coming up the hill and put the kettle on. Make us a brew, my love!" Campbell Aaronson's gaze turned from following the girl as she crossed to the stove to settle on Armour for a few seconds, as if trying to make up his mind about him.

"Japanese green is all I drink, Armour, I hope that will do. But don't read too much into the leaves. I'm not trying to make amends to the Japanese nation for the atom bomb, it's just what I prefer."

The journalist had expected Aaronson to be defensive about his role in the Manhattan Project, in the invention of the bombs that killed more than a hundred thousand human beings, but his host grinned broadly as he placed two hands on the table and levered himself to his feet in welcome – slightly stooped, but easily six foot three even after eighty years of carrying that enormous broad frame around. They shook hands. The old man's grip was politely firm, and lingering enough to betray that his skin was dry and rough.

"Sit down, Armour. My beloved Grizzel will bring us our tea."

For all his bohemian reputation and appearance, Aaronson spoke in the accent and commanding tone of the English upper class. Armour was offered an old bentwood chair at the table, although there were two comfortable couches facing the panoramic window that looked out towards the loch. At the back of the room a modern stainless steel kitchen, where the woman had set about making tea without demur, had been skilfully set against the curved timber wall. Out the corner of his eye Armour could see her standing there, shrouded in steam as she stirred. She'd thrown off her coat and was now revealed to him as slim, almost slight, with her jeans tight-fitting over a skinny, boyish backside. He couldn't stop his mind speculating on her relationship with the old man. Was she some sort of amanuensis? A carer? A groupie? His mistress? The journalist knew that Aaronson had flourished in the highly sexed sixties when his reputation as a cult composer and bohemian intellectual had been an irresistible attraction for many artsy young women. *The Herald* had a few old photographs in its picture library of Edinburgh Festival openings and parties, and those that featured Aaronson usually showed him with an attractive younger woman in tow. She must be, Armour found himself musing, in her late twenties or maybe thirty. Easily less than half the old goat's age! She called him "Campbell" and looked unflinchingly into his eyes when they spoke. He called her "my love", and his eyes often sought her out, even when he was speaking to Armour. It was oddly disconcerting to the journalist that this craggy oldster could be fucking her, and he tried to dismiss the thought from his mind.

Sensing that Aaronson was in the mood to talk, Armour quickly went through the formality of asking the old man if he minded him taking notes. A black-bound Moleskine notebook and a stylish aluminium propelling pencil with soft dark lead were produced. Tea was drunk. The journalist's heavy jacket was slung over the back of the bentwood chair. The old man spoke, and spoke on, in his cultivated upper-crust drawl, and Armour filled the first of many pages of his notebook in his partly learned, partly invented, shorthand script.

Aaronson was fluent, but guarded. He'd clearly decided in advance exactly what he was going to say. The old man had, Armour realised, a script – a score! There was to be no improvisation. The journalist quickly reviewed his tactics and decided to let Aaronson finish his performance, then double back with some hard, direct questions about the consequences and morality of building atom bombs. In this first skirmish, Aaronson simply skated over his work in the New Mexico desert with Oppenheimer, and spoke only briefly about his eventual disillusionment with science, of his depression and drinking and escape to a new life in Paris and the world of electronic music. He only became voluble when telling of his discovery of Calltain, of the other people who had come to work and settle there, of wind power and organic food, of how Western man no longer sees the stars because of the sludge of orange light that hangs over our towns and cities.

"I'll tell you this Armour, twenty-five years ago I went to Africa for the first time. I was going to a lot of places back then because I wanted to see them when they were still natural, before civilisation destroyed them. Intellectually I knew that man was fatally alienated from his environment, but I never understood that emotionally until I lay under the night sky in Southern Sudan. When I came back, I stopped just using electronically generated sound, and started incorporating drums and noises from nature into my work. People thought it was the African music that had changed me. Of course, I'd heard plenty of it when I was there. I sought it out! But it wasn't the music of Africa that obsessed me, but the stars. I knew when I lay there watching the sky that I was doing something that was a fundamental, natural, human experience for most of mankind's existence. Yet I, a graduate in physics from two great universities, had never done it before! I'd spent years in laboratories attempting to understand the fabric of the universe, yet I'd never seen the stars properly. I'd spent years as an artist exploring what it was to be a human being, seeking for something called beauty, yet I'd never truly felt the sense of awe that for millions of years was our ancestors' nightly experience. In just one life a traditional tribal man or woman would be confronted thousands of times with the majesty of creation ... and now we just watch fucking television. What a fucking waste of life!"

Aaronson thumped the table hard with the palms of both hands. The earthenware tea bowls wobbled precariously. The old man had by now worked himself up into a red-faced passion. "When I came back to Calltain I tried to hear the sounds of nature the way I'd seen the stars ... as if for the first time. From then on I began to use my music to seek and experience the sense of wonder that humankind has felt through most of its existence – that wonder that first animated our primitive brains and caused us to create religion and philosophy and art ... our sense of wonder, Armour, our instinctive compulsion to try and understand where we are within nature and the universe!"

The woman interrupted with more tea. Aaronson paused, fleetingly annoyed, but breathless. She poured without speaking and stood back behind Aaronson's chair. Armour felt her eyes upon him and glanced up. In one hand she held the pot, while with the other she made the gesture of patting down the air in front of her. He read her silent message.

Keep him calm. Don't let him get excited.

"Grizzel says I overdo things for a man of my age. She doesn't like it when I get molto agitato, do you, my love?" Aaronson said, over his shoulder. "She'd have me live my life with more Adagio and less Brio, but I always say, keep your head and your legs working and everything in between follows on." He laughed and gave Armour a wink as if to make clear a sexual implication to his motto.

"Look at these hands. Do they look like the hands of an effete musician?" He held them up as if in a gesture of surrender. They were large and powerful, but when he turned them Armour could see that they were dry and cracked, with painful looking hacks around the knuckles. Dirt was ingrained in the fissures and under the broken fingernails.

"I've become a horny-handed son of toil! I'm planting a wood, a hazel wood down by the shore of the big bay over there. I've dug every hole, raised every sapling from seed and planted them myself. When I first came here with Demarco in sixty-three there was hardly a tree on Calltain, just the odd rowan still growing outside the ruined croft houses to ward off witches and fairies. Yet this place was all natural forest before the first farmers came. They spent a few hundred years cutting down the mature trees with their bronze axes, and when iron came along they just got better at it. Then the deer, and later the sheep, chomped up the saplings and left Calltain to the heather and bracken. I've fenced off some patches down at Camas Calltain to keep the feral goats out, they're a bloody nuisance, and I'm slowly trying to undo what they and two thousand years of my fellow man have done to the place. Call it pissing against the wind, Armour, but it beats doing bugger all!"

"Well," said Armour, his head still bent over his notebook and furiously scribbling pencil, "if everyone did something like that we might beat global warming." He knew instantly that it sounded trite.

The old man snorted, indicating the pile of newspapers on the table in front of him with a flourish of his hand. "Look at all this newsprint. I'm as guilty as anybody! At least my Grizzel will re-cycle it into the stove, won't you, my love?"

When Armour had first entered the round tower he'd been pleased to note that it was *The Herald* that Aaronson was disembowelling. The composer had placed the article he had just snipped out onto a neat pile of cuttings. Aaronson now pushed the little pile towards Armour. Dates had been written on them in the blue ink of a fountain pen. The first carried the headline: **Deep water makes Calltain "ideal" for super-quarry**. Another read: **Geologists promise jobs boost**. Armour read them, uncomfortable in the certainty that Aaronson and Grizzel were watching his every twitch. The articles were cut from a variety of newspapers, but Armour vaguely recognised some of them from his own. The stories were all short on hard facts, but seemed to be about a proposal to dig a super-quarry at Calltain and ship millions of tons of aggregate down Loch Vallaig. The story was vaguely familiar, but it had never interested him much.

"So is this super-quarry going to happen?"

"Not yet, Armour. These stories are just kites in the wind. Argo Aggregates are using the local press to float the idea, to get it into people's minds ... soften them up by promising them new jobs and riches. They've had geologists dropping in on us by helicopter for the past couple of years now, but no official application for a quarry has been made yet. They're still at the stage of buttering up the local people and politicians. They're preaching so-called progress."

"What sort of impact would it have here?"

"Simply cataclysmic." The old man leaned towards him. Grizzel put her hand on his shoulder as if to restrain him. "They'd blow the whole fucking mountain away and cart it off to build more motorways to strangle the planet with. That's why we're going to stop it!"

"But if the plans aren't official yet, how can you ..."

"Haven't you been listening, man? These articles in the papers aren't just scuttlebutt. It isn't as if some reporter has bumped into a geologist who's spun him a line in a pub. They're being deliberately planted by a rich industrialist's propaganda machine. He's saying to people that Calltain is a piece of economically worthless land and that he'll make them all rich if they let him blow it to hell. Mark my words, Joshua Argo means to destroy this place." The old man leant back. Grizzel's hand stayed on his shoulder. He clutched at it and held it in his gnarled fist. "That's what you should be writing about, Armour, how this community of creative and valuable people will be swept away by capitalism ... how this landscape will be raped ... how another chunk of our environment is going to be destroyed. Don't you think that's more important than what I did nearly sixty years ago?"

"Yeah, but I'm the Arts Correspondent ... look, the paper has an environmental reporter. I could ..."

"This is an arts community, my young friend! I don't work alone here. Do you know Burgess the sculptor's work? He's one of the most creative people alive. There are two or three published poets here and half a dozen craft workshops. Have you seen Trail's books?" Armour looked at him blankly. "Well, anyway, he publishes books ... makes the paper from scratch out of seaweed and God knows what ... hand binds every copy himself. There are collectors in America who buy an edition of everything he prints just because they're so damn beautiful ... and he does all this in an upturned fucking boat for God's sake! Everyone in Calltain has built or renovated their own home ... and a guy who was a juvenile delinquent on the mainland put up nearly every wind generator in the place. There are people who've turned sodden acid soil into gardens that produce purer food than you'll get in any supermarket. We're energy self-sufficient. There's no crime here! Isn't that a creative community you should be writing about? Just living here is being creative, we're experimenting with alternative ways for humankind to survive and thrive."

"Listen Campbell, I've an idea." Grizzel's voice was low and soft, but had the timbre of authority. The old man fell uncharacteristically silent. "I think Mr Armour's come a long way to write a story about a man who once built atom bombs, but now composes weird music and preaches world peace. I think that's what he might call a scoop ... isn't that the word?"

Armour nodded, although he'd never met a journalist who used the expression except jokingly. She went on, "Why don't you tell him what he wants to know, Campbell? You could even give him the photograph of you and Oppenheimer together in Los Alamos. The deal would be ... that he comes back and writes about what really goes on here."

Her words were spoken to the old man but her gaze, and her offer of a deal, were aimed directly at Armour. "It's an amazing place with some amazing people ... I could show you around if you like. Have you heard of Caleb Burgess? Caleb is a bit of a recluse these days, but I'm sure he'd speak to you if I asked him."

Caleb Burgess. Severed heads. Pagan wells. Sculpted stone monoliths. Half-remembered neo-pagan images from an exhibition he'd once covered for *The Herald* came flickering into Armour's mind. Armour had been convinced that the American-born sculptor was going to be a leading figure of late twentieth-century art, and had often wondered about the man's sudden disappearance. Even now, more than twenty years later, a framed poster advertising Burgess's 1979 exhibition still hung in the journalist's study at home. As well as being a startling image – three bloody severed heads impaled on posts – the poster had strong sentimental value to Armour. It was partly on the strength of his article about Burgess's exhibition that Armour had started along the promotion trail from general news reporter to feature writer and eventually the job he really wanted, Arts and Culture Correspondent. Burgess's exhibition had profoundly impressed the young journalist, but the artist had vanished from public view after that.

"I'd really like to meet him. I saw his exhibition in Edinburgh years ago, but I've never met him. I had no idea ..."

"That he was alive?"

It was what he meant, but instead he managed to blurt out: "No, no ... that he was here ... here in Calltain."

"Is it a deal?"

And, of course, it was.

Throughout the late morning, Armour carefully filled pages of his notebook with the story of Aaronson's work on the Manhattan project. The old man described how, in the first weeks of 1943, the remote Los Alamos Ranch School was flooded with scores of American, British and European scientists and thousands of construction workers, all driven by the fear of a Nazi super-weapon.

"People often thought Oppie was arrogant ... well, I suppose he was, but it was fear, not hubris, that brought us to that godforsaken place."

Aaronson insisted that it was no secret that he'd worked on the atom bomb with the man he called Oppie. An artist, he insisted, was the sum of his contradictions.

"Do I wish that the atom bomb had never been invented? Absolutely. Do I wish that I'd never been part of the project? Most certainly! It's a lucky man indeed that has nothing in his past to regret ... either a lucky man or a psychopath. Don't tell me you don't have a memory that makes you unhappy ... a place in your mind that you don't care to visit too often?"

"Yes ... I have that."

"Well, Los Alamos is mine. I've never denied my part, but it's a painful memory that I don't choose to dwell on every day. It will always be with me, but I've learned how to use that bitter experience-e creatively. That's what an artist does ... uses the pain and contradictions in his life."

The old man's biographical details were recorded in Armour's spiky shorthand, while phrases like "HIGHLY ENRICHED URANIUM-234 PLUS PLUTONIUM-239" were carefully printed in capital letters.

After a lunch of omelettes, dutifully prepared by the girl, Aaronson announced that he wished to continue the interview while he took his afternoon walk. Grizzel took down an ancient waxed stockman's coat from a wooden peg and helped the old man on with it. It looked like the great-grandfather of the one she had worn when she met Armour at the jetty. It was frayed around the cuffs and collar, yet it was still glossy. Armour thought he smelled linseed oil.

"Don't stay out there talking till you're frozen," she scolded.

"My love," Aaronson intoned as he leaned forward to kiss her on the forehead, "remember that talking and walking upright is our evolutionary birthright. We just can't help it!"

The steep path which had brought Armour from the shore zigzagged on up past the round house, through a bleak landscape of peat hags and scrubby vegetation. The two men hiked it steadily for twenty minutes or more until they reached the *bealach*, the pass that took the track over Calltain's rocky spine and down towards the peninsula's northern coast. They were welcomed at the summit by a blast of chill wind and a panorama of blues and greys, of sky and sea, rocky headlands and distant islands. It was beautiful and exhilarating, although Armour was now shuddering under his thick jacket. He remembered that it was the first day of September. Summer had slipped away without him noticing.

"Every time I reach here it's a revelation," shouted the old man above the wind. "We'll keep walking till we get to Kilmailin. Come on Armour, presto! We'll be out of the wind there." They walked presto down the hill, as Aaronson commanded, towards a small horseshoe inlet. As they descended, Armour could see two great lines of standing stones close to the shore. Twenty monoliths, each about eight feet high, formed an avenue that led from the rough track on which they were walking to a green mound on the raised beach that fringed Kilmailin Bay.

Armour searched his memory for any of the smattering of facts about Calltain he'd picked up from a guidebook. "Are these the famous Neolithic remains?"

"Neolithic my arse." The old man snorted in amusement. "That's Caleb's back door, we put these up fourteen or fifteen years ago after he'd finished excavating his house. That hill is hollow. Caleb's a fucking troglodyte! His studio is a hole in the ground ... I know, I helped dig the damn thing because we couldn't get a JCB over here in those days, but the front's all glass and faces the sea. You'll see it from Kilmailin Chapel."

The ruined chapel was a low roofless building, but its walls and gable ends sill stood high. Close to it, a few rough rocks stood upright, evidently an ancient burial ground.

"Look at that." Aaronson pointed to a broad, recumbent boulder. It was covered in grey lichen, except where there were three circular pools of water, each perhaps three or four inches in diameter.

"Cup markings?"

"Yes Armour, Stone Age. This was a holy site long before a chapel was built. Imagine! What rituals here!"

"How old is the chapel?"

Aaronson didn't reply until they had entered the ruin. Against one wall were propped two carved Celtic crosses taller than a man. Out of the buffeting wind it seemed a place of calm. The old man caressed one of the crosses with the palm of a hand. "They say this place dates back to about the twelfth century, but there almost certainly was a church here for hundreds of years before that ... and it was probably built on the site of a pre-Christian temple ... hence the cup and ring markings." Aaronson gestured through an arched window space to a hundred-yard stretch of sand that lay below. "That beach is one of the few places on Calltain's north coast where you can land a boat. When the first Christian monks came ashore here they must have found pagan worship going on. They recognised that this was a sacred place, and what they did was just superimpose their own religion onto it. With their religion ... came their aesthetic." Aaronson approached the more ornately carved of the crosses and ran his fingers over it. "These beauties lay outside for seven centuries until the National Museum announced that it wanted them moved to Edinburgh. We'd a hell of a fight keeping them, but eventually the museum agreed to leave them here, as long as they were moved inside the walls to keep them from the worst of the elements."

Armour gazed down onto the pale fringe of sand where the waves crashed. Man and climate change may have swept away the forest that once covered all but the rocky bones of Calltain, he mused, but the rhythm of the waves and sand was timeless. "It's amazing to think of," he said, "Celtic art and religion, turning up on the beach here in a skin-covered coracle."

"Art AND religion?" Aaronson put his emphasis on the conjunction. "To my mind, Armour, they're the same thing, or at least they spring from the same source, just as magic does.

Saints, prophets, Shamans, ritual, metaphysical poetry, Yeats, Miró, Mozart's Requiem, cup and ring markings – where does religion end and art begin? Look at Miró. He was one of the greats, yet he once said that painting disgusted him, and that all he was interested in was pure spirit!"

"So you don't believe that there is an essential difference between the aesthetic experience and the spiritual?"

"Absolutely not! Look, for hundreds of years our society has taken seriously the concept that people have had divine inspiration to write music or poetry, but there are plenty of stories here in the Highlands and in Ireland of pipers and fiddlers who learned tunes from the fairies. Creative people have always fretted about where their inspiration comes from and have often resorted to metaphors to explain it. Frankly it doesn't matter a damn if you think the art you've created came from God, or the fairies, or magical powers, or little green men, or some great Jungian collective unconscious. If music or a painting moves me, if it inspires me or lets me see things differently, it doesn't matter to me where the artist thinks he got it from. You can be moved by a haiku or by Verdi's Requiem without the pain in the arse of being a Zen monk or a Catholic. God forbid! Art comes from artists ... that's all. That's what artists are for ... creating the transcendent."

"Do you not think that the modern concept of the artist as someone with some sort of special mystical insight is relatively new?" Once he'd spoken Armour feared he'd said too much. He had no wish to fall out with the old man, at least until he had all the material he needed for his article. He went on, choosing his words carefully, "What I mean is that in medieval times an artist and an artisan were the same thing. They could paint or sculpt or play music or make you a suit of armour, but they weren't given any special spiritual status ... all that came along with the Romantic Movement."

"The Romantic Movement and the Democratic Movement, you mean! You don't think that all these old kings and popes and potentates were ever going to admit to the possibility of an ordinary individual experiencing the transcendental, do you? They, and they alone, had the direct line to the divine ... and they weren't going to share it with a rabble of lute players and limners. But look, Armour, basically I agree with you.

Being an artist isn't all that special, it's like being a chef or a long jumper – it helps if you're born with a knack for it, but you've got to have the dedication to give the best you've got, if you want to be any good. I'm an artist, and it's part of my nature that my ego drives me to be the best I can be. But I make music first and foremost for myself. That sounds entirely elitist, but it's true ... frankly I don't give a damn what the public thinks or what the critics write ... but while I make music for me, I absolutely do it in a social context. Everything I've produced comes from being not just an artist, but an artist in society. I may hate and reject that society, I may take care never to allude to it in my work, but even the rejection of society is a profoundly powerful response to it. Artists devote their lives to expressing themselves. They may get well paid for that devotion, or they may pay a terrible price for it, but either way they've got the time and space to delve deep into themselves ... and just sometimes they get to places in their heads where all of society is heading, but just hasn't realised it yet. Artists might not be conscious of that. They may even resent people interpreting their work in certain ways, but nevertheless that's the role they have in society. I see my music as being like the wind chimes I've made. Sometimes I don't know that the wind is getting up, but the chimes are sensitive to the lightest breath and as soon as I hear them I fancy I feel the wind on my cheek. It might be just a breeze or a storm that's coming, but whatever it is, it's the chimes that alert me first. I hear them. I look up at the sky. I see the storm coming ... I run to tell my neighbour."

"But you do more than that," interrupted Armour, "you're not just a weather forecast, you instruct. You propose a way forward. That's surely what the Gaia Symphony was about ... and planting your hazel wood?"

"Mea Culpa," the old man laughed, "but I've already told you that I've inherited a Utopian gene. "When the lovely Grizzel gets tired of my lecturing she calls me 'Old flip chart'! You're very welcome to use the phrase when I go on a bit. Yes, I admit it, I think modern society stinks, and that we, as a species, have to start living differently in the world while there is still a world worth living in. But I don't just want to tell people that they're on the road to hell. I'm arrogant enough to want to save them too. For me, Armour, art is about the process of healing the world as well as understanding it."

Sheltering within the broken stone walls Aaronson spoke long and earnestly about the capacity of art to make the world anew, until they realised that the cold had seeped into their bones. They stepped outside and stood in the wind for a moment as Aaronson pointed out the concave terrace on the raised beach and the glass front of Caleb Burgess's underground studio. "Told you he was a damned troglodyte. Let's go before we freeze our arses off!"

They walked back briskly to warm themselves, Armour in breathless admiration of the old man's vigour.

"Do you want tea before you go?" On the lips of the witch woman this seemed more an instruction to leave than an invitation to stay, but Armour hardly minded as he could see that the old man was tiring. To his surprise she produced a box-file full of photographs. As she shuffled through the prints Armour saw a colour one of her and Aaronson, arm and arm on a beach, laughing together. She found a small black and white picture. Dressed in jeans, an open neck shirt with rolled up sleeves, and his trademark pork pie hat, the great Robert J. Oppenheimer stood smiling as he formally shook hands with an awkward beanpole of a youth who wore baggy trousers too short for him.

"Welcome to Los Alamos, son, and who the devil are you?" quoted Aaronson in a fake New York drawl. "Took me to his cabin and made us great vodka martinis. Well, my parents had brought me up believing that booze was a capitalist plot to keep the proletariat docile, so that was the first drink I ever had. But, apart from getting me hooked, Oppie was the smartest man I ever met. Masterminded the atom bomb and yet was immersed in Hindu mysticism. Do you think that's a contradiction?"

"I know that he quoted Hindu scripture when the first experimental bomb was exploded ... something about becoming death."

"Oh yes, Armour, you're right enough there! 'Now I am become Death, the destroyer of worlds' ... he said that all right ... but did you know that Oppie read Bhagavad-Gita in Sanskrit? Did you know that he knew pretty nearly every damn thing there is to know about classical Greek architecture ... or that he loved to ride a horse in the desert, and was pretty handy in a sailboat? Remember, what you perceive as a man's contradictions may just be complexities that you aren't equipped to understand." He fixed Armour in a gaze that was uncomfortable and yet compelling. "Oppenheimer wasn't just a great scientist. He was an extraordinary human being. He was a complex, arrogant bastard! But he was also thoughtful and progressive ... a radical. Did you know that Kitty, his wife, had been married to an American Communist who was killed in the Spanish Civil War? When we were at Los Alamos we were fighting Fascism, pure and simple ... it was a cause, and we saw it as a noble one. Your generation, my young friend, blames the bomb for the Cold War, but we had a hot war going on. Nietzsche once warned that he who fights monsters must take care not to become a monster himself, but I can tell you ... Nietzsche wasn't exactly fashionable at Los Alamos back then. Oh, I know that he was no anti-Semite, but the Nazis loved him so we didn't. Oppie was a Jew. I'm a half-Jew ... have you any idea what that meant in 1943? A lot of our guys came directly from Nazi-occupied Europe ... Rotblat's wife died in a concentration camp, Otto Frisch's father was held in Dachau, Bill Penney's wife was killed in the Blitz and Niels Bohr was a half-Jew who'd escaped from occupied Copenhagen. They knew that Nazism was evil to the core. But the Nazis had Heisenberg. He was a Nobel laureate for God's sake! We reckoned that if anyone could build a bomb it was Werner Heisenberg. Can you imagine what Hitler's foul regime would have done with such a weapon?"

The old man firmly pushed the small photograph across the table, signalling that the interview was over. The woman looked relieved.

"Take it, Armour, before I change my mind." The journalist thanked him, slipped the photograph into his notebook, and promised he would return it. He knew from Aaronson's sudden arms-crossed withdrawal into himself that there was no more to be got from him that day. He was surprised when the woman said she would walk him to the jetty.

After the goodbyes – Aaronson standing rather formally to make his – Armour and the woman stepped outside. The wind chimes were ringing frantically. Lean saplings growing in recycled plastic food containers bent in the wind. He assumed they were hazel. They walked quickly down the rough road towards the shore. White horses were breaking the lead-grey surface of Loch Vallaig.

"I'm glad we've got you to the boat before the wind gets any worse. I hope Campbell didn't get cold when you were out."

"I don't know about him but I was frozen. He seems pretty tough though."

"Yeah, as old boots, but he's getting on. We all keep telling him to take it easier, but he still works flat out. Sometimes he's in the studio twelve hours a day, as well as spending two or three hours on his bloody trees."

"Wow ... "

"Yes," she blurted out, as if anxious to make her point, "you're really honoured to have got so much of his time. Normally he would have been downstairs at his computer with headphones clamped to his ears ... either that or walking alone on the shore for hours with his Dat recorder and microphone. It's worse during the winter. He likes to get outside during the few hours of light, so he ends up working half the night."

"Twelve hours is a long stint for anyone, let alone someone his age. He's got amazing energy."

"That's pretty common among creative people. They're somehow very driven, especially if they have a history of depression. It seems their way of keeping their neurosis at bay ... you know, throwing yourself into your work. Campbell likes to say that he and Winston Churchill got their Black Dogs of depression from the same litter, but it was himself that got the bitch."

"Of course! *Black Dog Bacchanalia* ... the piece with the howling sounds and the samples of drunks talking ..."

Armour was suddenly worried that he'd missed an important part of Aaronson's story. "He didn't really talk about depression much at all. He just mentioned in passing that he'd had some kind of breakdown when he returned to England after the war, and that he'd hit the bottle a bit. Is there more to it than that?"

She looked at him coolly, as if judging whether she should trust him. "He's been battling depression all his life, but he doesn't go on about it. He's not ashamed of it or anything. It's always been with him, so he doesn't think it's remarkable ... he just throws himself into life and gets on with it. I think that the idea that you have to be mad to be a genius is pure bollocks, but I know that Campbell's depression has made him very tolerant of eccentric and unconventional people. He thinks they've got something special to offer, so he's always been a sort of guru for off-the-wall creative types. He just wants everyone to live as rich a life as he does. He's like ... a remarkable life force." She stopped abruptly, and he had to turn and take a few paces back along the path towards her. She stared at him now, as if trying to make up her mind if he was friend or foe. "We all love him, Mr Armour. Don't write anything to hurt or humiliate him."

Armour could hear the emotion in her voice, and thought she was going to cry. He wanted to hug her. "I really respect Mr Aaronson," he said gently. "I'm sure he'll be fine about what I write." He stared at the ground and kicked a small stone, giving her time to collect herself. "He's pretty much the main man round here, isn't he?"

"Christ, he'd hate to hear you say that!" He heard the relief in her voice at having something else, something less personal, to say. She suddenly seemed strong again. "This is a very laid-back community here, we're all anarchists really. We have meetings in the school and vote on stuff, but everyone lives pretty much as they please. But, yeah, everyone loves Campbell. He and Caleb are the longest residents here and everyone admires the work they do, although they sometimes get teased about being the Tribal Elders. That really pisses them off, but people here really do respect the committed and the creative."

"So what's your role in this creative community? Are you a musician like Aaronson?" He was fishing for the connection, for the nature of the relationship.

She laughed, burying her head in the upturned collar of her coat and letting her windblown hair hide her face, as if better to enjoy some private joke. "No, not yet."

"So ..."

"I'm joking. I'm a physicist like Campbell was, but I've no intention of becoming a composer. Mind you, neither did

Campbell when he worked on the Manhattan project ... but somehow I don't think music's for me."

"A physicist? So you don't live here."

"No, Matt's mastered building windmills, but he hasn't quite cracked a radio telescope yet." She smiled, waving her arm theatrically in the air. "Actually I'm an astrophysicist ... you know, stars, galaxies, red dwarves, quasars, that sort of thing. I work for the Clerk-Maxwell Institute. It's a part government, part university research place near Oxford, but I spend as much time here as I can. I'm working for a PhD ... alongside doing research, so I've got a lot of reading and thinking to do. Calltain's ideal. There's peace here ... and I have Campbell."

So he is fucking her, thought Armour. He remembered the old man talking about keeping the head and the legs active and everything in between following on. The lucky old goat.

"We'd best get a move on," she said, "or you'll miss your train."

The *Ran* was lying alongside the jetty, its engine idling.

"Well Mr Armour, it's goodbye until your next visit."

"Thank you ... Grizzel." He felt awkward pronouncing her ridiculous name. "And it's Jon, Jon Armour." She held out her hand to him. As he took it, she gazed directly into his eyes and mouthed his first name silently; her lips pouting round the single syllable. It was as if she was struggling to fix his face and name in her mind, but nonetheless he found the movement arousing.

"I'll come back as soon as you've cleared things with Caleb Burgess. Mr Aaronson pointed out his house to me when we walked to the north shore ... it's quite a place ... I'd really like to meet him. I write some articles for an arts magazine as well as *The Herald*, and I'm sure they would let me do an in-depth piece about Burgess. I'll give you my card and you can ring me when you've spoken to him."

"That's OK, Campbell has your details." She turned from him. "I'd better be getting back to him, and Matt will be anxious to go."

Tyler was unhooking the bow rope. Armour stepped aboard and watched Grizzel walk briskly down the jetty, hurrying back to her ancient lover.

"So, Campbell took you to Kilmalin and told you how to build an atomic bomb then?"

"News travels."

Tyler shrugged. "Grizzel mentioned it." He ducked into the cabin and, with an aggressive surge of the engine, headed the vessel towards Vallaig. Matt Tyler, Armour mused, must know everyone and everything that comes in and out of Calltain. It's him and his daft little boat that make the place viable. Aaronson, Burgess, Grizzel – they all depended on this laconic lout!

Instead of sheltering in the tiny wheelhouse the sole passenger sat huddled and chilled at the stern, watching the boatman, strong and confident, steer his vessel over the choppy loch. His legs and body rode the pitch and swell of the deck as his deft hands spun the wheel. Fit and not yet forty, Armour decided. A sour shot of jealousy slipped through his veins.

The Herald 4th September 2000

Cult composer helped build atom bomb

A *Herald* exclusive

by Jonathon Armour

A cult composer and environmental activist now living in the Scottish Highlands was one of the brains behind the atom bombs that destroyed Hiroshima and Nagasaki.

Campbell Aaronson (80), who lives in the "alternative" community on the Calltain peninsula in the Western Highlands, has revealed that he was a key member of the Manhattan Project – the team who built the bombs that forced Japan to surrender and ended World War II. A brilliant young Oxford physics graduate, Aaronson caught the attention of Robert Oppenheimer while doing research in Chicago. In March 1943, when Oppenheimer began to assemble the team that would build the atom bombs that would destroy two Japanese cities, the young Aaronson was one of the first to be called to his Los Alamos laboratory in New Mexico.

"It's no secret that I worked with Oppie," he told me in his home on Calltain. "Germany had produced some of the greatest nuclear scientists in the world and, whether they liked it or not, they were working for the Nazis. Can you imagine what Hitler's filthy regime would have done with such a weapon? Even after

Germany was beaten we thought that we were saving the world from a long-drawn-out, bloody war in the east that had already killed millions of people. We had no concept of the Cold War, no idea that what we were making might destroy all mankind."

Asked if he was ashamed of his role in building the bomb Aaronson said: "All creative people are the sum of their contradictions. The spark of invention I showed back then is the same spark that allows me to be an artist today. I really don't know what the fuss is about. I've never denied my part in the Manhattan Project."

But a search through Aaronson's listing in *Grove's Dictionary of Music and Musicians* reveals no reference to his work with Oppenheimer, nor can any be found in the potted biographies on the back of his record and CD covers. Aaronson denies any cover-up and points to an article he wrote for the small circulation eco-magazine *Resurgence* four years ago where he recalled his days at the Los Alamos laboratory. In it he wrote: "Our dream was freedom from the fear of a world dominated by fascism. I don't lose sleep over that. What worries me is that today there is no dream, no vision about what can improve the condition of humankind. Out there in the New Mexican desert half a century ago we shared a vision of a world made peaceful. Imagining a better world and trying to achieve it is part of what makes human beings human. I believe in the existence of a Utopian gene which might yet save mankind."

A spokesman for the Campaign for Nuclear Disarmament, of which Aaronson is a member, admitted that she did not know of Aaronson's connection with the first atom bomb. "I'm surprised," she admitted, "but who better to condemn weapons of mass destruction today than somebody who helped create them. He knows only too well the danger to mankind."

A Londoner by birth, Aaronson forsook experimental physics after the war and studied electronic music composition in Paris and Cologne. His first significant work, *$E = H.\ G.\ Wells^2$*, was recorded and released as a record in 1955. Although his work is usually thought to be obscure, he has built up a reputation as a cult figure for many musicians working in the contemporary "dance" music scene. Aaronson's work was featured in a concert of contemporary music at the Edinburgh International Festival in 1964. From then on he began spending more and more time in

Scotland, finally settling in Calltain, which has had a reputation as an alternative or "hippy" colony since the late sixties.

Aaronson is the son of the late Scottish chemical industries heiress Margaret Campbell, whose father Sir Hector Campbell made his fortune as an arms manufacturer during World War I.

Aaronson is second generation Awkward Squad. His mother turned her back on the ostentatious wealth of her family, and he on a brilliant early career in atomic physics and the development of nuclear weapons.

Aaronson describes his parents as "true bohemians". "My father was a real cosmopolitan, a Jewish socialist with very avant-garde views. He read all the new writers and thinkers in at least five languages, and as I was growing up there was never just the family at home, we always had a few penniless European writers or political exiles about. On the face of it, Mother was Scottish and much more down to earth. She had lots of progressive and artistic friends, but it was due to her that we all got fed, including the poets and anarchists, and anyone else who happened to be around. I remember someone saying to me back in the sixties that it was easy for my mother to be a bohemian because of her father's money. But she had the spirit to break free from that world of privilege. I'm not sure if my father would have been such a radical if he had been born a Krupp and not an Aaronson."

After the war Aaronson returned to Oxford disillusioned, and on the condition that he did no research but just taught. "Intellectually, we had a good idea what the bomb would do, but I was crushed when I saw the result. There was no need to drop the second bomb, the one on Nagasaki. One bomb was enough to convince the Japanese they were defeated, the second was nothing less than a war crime." Back in Europe the call of intellectual and artistic Bohemia was strong. After a bout of depression and heavy drinking he began frequenting the Musique Concrète Studio in Paris, where he met Karlheinz Stockhausen and Pierre Boulez. The following year he resigned his teaching post and moved to Cologne where Herbert Eimert had opened an electronic music studio. Aaronson quickly established himself as a leading composer of electronic and "sampled" music, although it was not until a decade later that his work was broadcast in his home country by the BBC Third Programme. In 1964 Aaronson was invited by Richard Demarco to lecture on, and host performances of, his work at the Edinburgh Festival. Exhausted after a frantic season of organising events and exhibitions, Demarco planned a "battery-charging" visit to the most important Neolithic sites in Orkney and the West Highlands and invited Aaronson to join him. At Calltain the pair found that some of the recently deserted crofts had been occupied by a hippy colony. Aaronson became a regular visitor to Calltain throughout the sixties, a period that saw the place evolve from a loose commune of itinerant dropouts into a stable community of artists, craftsmen, and organic smallholders. In 1972 Margaret Aaronson died and her son used what remained of the family fortune to buy and enlarge the croft house he had been squatting in each summer. His mother's money gave him the artistic freedom to experiment musically and to involve himself in pacifist and environmental issues.

Aaronson's musical direction changed around about the time he moved permanently to Calltain. From then on he began to incorporate sounds from nature – wind, the sea and animals – into his work, building up rich and complex soundscapes with them. He also began to experiment with primitive instruments and chanting. "The more primitive the better, skin drums, reed flutes, that sort of thing. At first I was using some sampled African chanting, but it worried me that although I myself didn't understand the language of the chant, it did have a linguistic significance to someone somewhere on the planet. I wanted to make music for the human voice, but for it to come from somewhere beyond, or before, language, so I started writing my own chants, phonetic sounds that carried no meaning other than what they were. I recorded them here at Calltain using the people around me. We often have music here, usually rock or folk stuff, so there's a tradition of the community getting together to make or listen to music. I've tapped into that in the same way that I've tapped into the sound millions of pebbles make when the surf drags them up and down the shore, or the cries of the oystercatchers that wake me up every morning."

I asked him if he saw a distinction between science and art or if they both came from the same creative core. "Who knows where they come from, but I suppose they may do. As a trained scientist, what first attracted me to the art of electro-acoustics was scientific curiosity. I could hear that it worked on an emotional and intellectual level, and I wanted to unravel it and understand what it was that made it work. I've never succeeded in that, but in music I've found great beauty, wonder and meaning in a world full of cruelty and suffering. If we as a species can make art, I believe that we also have the capacity to make the world anew."

In 1992 Aaronson was widely accused of sensationalism and political posturing for contributing a piece of music with an obscene title to an album compiled by rock musicians in support of anti-whaling charities.

"I've no problem with mixing art and politics. If a spirit of creation is what drives you, how can you do anything but stand up against wanton destruction? Artists have even more responsibility than most to speak out about cruelty. Every life is fragile, society is fragile, and so is life on our planet. I was always a foot soldier in the peace movement. I never became an organiser, but I marched a lot, signed petitions and made donations when I could. Lots of people knew that I'd worked with Oppie. I never tried to hide the fact. We are all the result of what we have been in the past. I don't speak on platforms or write to *The Times*, because words are not the medium I best express myself in. A lot of my thought is non-verbal. I have to look for a language of sounds to express what I feel. I've been arrested a few times for sitting on my arse at demonstrations, but nothing that I've ever done politically comes near to expressing my feelings in the way that my music does. I believe that making art matters, and that it is art that can heal the world. People have grown disenchanted because there is no dream, no vision. It's the artist's job to dream a better world into existence." He laughed loudly. "I realise that whatever you write will make me sound like the Easter Bunny. If your readers really want to know what I think, get them to listen to the *Gaia Symphony*, it's all in there, all the product of the Utopian gene."

He broke off from his tirade into sudden hearty laughter. I must have looked puzzled, for he struggled to control himself and told me, "I visited my mother in London shortly before she died in '72 ... she was nearly 80, younger than I am now, but she was quite frail. She asked me who this Bob Dylan was that she kept hearing about, so I went and bought an album and played it to her. She'd never listened to anything like that in her life before, but she really loved Dylan's *Masters of War*. She was quite ill by that time, but still as sharp as a tack. Halfway through the song she began to laugh. I was really worried because I thought she was losing her marbles. Then she turned to me and said: "Oh dear, Campbell! Your Grandfather would have been very disappointed in us!" And then she laughed again. Of all the sounds in the world, the most beautiful I ever heard was my mother laughing at that moment."

Calltain: The Second Visit

She phoned him a week after they met. Seven days. Not too soon, not too late, according to dating etiquette. Not showing any urgency on her part, although he had been waiting in unaccustomed anticipation. Her call came two days after his article about Aaronson had been published. He'd hoped she might have been in touch the following day, but she had waited two. She'd liked his article, she said. Aaronson had too – largely. The old man had written to him. Had he got the letter yet? He hadn't.

As Grizzel spoke, he tried to imagine her as he first saw her, striding towards him on the pier at Calltain with her coat-tails billowing behind her and her hair crazy in the wind. He found himself not just listening to her words, but tuning into the very sound of her voice, as if attempting to discover something about her by sifting through the layers of accent, influence and inflection. Her voice was low and there was a strain of transatlantic twang and a scattering of "yeah" and "like", but underneath was the unmistakable tone of middle-class England that Scots call "pan loaf". It was not an accent that Armour would normally have found attractive.

She was much more friendly on the phone than she had been when they'd met, but he knew she was only calling because it was payback time. That was OK by him. He thought she was sexy, interesting, and almost certainly the only way he had of getting to Caleb Burgess. He intended honouring the deal they'd made, and had already sold the idea of an article about Argo Aggregates and the threat it posed to the Calltain artists' colony to the paper's features editor, his friend Harry Urquhart. He had also decided to write about Burgess at greater length in his occasional column for *art*WORK. It was a cheaply printed but well-informed culture magazine. It didn't pay a lot, but it did let him do in-depth stories that *The Herald* didn't have the space for, and writing for it upped his profile in the arts community.

He had done his homework, reading the old cuttings about Burgess's last big exhibition and picking the brains of Rob, the Environmental Correspondent, about Josh Argo and his aggregates business. He'd been busy all week, filing at least an article a day as well as gathering material for his Saturday column. Apart from the piece he wrote about Aaronson, none of the stories he had covered seemed to mean much, and he found himself thinking about Grizzel a lot. It occurred to him that she'd been pulling his leg about being an astrophysicist. After all, a girl who shacked up with an old man nearly three times her age was obviously a weirdo.

She was chatty on the phone, as if she'd known him a while. He was to go to Calltain on Saturday and stay overnight. There would be a bed for him somewhere, and she'd feed him. Burgess didn't remember the piece he had written about his exhibition back in '79, but it had been a long time ago, so why should he? Yes, he was willing to talk, but Armour wasn't to bring a photographer or a camera. Caleb might eventually agree to some work being photographed, but only when he knew Armour wasn't – she put on a full-blooded American accent to tell him – a complete asshole. She'd show him around. He'd meet some of the poets and potters, eat organic and see the windmills. Matt Tyler would be waiting at the pier.

And so he was. Two days after Grizzel had phoned, Armour took the train north to Vallaig and once more made the ninety seconds' walk – Allegro! – along the pier to where Matt Tyler's boat lay moored. Armour was to see a lot of Matt Tyler that weekend, because it was Tyler, not Grizzel, who was to be his guide to Calltain. It was Tyler who had been delegated to take him to meet Caleb Burgess, introduce him to the poets and potters, and show him the miracles of organic vegetable plots, windmills and composting toilets.

Armour would have sworn that Tyler was grinning with pleasure when he announced that Grizzel's professor had summoned her back to Oxford. He had taken an instinctive and irrational dislike to the boatman on their previous meetings, but the next twenty-four hours would give him the time and space to develop a proper, well-considered and deep animosity to the man.

"Wind's getting up," Tyler stated, more to himself than to his passenger, as he headed the *Ran* for Calltain.

After the two men had disembarked and walked swiftly and in silence for an hour, Tyler delivered Armour to Kilmailin and the end of the path leading to the now purple heather-covered mound beneath which lay Burgess's studio.

"Ah have to get tae the lobsters now. Be at the pier at six and I'll take you somewhere to eat. You'll be crashing at my place by the way." With that Tyler turned to go. Armour resisted the temptation to mutter some bland polite "thank you" and stood watching him trudge back up the hill. "Dour bastard," he muttered. The prospect of staying overnight with Tyler further disheartened him. He was already suffering. He was, after all, almost fifty, clearly a decade or more older than Tyler and a lot less fit. It must have been obvious to the boatman that he had been struggling as they climbed up the hill to the *bealach*, yet the man had never slackened his pace.

Armour stood for a minute or two as if to catch his breath, while really trying to focus his mind. He longed to meet and interview Caleb Burgess, but he was still floundering about in the backwash of disappointment at not seeing Grizzel. The edge of anticipation and excitement that he always felt before a major interview had somehow been blunted. At last, he turned to walk down the avenue between the standing stones that led to Burgess's subterranean home, and found himself doing it self-consciously, like a talentless actor, out of his depth even in some low-budget horror movie. A pebble path curved round the green mound to the shore side. He tried to remember his schoolboy geography. Hillock? Drumlin? Moraine? Perhaps it was the burial chamber of some Bronze Age chieftain. His feet scrunched on the shingle as he made his way round. In front of the mound was the half-moon shaped terrace that he'd seen from the ruined chapel. Where the flank of the living hillside had been cut away, a semicircle of floor-to-ceiling plate glass windows faced out to sea. Behind the reflections of surf and sky lay a large oval room.

A small stone chimney jutted out from the grass and heather that blanketed the earth roof. A workbench built of old railway sleepers lay outside on the terrace amongst piles of rocks. On it was a rough grey slab of what looked like slate. The surface of the stone had been carved with circular dents a couple of inches across, and groups of shallow concentric circles. He knew the carving was recent, because there were smears of dust on the slab's surface, tiny chippings of rock that had been brushed aside by the hand or sleeve of the carver. Armour recognised the design at once. These were modern versions of cup and ring markings made by Neolithic and Early Bronze Age people about five thousand years ago, copies of the ancient ones Aaronson had shown him at Kilmailin Chapel only a few hundred yards away.

Of the sculptor, there was no sign. Armour slung his old leather shoulder bag to the ground and took out his propelling pencil and notebook. He looked at the stone slab carefully for some minutes and jotted down a description of it. Then he turned to the house, seeking more details to note and use to evoke the scene in his article. He looked carefully around, in case somebody was watching, before pressing his nose to a window. Behind the glass was a large area that appeared to be a combined living room, kitchen and artist's studio. Three doors led off the space, presumably leading to bedrooms and a bathroom that had been carved deeper into the hill. He realised at that moment that he needed to piss. The north wind, invigorating when he crossed Loch Vallaig in the stern of the *Ran*, was now achingly cold. The chill had crept up on him, stealthily overtaking his city-slack body before he was conscious of it. He thrust stiff frozen fingers into his pockets and stamped up and down, his temper beginning to fray, although his watch told him he was still a few minutes early for the appointment Grizzel had made for him. He still tasted the sharp tang of disappointment that he'd experienced when she'd failed to meet him. It's ridiculous to feel that, said the part of his mind that usually dealt efficiently with practical aspects of the external world. He was, after all, a reasonably well-respected arts correspondent on an assignment to interview an important sculptor. It was Caleb Burgess who interested him, not some skinny geriatric-shagging stargazer! If an old crock like Aaronson can have her, why can't I? replied the primitive in him. Jonathon Armour, his id and his ego, sheltered from the wind where best they could.

After he had been there half an hour, a movement on the rocky coast beyond Kilmailin beach caught his eye. He watched a tiny figure grow closer. The man, for he could see clearly now that it was a man, was making his way towards the house. Caleb Burgess was smaller than he expected but broad-shouldered and fit-looking. Armour knew the artist was fifty-seven, not that much older than himself, but he moved with ease and grace over the rough coastline. Burgess raised an arm in salutation. Armour waved back. He saw how the man's head moved constantly from side to side and up and down, as if scrutinising the landscape as he passed through it. He looked, Armour thought, comical, a bit like the nodding dogs people once used to have in the back windows of their cars. Burgess broke into a trot when he reached the sandy beach, and then ran up the thirty or forty rough stone steps that led to his house. Armour watched enviously. He knew he would have been left panting if he'd sprinted up these steps, but Burgess was unflustered. His lively darting eyes seemed over-large for his head, giving him a permanently surprised look, as if he constantly saw all creation anew. His face, partly covered by a stubbly grey beard, was weather-beaten and chapped, with prominent veins where the flesh was thin, and deep wrinkles round his eyes. Armour thought that he had an old man's head grafted onto a youth's body. The hands too were old; dark and gnarled like tree roots, or those of an ancient bog man preserved for centuries in the peat. A woollen knitted hat hid the fact that his hair, once long and dark and worn in a ponytail tied with a black bow, was now receding, grey and severely cropped. The artist regarded Armour momentarily, his restless eyes taking in everything they could about him. His deep voice, although clearly American, was no drawl, but clipped and urgent.

"You look frozen, man! You should have gone inside. It's not locked, you're in Calltain now."

The Pink Telephone Box (1)

Matt Tyler scowled as he watched squalls scarify the dark waters of the loch. The wind had strengthened, as he knew it would, and unless he sailed soon he'd be stranded overnight in the town. He stood waiting by the public telephone box, one of the traditional red ones that were rare these days. Most had been replaced by glass and moulded plastic efforts that looked like shower units in cheap chain hotels. This old box on Vallaig pier had been left because it afforded better shelter from the elements, or perhaps because it looked picturesque. The salt sea spray had bleached it a dirty pink, but at least nobody had pissed in it recently.

Within a few seconds of the appointed time, the phone rang, as he knew it would. She was, in his words, rock-steady. He stepped in and let the heavy door swing behind him before picking up the receiver.

"Hey Grizzly! How you daein babe?"

The caller had evidently no time for banter.

"Aye, it's cool. He arrived OK and ah've dumped him at Caleb's place. He's with him now."

He snorted some sort of laugh into the mouthpiece.

"Pretty badly. Really pissed off just to see me, but he'll live. You've made a click there."

The wind gusted. He had to listen carefully.

"Roger, heartbreaker, I'll call you as soon as he's gone ... nae problem ... I'll be here when you call. Don't worry Grizz, it's going just fine. Ah'm heading back to Calltain right now, before the weather turns really shite, and coz I don't want to keep ma new pal waiting now, do I?" He listened intently again for a few moments, his thin upper lip forming what stood for a smile. "Aye, you take care too. Over and out, babes."

The Hazel Wood

The boatman had not long tied up at the jetty and was loading lobster creels onto the deck of the *Ran* when Armour returned from Burgess's Hobbit house. The journalist looked at the spume-whipped sea and was almost glad he wasn't sailing that afternoon, even if he had to stay overnight with Tyler. After a fascinating afternoon with a man he believed to be uniquely gifted, he had experienced mild euphoria as he had hiked back over the Calltain ridge to the jetty. It had been the kind of day he'd imagined having when he was at university thirty years before, in the time he first dreamed about being a writer and critic, and at least the friend and confidant of great artists even if he couldn't be one himself. He'd seen little of Burgess's recent work, but the artist had spoken slyly of being in the midst of a major project. Armour had asked him directly for an exclusive preview, but the artist had been evasive although, Armour noted, not entirely dismissive. Burgess had spoken with conviction about why he'd dropped out of the visible art world of public exhibitions and critical scrutiny to work in obscurity, and of his own dark vision of where the rest of society was heading. In Armour's notebook there now lay the substance of a two-thousand-word essay he planned to write for *art*WORK.

As soon as he saw Tyler, the journalist's spirits sank. He'd hoped to spend the evening with Aaronson and Grizzel, but now he was in the hands of this surly specimen. To make matters worse, Tyler was now rubbing coarse salt into a half-full bucket of bloody fish heads. Armour thought fast.

"It's still light. If you were heading over to Vallaig I could come with you. It would save you having to put me up."

"Too late", said Tyler sharply. "Grizzel has fixed it for you to eat at Doug's. He's one of the local poets yer so keen to meet. Anyway, Campbell is expecting to see you tomorrow."

"What are the fish heads for?" Armour could think of nothing else to say.

"Bait. Salt them and they last longer in the creels. Got to get the bait right if you want lobsters. Look man, I'm fuckin busy. Why don't you put your feet up. That's ma place," he gestured to the shore-side cottages. "The green door ... it's nae locked ...just go in and turn right."

Tyler's place was in the middle of the row. It was an old, single-storey stone cottage that stood by the road opposite the jetty. It had a pitch tar roof, a squat wooden door and two small windows that gazed south onto the loch. It was like thousands of other little homes built in the Highlands in the nineteenth century for boatmen, gamekeepers and farm servants, except that this one had grown a small wind turbine and two solar panels on its roof. The door was closed, but unlocked. Armour pushed through into a tiny hall. Opposite him was an open bathroom door and next to it a doorless cupboard, a glory-hole of waterproofs, rubber boots, a tangle of ropes and bits of boats that looked like flotsam. The corridor to the left led to Tyler's room. Armour could see a dishevelled double bed. He turned right into the kitchen. It was clean enough, if Spartan. A couch had been made up as a bed. There was a tiny two-ring gas cooker, a table and two chairs. Armour slung his bag in a corner and went to the window, from where he could see Tyler bent over his creels on the deck of the *Ran.* He watched, weighing his dislike of the man against the obvious respect the community bestowed on him. An array of shells and twisted fragments of driftwood lay arranged on the deep window ledge. Armour turned to explore the place. Apart from the beach art, a Greenpeace poster of a leaping whale, and another with the caption "You Live Here" beneath a picture of the blue earth suspended in space, were the only concessions to decoration. Tyler had a wind-up radio, and some neatly made bookshelves built of odd planks of driftwood. On them, arranged higgledy-piggledy, were a couple of ragged Land Rover maintenance guides, some broken-backed electrical text books, a book about wrecks off the Scottish coast, and the modern paperbacks of someone who had come to reading late for anything other than practical instruction. There was a smattering of Tolkien and Herman Hesse, *Small is Beautiful* and *Zen and The Art of Motorcycle Maintenance.* Old hippy stuff. Armour was tempted to pry into the bedroom, but when he glanced out the window Tyler was stepping onto the jetty. The journalist was sitting on the couch writing in his notebook when the boatman came home.

That night the two men ate with a couple Grizzel had suggested that Armour interview. They were what Armour might once have called “hand knitted”, very earnest and New Age, but it was a relief to be in the company of anyone other than just the boorish Tyler. They were a middle-aged couple that anywhere else might have settled for early retiral to the golf club. Instead, they were trying to save the world. Doug Fowlie and his partner Ruth Sullivan lived in an A-framed timber building that they'd shipped in kit form over from the mainland and erected themselves on the grounds of an old croft, close to the shore. Over a meal, comprised of the very first of autumn's wild mushrooms and what Doug called “Ruth's farting lentil patties”, the couple told Armour something of themselves. They'd met while visiting a tiny folk festival on Calltain fourteen years previously, stayed, and stayed together. For Doug it was what he saw as the final stage of a lifelong journey that had taken him as far as Goa, Mexico and Alaska. He was a university law-degree dropout, a veteran of the early seventies hippy trail, and had survived the associated chemical abuses well enough to emerge as a lean, vegetarian, small-scale commercial herb gardener, and occasionally published poet. Ruth was a working-class Geordie, who'd been knocked around by an abusive husband. She spoke of her grown-up kids on the mainland and wished they'd visit her more often. Armour commiserated with her, and for a few moments they together lamented living in an age when kids didn't have time to keep in touch, although Armour told her he had no children of his own. Ruth doted on Beastie, the couple's mongrel dog which they had rescued from a pound and which fled from the room when Armour tried to pat him.

“We call him Beastie because he's such a timorous beastie until you get to know him,” said Doug. “The puir cratur must have been terrible abused.”

Armour thought Ruth and Doug were an eccentrically likeable couple, who scraped by mostly on what they grew, their love for the scenery around them and the companionship they shared. What really surprised Armour was how the graceless Tyler relaxed in their company. He didn't say much, but listened to the conversation, supping his beer steadily. In between stories, the loquacious Doug would command him from the top of the table, "Son, nip out to the shed and bring in a couple more home brews," and Tyler would do it cheerfully as Doug launched into another of his tales. "Trooper's turned out a good lad," Doug told Armour, "He was a bit of an alcho-hooligan when he first came here, but Ruth and I could never have built this place without him." Armour dutifully wrote down a couple of usable quotes of Doug's about the plan for the super-quarry. He'd listened to the same arguments from Aaronson and Burgess before, but it was good for his article to hear them expressed in the voice of someone who was a down-to-earth native Scot, not an intellectual Anglo or American incomer.

Doug talked of writing a history of the Calltain clearances and had tracked down and interviewed some of the old Gaelic speakers who had once lived there.

"I met a man who was born on this croft," he said, his eyes shining with the pleasure of drinking beer and telling a well-loved story. "The house is a ruin now, about half a mile up the hill, but we still use the old enclosure as our vegetable garden ... anyway, he told me that after a storm one winter his grandfather found a wooden barrel washed up on the shore. It had writing on it, but he couldn't read it because it was in Dutch ... however, he jaloused that it was a liquor barrel and, as it was full, he rolled it away to a hiding place among the rocks. That evening he went back to the hiding place with an awl and a bucket and bored a hole in the barrel. And what was in it? Pure Jenever ... Dutch gin! Well, all that winter he'd draw a pail of gin from the barrel every few days and entertain his friends in the evenings. They would ask him, "Where did you get the gin from?" but he never told them. Anyway, it was a very jolly winter, with him and all his neighbours contentedly pissed. Well, all good things come to an end and one day the old crofter went back to the barrel and nothing came out! He tipped it onto its side and, although it didn't feel empty, still nothing came out of it. So, the old boy went back to his house, got a hatchet and bashed in the lid. And what do you think he found?" Eyebrows dramatically raised, Doug stared at each of them in turn, although two of the party had heard the story many times before. "A pickled orang-utan!"

Doug collapsed back in his chair with laughter, which they all joined in, Ruth winking at Tyler. "It was a bloody specimen going back to some zoological institute in the Netherlands from the Dutch East Indies ... and the old boy had been drinking the stuff all winter!"

The home-brewed beer slipped down fine and Armour began to realise that it was stronger than it tasted. Doug, increasingly high on his own supply, became more garrulous, denouncing the planet's environmental ills in scraps of his own verse, recited from memory.

"I like that, Doug," said Armour in response to a few lines, turning in his chair to dig in his jacket pocket and extract his notebook. "Could you give me it again? If it was OK with you I might be able to use it in my article."

Doug rose and moved on unsteady feet to a chaotic and over-stuffed bookcase which he regarded short-sightedly. At last he reached forward and drew out a volume which he handed to Ruth, gesturing that she should pass it to their guest.

"Don't have my specs on. You'll find the poem in there. It's yours to keep, compliments of the house."

The volume was a slim but high quality paperback, its covers of thick black-green card the colour of seaweed and the texture of parchment. It felt good to hold. On the front, in gold lettering, was a single word in capital letters, WOLFSTAR.

"Thank you very much ... it's beautiful. You must let me pay ..."

"Bollocks! It's a gift. Write something bloody positive about Calltain and I'll be more than well paid."

Armour could feel all eyes on him as he turned over the front cover. The book's title was repeated on the frontispiece, but below it, somewhere about the middle of the page, were the words: *Thirteen Poems by Doug Fowlie*. At the foot of the page was embossed a curious swirl of a logo he vaguely recognised, and then he read the words below: Calltain Publishing Unlimited. He leafed though the rough-edged pages of thick, off-white and fibrous paper. Doug seemed to specialise in poems with many lines, but with very few words per line. Each of the long thin verses straggled over three or four pages, and the publisher had contrived to lay out the volume in such a way that the thirteen poems, along with a dedication to Ruth, an introduction written by Campbell Aaronson, an index and acknowledgements, more or less filled sixty pages. It was a slim but beautifully produced volume.

"Quality thought on quality paper," he remembered aloud.

Doug and Ruth cheered together.

"So you've met Trail then?"

"No, I'm sorry Doug, I haven't, but Campbell mentioned something about him. Isn't he the guy with the upturned boat for a house?"

"Yeah. He and Andy built it three years ago. The hull is a decommissioned fishing boat. Matt towed it with the *Ran* over here from Oban. It was a right bugger getting ashore. Well anyway, they got their place built and installed this old-fashioned printing press, and now they've published more than a dozen books. Trail's a poet and he wanted to control every aspect of his work, so he taught himself bookbinding and went to Japan to learn about paper making. The cover of my book is made from seaweed collected on the shore here."

"Campbell and MacDonald, eh?" Tyler had suddenly become noisy and animated. "Tell the reporter about that, Doug! He thinks he knows everyfuckinthing."

"What Matt's saying is that Trail's name is Trail MacDonald and his partner is Andy Campbell."

"Massacre of Glencoe!" Tyler shouted. "Now they're fuckin bum chums, eh? Is that right Doug?"

"That's right Trooper, they're a gay couple."

"That's hunky dory wi' me. Ah've got fuck all problems with that. Folks can shag whoever they like as far as ah'm concerned."

Armour had no wish to follow where the conversation was leading and kept his eyes on the pages before him. It was clear to him that Doug was no Seamus Heaney, but from a quick perusal Armour could see that the man was a minor nature poet who could coin a few neat lines and got steamed up over the environment. He found the poem that Doug had recited. It ended:

> And the old world turns.
> Turns a little madder,

Turns a little hotter,
Turns a little sadder.

"Doug, I really like these lines. Would you mind if I used them in an article?"

"No problem, that's fine with me."

"It's a beautiful book, and I'm very grateful for it. It's wonderful that something of such quality can be made in Calltain years after the place was abandoned."

"There's lots of good things happen here, Jon." Ruth had turned to smile at Doug as she spoke.

"I love this place," the poet said, wiping a dribble of beer with his sleeve. "There's no way Argo will be allowed to blow it to hell, no way."

"It's not just Calltain that's at stake, Jon," interrupted Ruth. "Destroying this little place may not seem such a big deal compared with what else is going on in the world, but the knock-on effect of blowing up Calltain will be horrendous. They'll use the stuff they quarry here to build more and more motorways. That means burning more petrol ... more pollution, more ... global warming ... that sort of thing." She tried to laugh, but tiny tears were forming like crystals in her eyes. She wiped them with the back of her hand. "If only Grizzel was here, 'cos I'm completely clueless about the science! She could quote you all the figures. But I do know that by fighting for Calltain we're fighting against all that stuff. People have got to learn that the motor car doesn't mean freedom, it means the destruction of the planet. And in any case ... this is our home. We've got nowhere else."

Armour was drunkenly moved by the sentiment, but couldn't think of anything comforting to say to her. He reached out and patted the back of her rough, tear-stained hand.

Tyler broke his silence. "What the fuck do you drive?" Armour turned to face his glare. The boatman had evidently crossed the line from the benign to the belligerent side of drunkenness.

"Me? I don't have a car. I don't drive."

Tyler grinned viscously. "Pished were you? Done for drunk driving?"

"No, I never lost my licence. I still have one, it's just that I don't drive."

"Why the hell not?"

"I just ... don't like driving ... anyway, I don't really need to."

"That's weird, man."

"Just call it carbon neutral."

"Shite!"

"Come on Tyler, you just don't like it that I'm greener than you are. I don't even have a boat."

"Fuck off."

"Oh come on Matt," laughed Ruth, "it's great that Jon doesn't drive." She turned to Armour, defusing the situation. "Good for you, Jon. Do you just use public transport?"

"Yes ... mostly. I must admit to a bit of a late-night taxi habit back in Glasgow, but usually I walk to fight the flab. I live in the centre of town, near the office, so it's easy. If I'm going any distance the train suits me fine. I can read and even write on the train."

"Hey man, you're one of us!" shouted Doug, unscrewing the cap of another bottle. "Let's drink to the victory of enlightened and informed citizenry!"

They drank Doug's strong beer till after midnight, when Armour and Tyler bid elaborate and rambling goodbyes.

"It's just a pity Grizzel wasn't here," said Ruth, "she's so smart, she could tell you lots."

"Nonsense," cut in Doug, throwing an arm round her shoulders. "Jon's bloody lucky Grizz isn't here. He'd have had to eat at Campbell's, and Grizzel is a rubbish cook. Not like you, Ruthie darling!" He kissed her cheek drunkenly, and the pair stood on the stone step shouting cheerios into the night as their two guests began their unsteady hike back to Tyler's cottage by moon and starlight. The home-brewed alcohol had loosened the boatman's tongue and inhibitions, and he wanted to talk, distracting Armour from his thoughts of the absent Grizzel.

"See that notebook of yours. You get it out now and I'll give ye a fuckin quote for your fuckin paper." Armour did as he was told. "See that mountain," Tyler waved drunkenly towards the humpback on the starry horizon that was Calltain's rocky spine, "it's millions of years old man, fuckin millions. I don't know how many millions. I'm no a geologist, but I know all about the sea. I've been hit by storms out on the loch there, so I know what it's like. I know about the power of it, man!"

Armour was losing patience. "Yes I'm sure it's very dangerous sometimes, but if you're going to give me something to write about it'll have to be about the super-quarry."

"I know fine why you're here. Grizzel told me all about you. But you're no listenin to me, I'm just the stupit fuckin boatman."

"I'm sorry Tyler, what was the point you were making?"

"It's this!" Tyler began pounding the palm of his open left hand with his right fist. "The sea has been fuckin smashing against these rocks here for millions of years. Millions! And what do you see? Calltain!" Tyler began to prance about theatrically, his hand held up to his forehead as if shielding his eyes from the sun while staring out to sea. "Calltain! It's still fucking here after being battered for millions of years. The sea has nae smashed it. And it's no going to be smashed by some capitalist scum like Argo. It's him that'll be smashed. The rocks of Calltain will smash him too ... I'll fuckin smash him! Stupit fucking boatman? Ah tell you pal, ah've killed men ... two fuckin grenades down the hatch ... nae bastard survives that. I'll smash that bastard Argo too! Scotland forever!"

Tyler took a wild swipe at the night air, lost his balance, teetered for a second and crashed into Armour, who instinctively flung up his hands to ward off the careering man. His notebook went flying while the tip of his metal propelling pencil caught Tyler under the left eye. There was a scream of pain. Armour stepped back.

"I'm sorry, I didn't mean ..."

"Bastard!"

Tyler's attack was furious. Lashing out with both fists he sent Armour reeling backwards. Armour grabbed at the front of Tyler's jacket but only pulled the flailing screaming man down on top of him as he collapsed heavily on the ground. He tried to roll the man off him but the boatman brought his knees up to Armour's chest so that he now straddled him. He grabbed at Armour's face, clutching him by the chin and began pounding his face with his clenched right fist. Armour tried to fend off the blows. He managed to grab Tyler's wrist with one, then both hands, but to no avail: the man used his vice grip on Armour's chin to pound his head on the ground. Armour shook his head in a violent spasm and for an instant his mouth connected with a knuckle on Tyler's forefinger. He bit down hard. Tyler roared, trying to wrench his hand away, but Armour, his mouth filling with blood, held on grimly. Tyler flung himself to one side, breaking Armour's bite but sprawling face down on the ground. Both men struggled to their feet at the same time. Tyler was younger, tougher, and used to physical labour, but he was smaller and he was drunker. He ran at Armour, fist flailing. This time the attack was expected and Armour's weight, reach and instinct for self-preservation told. He took a few wild blows but landed two powerful punches, one on Tyler's throat. It sent the man flying back wheezing and retching, but still standing, and raging. Armour pressed home, landing a kick on Tyler's ankle. Tyler lunged again, not punching but grabbing the heavier man in both arms as if to wrestle him down, all the time attempting to knee him in the testicles. They grappled like angry bears. Tyler landed a head-butt on Armour's mouth, splitting his upper lip, and Armour stamped down heavily on the bridge of Tyler's plimsoll- clad foot, and the man howled in pain. Armour could feel his left eye closing. It had taken several of Tyler's blows. His mouth was bleeding heavily. He knew he was just about holding his own, but he was tiring and the younger man's strength and fury were beginning to wear him down. He sensed that Tyler was an experienced brawler, and he knew that he was now fighting to survive. If he went down again, the enraged Tyler might beat and kick him to death. The brute lunged a head-butt at his face again and a blinding light caught Armour's good eye. For a fleeting moment he thought he'd been struck hard and was losing consciousness. Then he heard a voice, not the roaring and cursing of Tyler, but the urgent and anxious voice of the torch- bearing Doug Fowlie. Doug plunged in between them, straining to force them apart. Ruth was shouting in the background for them to stop. The timorous beastie was barking like a dog demented.

"The bastard stabbed me."

Armour now pushed Tyler with all his strength and Doug finally thrust them apart.

"For Christ's sake, what the hell are you bampots doing?"

"The cunt stabbed me."

"I didn't. The bloody idiot stumbled into me ... my pencil caught his eye."

Doug shone his torch directly into Armour's face, causing him to wince and cover his eyes with his hands. Doug roughly gripped a wrist, pulling it away from Armour's face.

"Christ, you're a mess." He turned to shout: "Ruthie, how's Trooper?"

Ruth was calming Tyler, holding both his forearms and talking soothingly. When he'd stopped struggling she took the torch and examined his face.

"Bloody nose and a nasty scratch below the eye, but he'll live."

"Hold on to the torch and take him home, Ruth, I'll deal with this one." He put his hand on Armour's shoulder. "You'd best come with me. We can't have you and Tyler killing each other. We'll have to attend to that eye."

In the morning, the bathroom mirror revealed the damage. Red, raw swelling had half-closed his left eye, and the puffy flesh around it was blue. Overnight his split lip had bled onto the pillow of the makeshift bed. He dabbed at the caked wound gently with a piece of toilet tissue dampened under the cold tap. The bleeding had stopped, but his mouth was swollen and his front teeth ached.

Doug made him instant coffee which he sipped with difficulty. Beastie gave him an even wider berth than he had done the previous evening. Ruth returned from visiting Tyler, and reported that she had changed the bandage she'd applied to his finger the night before. She was carrying Armour's overnight bag.

"Nothing wrong with your teeth, Jon, you gave him a good deep bite."

"He's lucky to still have teeth," Doug said. "His mouth took a bit of a battering."

"I brought your bag from Matt's place. Didn't think you'd fancy dropping in for it. Oh ... and I found your notebook and pencil on the path ... and this." From inside her jacket she pulled the copy of WOLFSTAR. Armour felt ashamed that he'd treated something obviously precious to her, something that celebrated the good life she had found there, so shoddily. He murmured thanks.

"Just as well it didn't rain last night," she said brightly. "By the way, he'll be going over to Vallaig at two thirty. He's expecting you to be on the boat." She smiled. "Don't worry, I've spoken to him. He'll be fine."

Armour didn't want to admit that he had actually been thinking of hiking the miles of rough path that hairpinned round the loch shore to get back to Vallaig. He certainly didn't relish seeing Tyler again, but if he took the ferry he'd have time to spend with Aaronson. He pocketed the notebook and propelling pencil and carefully tucked Doug's book of poems into his bag.

"Thanks, Ruth. I'll be on it. By the way, sorry about the pillow."

"Sobby abboub thib pbillob," imitated Doug. Armour winced as his mouth tried to form a grin.

Even wearing fresh clothes he felt shoddy, disreputable, hung-over, distinctly ill-used and seedy. He thought that a walk might do him good and stepped out into a cold but radiant autumn morning. The air was as sharp and chill as a nip of good Finnish vodka. The sky was as cloudless as it had been starry the night before and the morning light danced on the wind-whipped loch. From the doorstep he could see the jetty and the row of cottages where Tyler lived. There was no sign of life there yet, but rather than pass the place, and ruin his improving mood, Armour turned eastward on the track that would eventually take a hardy walker to the head of the sea loch and then round to Vallaig. He strolled for half an hour and, feeling better, turned and sat himself on a sea-smoothed rock to look back towards Doug and Ruth's A-frame. A wisp of peat smoke now curled from its blackened steel chimney before being whipped away by the breeze. He liked the couple. He'd found the man genuine, decent, even impressive, and his woman bright and caring. He sensed that they had led troubled lives, and had at last found some sort of contentment here. Calltain was, for them, what Grizzel had promised him, a peaceful place. Grizzel Gillespie. She kept slipping, without invitation, into his mind. One moment he was thinking about something quite different, and then suddenly, there she was, banishing every other thought and memory. He imagined her now, dressed as he'd first seen her in a long waxed coat, her hair tossed by the wind, striding down the jetty, coming towards him. With a jolt he remembered his appointment with Aaronson, and glanced to check the time. His wrist was bare. He must have left his watch at Doug and Ruth's. He didn't want to burst in on Aaronson too early on a Sunday morning, yet did want to spend some time with him before Tyler took him back to the mainland. He brooded on how to explain his mangled face to the old man. Not knowing what time it was made him uneasy and he began to make his way back.

Approaching him was a distant figure on the path. For a fleeting moment he thought it was Grizzel, just as he'd imagined her only minutes before, but as the walker came close, Armour recognised Doug. Minutes later the poet greeted him by cheerfully asking if he'd yet experienced the inevitable consequences of Ruth's famous lentil patties. Beastie kept a wary distance, but followed on when Doug turned to accompany Armour back along the track. From near the poet's house they could see the distant figure of Tyler moving about the stern of the *Ran*.

"We'd be stuck without Matt. He's a genius at keeping that old engine going. He was a real find."

"How did he get here?" And Tyler's story unfolded.

Matt Tyler had grown up feral on a city housing estate known for high unemployment, a higher crime rate and very low regard for society and the property of the middle classes. The teenager had fallen foul of the law for car theft and shoplifting, then graduated into housebreaking and dealing in pills and hash. Inevitably, he'd ended up in a young offenders' institution, but on his release tried to break free of his past by going on the road. He'd been hitchhiking somewhere in the Highlands when he encountered a stranded Campbell Aaronson. Aaronson's car had broken down on some lonely byway in Caithness, and Tyler had fixed it there and then. Aaronson had asked the young man where he was going and offered him a lift, and was taken aback when the youth told him that he wasn't heading anywhere in particular, but that as the weather was shite he'd be glad of a lift anyway. By then, Aaronson was in the process of moving to Calltain permanently and, recognising the youth's practical skills and can-do attitude, offered Tyler the job of converting his old blackhouse and building the round timber tower that was to be his studio and living area. Tyler used the money he earned from Aaronson to buy the old boat he renamed the *Ran* and started fishing for lobsters that he sold to a fish merchant in Vallaig. Somewhere along the line he'd become Calltain's ferryman. Tyler's ability to keep the *Ran's* old engine turning over showed him to be an instinctive mechanical genius and he began to build wind turbines and service the community's unreliable generators.

"When Ruthie and I started putting up the kit-house Matt came along to give us a hand," said Doug. "I'd studied the plans carefully and I thought that Matt could supply the brawn ... but the bugger ended up supplying the brains as well. We'd have been completely stuck without him." He looked at the house thoughtfully for a moment and then turned to Armour. "He was pretty feral when he first came here, a real lost boy. Campbell took him under his wing. I don't think he ever read a book until he met Campbell."

"Imagine if he'd had a different background and gone to university."

"Yeah, imagine. He'd probably be earning a fortune and living a miserable fucked-up life on the mainland."

"You might be right Doug, you might be right."

A sudden thought came to Armour. "Hang on, last night when he was raving on to me he said something about having killed men ... said he'd done it with a hand grenade. I take it he was just havering?"

Doug slowly shook his head. Armour could see that what he was about to say pained him. "Regrettably ... no."

The man looked up to face the journalist's puzzled stare. He shrugged, and went on: "Eleven or twelve years ago Matt took it into his head to join the army. He just packed his bags and vanished without telling anybody where he was going ... not even Campbell. Well, it turned out that he'd joined some tank regiment and a year or so later he was in the Gulf in time for Desert Storm."

"Scotland Forever," murmured Armour.

"What?"

"It's something that Tyler said ... it's the name of a famous painting of the Scots Greys charging at Waterloo. Their battle cry was "Scotland Forever". The regiment's still going, except now it has tanks and is called the Scots Dragoon Guards ... you know ... the lot whose pipe band had a Top Ten hit with *Amazing Grace* back in the early seventies."

"Aye well, whatever you call them they recognised his mechanical genius and soon had him driving tanks. Apparently his regiment came across a mass of enemy deserters in the desert, but there was this bloody big Iraqi tank in the middle of them ... sort of using them as a human shield. The British commander didn't want to fire on it 'cos they'd kill all these guys who were laying down their arms, so Matt saunters over to it and drops two bombs down the turret and blows it and its crew to buggery. Anyway, that's what he told me. Then after the war the regiment goes back to Germany where Matt fails a blood test and gets kicked out for taking cocaine. End of Trooper Tyler's distinguished military career. Next thing, he pitches up here again."

"So that's why people call him 'Trooper'."

"Yeah. It's kind of ironic ... this being an alternative community an' all that. We were just glad to get him back."

"Yes ... I can see that he's a useful guy to have around. Look Doug, I'd better get going, I have to see Aaronson soon."

He picked up his bag and his watch from the house, and somehow felt more comfortable and in control with the familiar face of the Swiss railway timepiece strapped to his wrist. He was sorry that Ruth wasn't around. Doug walked him as far as his garden gate.

"Thanks for last night, Doug. Sorry the evening turned into such a shambles. And thanks too to Ruth. I really enjoyed the food."

"Thank her yourself next time you're here." Doug turned with a wave and walked away. When he'd taken only a few steps he turned and grinned. "You'll be back. I can tell that. I told you last night that you were really one of us!"

Armour tramped along the coast. As he approached the jetty he could see Tyler working on his boat. He'd have to pass close to him, and he tried to look nonchalant and hold himself back from involuntarily quickening his pace. Tyler seemed engrossed, or at any rate made no acknowledgement of his presence. Armour turned up the hill towards Aaronson's tower house. The old man was in the garden, wrapped in his stockman's coat and a red tartan scarf against the wind, tugging saplings from plastic pots and piling them onto a wheelbarrow. He seemed absorbed in his work, examining each plant carefully before bending to select another. He was humming to himself, rather tunelessly for a composer, Armour thought.

Armour noisily scuffed some loose chippings with his boot before calling out to the old man, who straightened stiffly at the sound.

"Good morning and good timing, my young friend!" he boomed. "My old bones are beginning to seize up. If Matt's not taking you to the mainland till this afternoon, you've got time to give me a hand with these."

Armour felt the old man's eyes appraising the damage to his face.

"Matt Tyler and I ... eh ... got into a bit of a fight last night ... just a stupid misunderstanding ..."

"Yes, yes, I know. From what I hear, the propelling pencil, if not actually the pen, has proven to be mightier than the sword!"

How the hell did he know? The old man didn't say, and just smiled, as if faintly amused.

"To work, Armour, Allegro feroce!" He gestured extravagantly with his arm.

The job was to wrestle the wheelbarrow, laden with a dozen three-feet-tall saplings with muddy, heavy root balls, down to the loch side and along the rough footpath that followed the coast to the west. Aaronson shouldered a spade and walked ahead, occasionally stopping for the younger man to catch up. Going down the hill was easy, but pushing the barrow over the gnarled shore path was hard work, and Armour found himself having to use his stomach as well as his arms to drive it forward over rocks and tufts of heather. After about a mile they came to a small bay that bit deep into the coast. The land behind it rose gently and Armour could see from the contours of ancient run rigs that it had been cultivated in the past. This, announced Aaronson, was *Camas Challtain*, the Bay of Calltain, once home to a small community of Gaelic-speaking crofters, but now just a sheltered place for yachtsmen to anchor overnight. On the bracken-covered slopes were clumps of young trees, the beginning of Aaronson's hazel wood. The composer glowed with pleasure.

"Some of these are fifteen years old. They've already begun to regenerate themselves, but I grew every one of the first generation from seed in old yoghurt pots."

He strode ahead to a patch of blackened ground. Armour found it easier now to turn the wheelbarrow around and pull it over the bracken. By the time he'd caught up with the composer Aaronson already had the first hole dug.

"Ideally it's best to plant them in the spring in a windy place like this, and give them some time to develop a root system that'll withstand the winter storms." Aaronson had planted a sapling, filled the hole around it with soil, and was firming the ground around it with his boots. "But these are good strong plants and they'll be fine if we tread them down firmly enough." Armour dug the next hole. The earth was heavy and fibrous and the effort made him realise how remarkably fit the old man was. They took turns after that and in an hour had the dozen saplings planted.

"Why hazel? Why not ... oak, ash, Scots Pine ... whatever?"

"Linguistic archaeology, that's why, Armour. It's because this place Calltain is a corruption of the Gaelic word for hazel. There can't have been a hazel tree in these parts for centuries, but when Gaelic-speaking Celts first arrived here in about the sixth century the name they gave the place was ..." at this point Aaronson spoke slowly, enunciating each syllable "... *Camas nan Chaltain*, the bay of the hazel trees. Before I die it's going to live up to that name again. Did you know that hazel woods might even be the reason why Neolithic people first came here? Their middens show that they gathered the nuts, probably because they could store them over the winter. Hazel nuts were the wheat of the Stone Age. They may have made a gruel out of them, or even have baked them on a hot stone into some sort of bannock or biscuit."

The old man breathed deeply of the sharp salty breeze. He seemed to the town-bred Armour to inhale a joy and self-confidence from the wild coastline that made him appear half his age.

"When Demarco first brought me to the Highlands I thought the barren hills were untouched and beautiful. I thought that this was a natural landscape, but then I learned that the Scottish wilderness is man-made ... or rather man-unmade! You see, it was once densely wooded and teeming with all sorts of animals we've hounded to extinction ... beavers, lynx, wolves, bear and wild boar. Remember, Armour," he said, without a hint of irony in his top-drawer English accent, "I may be an old Jew, but I'm a true Argyll Campbell on my mother's side, and our crest is a wild boar. The old clansmen didn't pick their symbolism out of a picture book ... they took their tribal totems from the world around them.

"Where we're standing was once the most westerly fringe of a vast forest that stretched unbroken from Asia, right through Russia and Scandinavia. Today only fragments of it exist, but I've been giving it a hand here in Calltain. Every year I burn-off an area of bracken and plant more young native trees, in my small way helping the forest to come back. There must be five or six hundred hazels here now. I've put in a few birch and oak and rowan and Scots Pine for variety, but it was the preponderance of hazel that gave the place its name, so that's mostly what I plant. Listen to the wind in these trees! Forests are where humankind has done most of its evolving, so we instinctively feel at home in them ... not in cities my young friend, never in cities."

They stood quietly for a few moments listening to the breeze blustering amongst the saplings as they contemplated Aaronson's work. Armour calculated. The old man must have filled nearly a thousand recycled yoghurt cartons with home-made compost, watered and tended the seedlings for years and made ... what? ... a hundred such journeys with his barrow and spade? Aaronson seemed to sense the journalist's thoughts, and turned to fix him with a watery stare.

"I'm an old man now. I don't suppose I'll be doing this much longer, but I just can't shake off the habit of trying to change things ... of always wanting to do what I see as right. It's a tiresome habit I inherited from my parents." Armour averted his eyes from the old man's gaze. "Ha! I can see you think I'm bonkers, but you must admit that planting trees is harmless. I can tell you, my young friend, that once you've built a nuclear bomb in the belief that you are saving civilisation, you learn to be very careful about doing the right thing. Doing the right thing ... harming nobody ... of course it's hopelessly utopian, but I for one don't want another scorched human being on my conscience."

It was the first time Aaronson had actually admitted to him that he did have the Hiroshima dead on his conscience, but Armour remained silent. He kept his eyes fixed on the young trees, listening to the wind and waiting for further revelations. At last the old man spoke again.

"Has it ever struck you, Armour, that our species is very lucky in the way that each of us is fully conscious of that fact that we must die?"

"Well, I suppose that's what makes us unique ... the fact that we're conscious of our consciousness ... but I'm not sure contemplating our certain death makes us lucky. Surely it makes us fearful, superstitious, gullible ... religious?"

"Ah, Armour, I applaud your rationalism! But look at the drive for creativity that our certainty of destruction brings." He waved an arm extravagantly towards his trees. "This living, self-regenerating organism that I have planted will remain when you and I, and all our other works of hand and brain, are long forgotten." A look of triumph lit up the old man's face. "In a hundred years it will look as if the human race had never set foot here. It will be like the world anew, a better world, before the time of mankind."

Aaronson's bucolic fantasy of a planet without people irked Armour. He now knew more about the Manhattan project than he had done when he'd first interviewed the old man. There was a question he should have asked him then, and he felt goaded into demanding an answer now.

"When we spoke a couple of weeks ago, you mentioned Joseph Rotblat." Aaronson turned to stare at Armour as if he knew what was coming. "Rotblat left the Manhattan Project when it became clear that the Nazis didn't have a bomb and were almost beaten. Why did you stay on with Oppenheimer? Nobody ever thought the Japanese had a bomb."

Aaronson stood, motionless and unblinking. The journalist was ready for this and held his gaze until the old man spoke.

"At last, my friend. That's the question I've been expecting. It's the one I've asked myself many times. I think you can say ... that we were contaminated ... not contaminated by radiation, although a few of us got a dose of that. We got a fatal dose of hubris, Armour ... pure and simple arrogance. We were the best minds the allies had and we were working on the frontiers of science ... like Prometheus, stealing fire from the gods. We thought we were so damned smart. Yes, arrogance ... we were blinded by the brilliance of what we were achieving. The politicians and the military gave us everything we demanded. They wanted a big stick to shake at the Soviets. As for us, the so-called geniuses ... God help us ... we were horribly fascinated to see what would happen when the bombs fell."

artWORK, September 2000

TWILIGHT OF THE GODS
The Neo-paganism of Caleb Burgess

The American artist Caleb Burgess is chiefly remembered for a major exhibition held more than two decades ago. Yet the reclusive sculptor – long resident in the Scottish Highlands – is as energetic and creative as ever. *Jonathon Armour* rediscovered Burgess in his home on the remote Calltain peninsula – and found a man equally obsessed with the distant past and far future.

Admirers of *The Well of the Heads*, the most outstanding work from the artist's 1979 Edinburgh exhibition, often assume that its sculptor, Caleb Burgess, has died, or possibly moved back to the USA. How else could the creator of one of the most important contemporary modern sculptures in the national collection have vanished from public view?

Twenty-one years ago his exhibition *Liminal Landscapes* was the "must-see" art show of the Edinburgh International Festival. While critical acclaim was not universal, the exhibition attracted large crowds and for months newspapers and television arts programmes made much of the American bohemian who made art inspired by Celtic myth and symbols. For a time Burgess was being talked about in the same awestruck tones as Anthony Gormley and Andy Goldsworthy are today. The Museum of Modern Art in Edinburgh purchased *The Well of Heads.* In this sculpture – an echo of the ancient Celtic cult of the severed head – Caleb Burgess carved faces derived from primitive art on human-head-sized boulders and piled them up like the ghastly aftermath of a massacre. A stream of water emerged from high on the pile and flowed down over the faces, many of which had bulging eyes and gaping mouths. The effect was – and remains – striking. *The Well of Heads* always draws a gaggle of viewers, attracted and probably mystified by its power. But despite its popularity, *The Well of Heads* is one of very few examples of the sculptor's work on public exhibition in Britain. This is all the more surprising given that Burgess has lived entirely in Scotland since the early 1970s.

Like many others, I retain a strong memory of *Liminal Landscapes* but had forgotten the fashionable acclaim that surrounded its creator. Even Burgess himself had slipped from my mind. It was only recently, while visiting Calltain, that I found Burgess alive, well, and as creative as ever. I had travelled to the peninsula to interview the composer Campbell Aaronson. During my visit Aaronson had pointed out to me an avenue of "modern" standing stones leading to a house that had been dug into the side of a small hill. The man who erected the megaliths and lived underground was Caleb Burgess, and the man I was interviewing turned out to have been Burgess's un-credited musical collaborator in the *Liminal Landscapes* exhibition. The action of simply walking to the artist's studio home was heightened by the experience of journeying down a *faux* Neolithic avenue. Even dropping in for a cup of tea became a significant ritual entry into the artist's world and imagination. I was struck by the similarity to the centrepiece of *Liminal Landscapes* in the way that the avenue of standing stones boldly confronted the modern viewer with the undoubted power of pagan ritual and symbolism.

Also featured in that exhibition was *Processional*, a massive work that filled an entire room of the Museum of Modern Art. A beaten red-earth path ran between two rows of wooden stakes on each of which was impaled a moulded, but graphically realistic, severed head, the blood represented by a scarlet cloth that "poured" from the neck and entwined itself around the stake. The room was dark, with each head lit by a spotlight. The "pagan" experience was heightened by a continuous sound loop of drumming and chanting. Passing through *Processional* was an unsettling but unforgettable experience. I left with a feeling that some great and terrible event had happened or was about to happen or, more banally, that I had strayed onto the set of a production of Peter Brook's *Mahabarrata*. Doubtless this was Burgess's intention, for he gave *Processional* the subtitle *Setting for the Extraordinary ...* Extraordinary what?

Eerie and creepy? Certainly. But *Processional*, some critics claimed, was not entirely successful – leading us somewhere without quite delivering us. It was as if – and the subtitle certainly supports this – Burgess was not exhibiting an artwork, but a theatre set, as yet devoid of performers. One half-expected dancers to perform *The Rite of Spring* – but was left contemplating an empty stage. In retrospect, I wonder if I and other critics of *Liminal Landscapes* missed the point. Was *Processional* not the artwork, but only created as a "setting", a sacred site for initiates – the exhibition's visitors themselves – to be touched and moved by the music of Burgess's collaborator? Whether the sculptor was playing second fiddle to the composer or not, the work of Caleb Burgess almost entirely vanished from public galleries after that exhibition.

Since then the sculptor has created only a handful of site-specific works, and some small-scale carvings commissioned by private collectors.

When I returned home from interviewing Aaronson, I looked out the cuttings file on Caleb Burgess in *The Herald* library. The more I read, the more I was astonished at his virtual disappearance from the art scene. I had not been alone in believing that Burgess had been on the point of breaking through as a major artist. While Calltain had its share of potters, poets, wood-turners and tie-dyers, it seemed to me that it was an extraordinary place that had not one but two genuine, if reclusive, geniuses.

A few weeks later I travelled once more to Calltain, landing from an open boat at the small pier and trekking the two-mile rough path that led to Kilmailin on the north side of the peninsula. Once there I "processed" down the avenue of standing stones to Burgess's house. The artist was shorter than I expected, but broad-shouldered and fit. His voice was still clearly American, but his pronunciation of local place names was that of someone who'd lived long in these parts. He was not what I was expecting from a recluse. He was loquacious, even funny. "The north wind is always cold, no matter where it comes from," he said, watching me with curiosity.

In Burgess's large semicircular living and working space, pieces of rough-hewn wood and rock lay in piles. There were shelves of books and racks of tools, and everywhere was evidence of Burgess's ceaseless creativity – drawings, carvings, driftwood constructions. On wooden posts were three of the bloody severed heads from *Processional*. They gave me the opportunity to talk about *Liminal Landscapes* and the fact that it was more than two decades since the public had seen his work.

"I don't care to exhibit," he said simply. I asked him to explain. "I'm no longer prepared to perform in the circus. I don't do gallery art. I take rocks from the mountain here, carve them, and then return them to the mountain. My work is all over Calltain, it's here to see for those who want to see it. If people want to find it, that's cool. If they come across it unexpectedly, that's even better."

I asked him how it was possible to make a living this way. "Yeah ... OK, sometimes I whore a bit. There are some collectors who really get the cup and ring thing. Private collectors. I make a few pieces each winter. If there were still wolves here, the work I sell would just about keep them from the door."

Burgess revealed that his early obsession with Celticism and the Neolithic has been increased rather than exorcised by *Liminal Landscapes*, and that he had moved to Calltain having sold enough works to build his earth-house and reflect more deeply on the source of his art. "I'd found a creative community here at Calltain and I wanted to live in such a place. The earliest people to settle here built stone and turf roundhouses. I've done that too ... only I've used steel and glass as well as earth and turf. I was first attracted to Kilmailin because of the ruins of the chapel. You can see why Celtic monks settled here ... there's a bay to land a boat in, there's fresh water. But when I was looking for a place to build this house I began to read the landscape differently. There were Stone Age people living here for thousands of years before the Celts showed up. They must have known every rock, every fissure. Sometimes they decorated these rocks with carvings. They were artists, man! Art started in places like this. They weren't taking their art to some f****** Stone Age art gallery. This was their gallery ... this was their canvas. The landscape wasn't just where they lived, it was their cathedral! A rock face wasn't just a neat place to stick a picture on. Their art was what we'd now call site-specific – it grew directly from the interaction between the people and their environment. This concept is still second nature to the Aborigines. It's like a piece of plaid. The Landscape was the warp and their myths were the weft and together they made sense of the world. Their culture was like an encyclopaedia, something to refer to when they needed water, or the best place to find flint or a cave to shelter in. They didn't just f****** occupy and dominate the landscape like we do, they were part of it. Human consciousness, animals, plants, rocks, the stars in the sky, the wind, the rain – every damn thing all the same damn thing."

Burgess believes the destruction of the environment is comparable with taking a sledgehammer to Michelangelo's David or a knife to Da Vinci's Mona Lisa. Two decades ago one London critic criticised *Liminal Landscapes* for its "phoney Celtology", and it would be easy to dismiss Burgess's current obsession with the supposed spirituality of the Neolithic as naive New Ageism, but there is no doubt that he is sincere in his belief that it is the dislocation between man and nature that is the cause of the world's ills.

"Living here changed my consciousness," he told me. "Calltain has been occupied for thousands of years, and in all that time man has lived with nature. Culture and landscape evolved together. The first settlers moulded the landscape slowly, and they in turn were moulded by the landscape. There was a harmony because they couldn't rip the place apart like we can today. We need to get back to living with nature, not dominating and destroying it." At this point Burgess waved expansively, taking in his earth- house and surroundings with a sweep of his arm. "It's happening right here. That's what I'm part of ... a community in harmony with nature. It's places like this, not in parliaments and boardrooms, where the world will be saved."

I told him that I'd seen his *Liminal Landscapes* as more spiritual than political. "There you go, man! Spiritual ... political ... man ... environment ... work ... art ... it's these divisions that's f****** up the world. We have to go back to the ancient ways of thinking if we want to heal the Earth. Suppose the Neolithics had destroyed their environment? The entire human race would have perished!"

I countered that Stone Age people didn't have the technology to destroy their environment, and that their living in supposed harmony with nature didn't imply that they had any greater spirituality than we have. And as for cave art ... perhaps, I suggested, our ancestors just liked to doodle.

"That's garbage!" he retorted sharply. "The archaeology tells us that Palaeolithic art in Europe blossomed during the last ice age. These people survived in an environment that would snuff us out. Why carve when you have no metal tools? If you want to just doodle, you can do it with a burnt stick. That incised stuff meant something important." He was becoming exasperated with my line of questioning, and I changed the subject by asking him about his current work. He told me he was busy on a big project, but when I pressed him on it, he simply stated that it was "too early to verbalise". He seemed distracted for a moment and then suddenly went to an old table and took a sheaf of drawings from it. "These don't look much, but they may be the most important work I ever do."

I stepped over, expecting to see something extraordinary – and was initially only disappointed and perplexed. The topmost work depicted a desert landscape in which two tiny human figures stood in front of a group of immense spiked pillars. The pillars were geometric wedges, obviously man-made with no attempt to give them an organic shape or make them sympathetic to the landscape. Scribbled on the drawing were notes about the dimension of the pillars, so it was clearly a preliminary sketch for a sculpture. Burgess slipped the drawing aside to reveal another. This was a detail from the first, showing one of the faces of the pillars. On it was a drawing of what looked like a science textbook illustration of an atom – complete with nucleus and revolving electrons. In a corner he had also drawn the conventional sign for radiation and a cartoon of an anguished face based on Munch's painting *The Scream*. He shuffled the papers again, revealing another sketch. Crude, hardly more than a matchstick man, this one was of a primitive horned figure that appeared to be dancing. It had a long, downward-pointing, triangular body and short spindle legs jutting out from the acute angle. Arms stretched out from the shoulders, and bent at the elbows with one forearm held up and the other down. The fingers were clearly splayed in some vital gesture. The figure had a preposterously long neck and a tiny head. Great antlers sprang from this, and two objects dangled from it like great pendulous ears or part of a headdress.

"Do you know how fast language decays?" I must have shaken my head, for he plunged on into his argument. "Every thousand years about twenty per cent of the basic words of any language change beyond recognition. In ten thousand years people would only understand a fraction of our conversation here, if anything at all. Yet all over the world we're burying nuclear waste that will be lethal to all life forms for millions and millions of years. We fuse it into glass, bury it in an old salt mine, pour concrete down the shaft and call out the National Guard if someone goes near it. But for how long? We've no idea what civilisation will be like hundreds of generations from now. What kind of language will they speak? How can they know what kind of s**t we've left behind? Our records will have crumbled. They will have no means of knowing what dangers lie under the earth. Suppose they want to mine there? Sure, the location of these dumps might be handed down the generations, but suppose there is a cataclysmic disruption in human history? Suppose plague or war reduces man to a primitive state and we have to start building again? Any knowledge we have, even the skills of reading and writing, may be swept away."

I asked him about the little dancing figure. "Shamanistic," he said. "Native American. I'm still trying to figure out what he's trying to tell us, but I'm sure as hell it's bad news."

Standing in Burgess's presence it all made some sort of sense. He was attempting to develop a symbolic language – a permanent "Danger!" sign that, in his words, would "defy the teeth of time" and be understood by the speakers of every tongue that might ever be be spoken on earth.

I had come to Calltain curious about an artist who hadn't exhibited for twenty years, and found a man who thinks in terms of ten million years. I'd expected to meet an eccentric recluse hiding from the world, but I had found an eminently sane – if unorthodox – man whose mission was to save it. I left Caleb Burgess's earth-house and took the track back towards the jetty. I knew that climate change and hundreds of years of human habitation had changed the landscape through which I walked. But I swear that I saw the bare rocks of Calltain with a new – or perhaps very ancient – eye.

The Herald, 16th September, 2000
Super-quarry threat to artists' colony
By Jonathon Armour

Argo Aggregates – the latest venture by Scots multi-millionaire Josh Argo – is to seek planning permission for a super-quarry on the Calltain peninsula on the north-west coast of Scotland.

The £60 million project would provide material for road building over a period of forty years, and become a major employer in the area. Seven million tons a year of hard granite-like rock would be blasted from Calltain and shipped away from a newly built harbour on Loch Vallaig. A spokesman for the company said last night that two decades of quarrying would, "virtually remove the hill that dominates the west of this sparsely populated and economically unproductive area. The development will be a major boost to the town of Vallaig and the surrounding region which have fallen on hard times since the decline of the fishing industry."

Argo Aggregates is the brainchild of banker and entrepreneur Josh Argo. Argo made his first million by turning his late father's fishing boat business into a shipping company supplying specialist vessels to the North Sea oil industry. Backing a hunch, he borrowed heavily to found Argo Exploration, which became one of the most successful independent oil production companies in British waters. Industry insiders see Argo's new aggregates venture as a logical step for a group of companies with both mineral exploration and shipping interests. The rock removed from Calltain would be used for motorway construction in the UK and abroad.

The Calltain peninsula was abandoned by the last of its native community in the 1960s, but has since been resettled by a colony of artists, craftspeople and exponents of organic farming and self-sufficiency. More than 80 people live there and the community supports a nine-pupil primary school.

Caleb Burgess, an American born sculptor who has lived on Calltain since the mid 1960s, described the Argo Aggregates plans as "grotesque and insane". Standing outside his studio on the north shore of the peninsula, Mr Burgess said: "As far as we can tell Argo's surveyors spent less than a week here, flying in by helicopter every day. They only looked at the rocks. They never spoke to the people. On the strength of that, they want to blast the place into oblivion. There's more to Calltain than just geology, and they're going to have to learn that."

Doug Fowlie and Ruth Sullivan opted for the self-sufficient life on Calltain a decade ago. Ruth says that they've sunk all their savings into building their comfortable home. They have only crofters' rights, and do not own the land they've built on, so if the quarrymen move in they'll lose everything they own, and are unlikely to be in line for compensation. "They'll destroy this place," says Doug, "and use the rock they blast here to build roads that will wreak destruction up and down rural Britain. This is not just a local issue, it's an environmental issue for the whole country." A published poet, Fowlie laments: *And the old world turns./Turns a little madder,/Turns a little hotter,/Turns a little sadder.*

Matt Tyler, who runs the tiny passenger ferry to the community from the fishing port of Vallaig, is adamant that Argo Aggregates plans for Calltain will be resisted. "The sea has been smashing against the rocks here for millions of years now, and Calltain is still there. It's not going to be destroyed by a capitalist like Argo. The rocks of Calltain will smash him too."

This is the second controversial scheme Argo Aggregates has embarked on since it was launched eighteen months ago. The company has also been surveying throughout the Highlands for potential sites for the underground storage of nuclear waste. Argo Aggregates is understood to have been in talks with the Government over plans to safely store Britain's growing mountain of radioactive waste – the product of the country's nuclear power programme. Some of the waste will remain dangerous for hundreds of thousands of years. While the Department of the Environment has described any plans to bury waste as being "in a very early stage", environmental groups have promised a campaign of civil disobedience against the burying of nuclear waste anywhere in the Highlands.

Café Sarti (2)

When I was still employable, I used to walk here from *The Herald* office in just five minutes. Not that I was a regular back then the way I am today, it was just a place to escape to occasionally, and find the space to scribble in pencil the first draft of an article that required more concentration than I could muster in the busy office. Nobody else from the paper used Sarti's, so it was here I brought Grizzel when she phoned out of the blue and asked me outright to buy her lunch. My article on the super-quarry threat to Calltain had been published a couple of days before. She said that she'd quite liked it.

I arrived early. She was on time. Grizzel wore a faded denim jacket streaked dark with rain. When she peeled it off she revealed a white top that looked like an old-fashioned vest with lace and pearl buttons around the neck. It was pretty and feminine, but I remember that she wore it with deep-pocketed cargo pants that were ragged and wet to the ankles from trailing on the ground. Her face was long and pale, and framed with wet rat-tails that slowly dried into ringlets. Her eyes were the deepest blue, and she fixed them on me, or rather on the still angry bruise under my left eye. She wasn't what I would call pretty, her face was too long, her eyes too deep set. I thought she was beautiful. Close to us, a noisy table of young suits eyed her up curiously, as if trying to work out if she was fanciable. Any man in his right mind would be crazy not to fancy her, I thought, my heart soaring.

Nowadays I always sit at one of the bar stools in the window, but that lunchtime we were shown to a table deep inside the cellar restaurant, close to the busy kitchen and the pizza oven. Grizzel said I was a genius for knowing that she loved pizza. She asked me my star sign – Cancer actually – but I'm certain I didn't tell her. I clearly remember play-acting incredulity that she believed in such nonsense. She countered that she only believed in astrology's existence, not its veracity, but that at one time her mother had partly supported the pair of them by reading people's palms and star signs in Brighton.

"The astrology brought in a few bob, but for years she managed to screw the state for every benefit going ... I can't even begin to remember the various names and addresses we had! We'd just ... like ... up sticks and move on. Then we lived on some Greek island. One time my mother rented a house that didn't even have electricity, so I got to know the stars quite well, even if I also heard lots of wacky stuff about astrology. Mum is the last of the old hippies," she explained, raising her eyebrows in the way teenagers do when mentioning embarrassing parents. "In fact, I only started calling her Mum when I was eleven. I'd called her Isis until then. Her name's really Annette, but she'd-been going through an Egyptian phase when I was born."

The waiter was hovering, so we ordered. She didn't want a starter, just pizza. I ordered pasta and we agreed on Chianti. As the waiter hurried off, she apologised for not being in Calltain when I visited Burgess. Then she smiled mischievously and said that she'd heard that Matt Tyler had "looked after me".

"Oh yeah, we got on just great. He's my best mate now."

She stifled a slightly hysterical giggle behind her hand. "I'm really sorry about that too. Matt's got a bit of a temper, but he's really a good and caring guy, I've known him for years. He can just get a bit ... like, obnoxious when he's had too much to drink. It was my fault for not being there ... after all, it was me that promised to take you to Caleb's."

"Look Grizzel," I said, deliberately using her name, "it was just one of those things. Anyway, I'm old enough and ugly enough to look after myself."

She'd been "distracted" by her work, she explained, "astrophysics is like that. You kind of get drawn in and forget sometimes to come out again." She said I should visit again soon, just for a holiday. She and Aaronson lived in the blackhouse, but there was a fold-down bed in the tower that I could use. She was being very friendly, even slightly flirtatious. Of course, I already fancied her like mad and I couldn't help wondering about the sleeping arrangements in the blackhouse. I still wasn't even sure that she wasn't just taking the piss saying she was an astrophysicist, so I asked her to try and explain what she did in a way that a non-scientific-artsy-kind-of-guy could understand.

"O...K," she began thoughtfully, drawing a breath. "Well the bad news is that the universe is expanding way out of control. As galaxies fly apart the temperature of the universe is going to fall to absolute zero ..."

I watched her, rather than listen, appropriating Einstein, the Big Bang and supernova explosions as my reasons for gazing attentively into her face. Lightly, but carefully applied, make-up. High cheekbones, faint creases round her deep-set eyes, teeth not quite straight but a mouth that I can only revert to the rosebud cliché to describe. The bottom lip slightly fuller, highly coloured in contrast to her pale complexion, perhaps a touch of gloss, it was a mouth that provoked in me an urgent desire to kiss. When the food came, she would stop talking for a minute or two at a time to eat hungrily. I was hardly listening to a word she said, but I was captivated by the sound of her voice and the way her face and hands were animated by the ideas fizzing in her lovely head. When she began to talk about "Dark Energy" I broke in to tell her that it sounded like a Phillip Pullman novel. She stopped talking, and looked at me blankly for a moment. Then, the spell broken, she changed the subject completely and said I should be writing more about Joshua Argo and his plans to blow up Calltain and cart it away in boatloads. I teased her by telling her that I wanted to write about an astrologer's daughter who was now studying astrophysics. She asked me if it wasn't more likely that she got her knack for science from her father. That was the word she used, a "knack". I asked her what her father did. She looked at me curiously.

"Campbell. You know ... Campbell Aaronson?" There was a long, embarrassing silence during which she gazed at me intently, reading my face like a book. "Didn't you know that?" As my idiotic misapprehension dawned on her she started to laugh out loud, quickly covering her mouth with her hand, her eyes wide in incredulity. "Didn't you know? Did you think I was some sort of cult music groupie? For fuck's sake ... you didn't think that I was his latest squeeze, did you?"

It was ridiculously clear now. So simple. So stunningly obvious. I marvelled at my breathtaking stupidity. "A ... a family friend," I head myself lamely stutter, "I thought he was a family ... friend." Aaronson, I knew, was eighty. She probably wasn't thirty yet. How could I have been so stupid?

But of course, now that I knew the truth, at that moment I also knew that I wanted her myself. For some reason I had found a way to put her off-limits until then. The fantasy of her having some sort of sick relationship with an ancient, but possibly Viagra-fuelled, lover was easier for me to accept than the reality of her being free, yet very unlikely to get involved with a middle-aged hack with a truck-load of emotional baggage, an expanding waistline and a fondness for alcohol. In my imagination I had given Grizzel a sex life that made her a weirdo, a star-fucker, although probably more a geriatric nurse than lover. Crazily, that had been easier for me to imagine and accept than the idea of Grizzel just having a steady boyfriend in Oxford. For all I knew there really was a steady boyfriend in Oxford, a smart young scientist with whom she enjoyed sex and supernovas, possibly both at the same time. How could I tell her that I thought she was fucking her eighty-year-old father? But sitting in the restaurant, with a stupid look on my battered face, I felt the embarrassment at my credulity giving way to elation. I'd already had two glasses of Prosecco before she had arrived, and had drunk most of the Chianti on the table, and I suddenly found myself alcoholically emboldened enough to flirt with her.

"But it really is a great story for a feature," I told her. "The astrologist's daughter who became an astrophysicist!"

"What, an article about me ... like ... for a newspaper? No way!"

"It would be great. It wouldn't really be about you, but about the triumph of science and reason over superstition and ignorance. It's your scientific duty! And hey, you're very photogenic. We could use a picture of you."

She airily brushed my compliment aside with her hand. "So, Mr Big Wig Reporter, what sort of questions would you ask me?"

I stroked my chin in pantomime thoughtfulness and put on an old-fashioned BBC voice. "Miss Gillespie, what is it that drives you to seek the meaning of life, the universe and everything?" She laughed out loud, stifling the noise with her hand. I went on in the same ridiculous tone, "Are you motivated in the same way as your distinguished father the physicist and composer Dougald Campbell Aaronson, or are you perhaps an apostle of enlightenment, attempting to banish the superstition you imbibed with your mother's milk?"

"You mean am I a depressed psychotic with Freudian hang-ups, or just an angry brat?"

It occurred to me that that was exactly what I was wondering, but I just laughed and raised my glass to signify game over. To my surprise she continued.

"Well there's not much sign of actual manic depression so far. Oh, I have my down-in-the-dumps days I suppose, and I certainly put in long workaholic hours sometimes, but that's just part and parcel of being a research scientist. We're all groping in the dark, but astrophysicists do it more literally than others, so being gloomy now and then is an occupational hazard. So ... yes, perhaps just a touch obsessive."

"I suppose you and ... your father", this was a concept I was still adjusting to, "are living, genetic proof that art and science are two sides of the same creative coin."

She laughed. "Campbell never tires of telling me that scientists just discover what's already there, while artists create something new. What I do know is that I have a brilliant and creative father who likes to scrutinise and analyse everything, and a feckless fruitcake of a mother who believes any old hocus-pocus. I just hope the two of them cancel each other out and make me normal."

"Normal, very attractive, young astrophysicist – I meet them every day." I knew I was chancing my arm with the compliment, but reckoned that the joke would carry it off.

"Yes, well ... thanks."

"Look, I really would like to do a story about you. You've read the kind of stuff I write, so I think you know me well enough to know that I won't take the piss."

Well, I won her round. Over coffee, she said she wouldn't mind talking to me about her work if I thought it would make an article, but that it was really much more important for journalists to scrutinise the schemes and scams of big business. I particularly remember her expression, "schemes and scams".

We made some sort of deal there and then. Once again she'd done a trade-off. In exchange for writing the article I wanted to write, I also wrote the article that she wanted written. Of course, I'd taken no notes about the kind of research she did or ideas she had. But that was fine. She was heading back to Calltain on the afternoon train, so there wasn't time for her to give me enough material for an article. I would have to go to Calltain. There was, she said, an evening train from Vallaig so I could get there and back in a day. I was sorry that she didn't mention the fold-down bed again. But before I could go, I had to schlep up to Fraserburgh.

That table for two is still there, like a monument to my lost happiness. Sometimes I pass it on my way to the toilet, so I try not to go for a piss when I'm in Sarti's.

The Herald, 25th September 2000

Voyage of the Argonaut

Self-made tycoon Josh Argo has won more respect than friends – as *Herald* writer Jonathon Armour discovers in the multi-millionaire's home town of Fraserburgh.

The harbour front at Fraserburgh is a long way from the boardrooms of the banks, oil companies and shipping lines where Josh Argo made his millions.

What was once one of the busiest fishing ports in Europe is today caught in a spiral of economic and social decline as the town's main industry shrinks in the face of over-fishing and European quota legislation. In the past year the town's economy has contracted by 50%. Groups of unemployed men now hang around the once bustling harbour. Many shops have closed and now lie boarded up. Fishermen and fish merchants once made fortunes here. Today drug dealers are the ones to prosper. They moved in for the rich pickings when the town was thriving, and have added drug addiction to the community's increasingly bleak economic and social future. There are now an estimated 400 heroin addicts in Fraserburgh.

Fewer boats operate from here than ever before, and those that do scarcely land enough fish to keep the community's economy afloat. Today, Fraserburgh's greatest success story lives a hundred and fifty miles away in the heart of Edinburgh's financial district.

John Joshua (Josh) Argo was twenty-five when he inherited his father's fleet of six North Sea trawlers. It was never meant to happen, but 1968 was a devastating year for the Argo dynasty. Brother Andrew, four years older than Josh, was killed in an accident at sea, and James, two years older, died in a car crash. Their father Zander (Alexander) suffered a fatal heart attack only days after James's funeral.

Born with a minor physical disability, the young Argo did not follow his father and brothers into fishing, but excelled at school and went on to win first-class honours in Economics at Aberdeen University. He attended business school in Texas, and returned to Scotland as an economist at the Royal Bank.

When Zander Argo died, only Josh remained to take over the Fraserburgh empire of six trawlers and their precious fishing licences. In Fraserburgh the story goes that Josh was born with a club foot and that his father made it clear from the outset that his youngest son was not cut out for fishing. One fisherman, who had sailed with Zander Argo as a young man, told me that the boy's father had been ashamed of Josh's disability. "Zander didn't think university was a proper job," he told me. "He was very proud of the older boys and I think when they were killed, it broke his heart. He just lost the will to live. It didn't matter that Josh was doing well. It was the other boys he doted on." Josh Argo had already gained wide economic and business experience – including knowledge of the US oil industry – when Argo & Sons became his. Skipper Jim Fairbairn, who was at school with James Argo, said that Josh had taken the town by surprise.

"We knew he was in banking, that's all. He'd never even been on a fishing boat as far as I know. But within weeks of his father's death he'd chucked the bank job and come here to take over Zander's boats."

The town was not surprised when the sole survivor of the Argo clan sold the six boats and their licences, but they weren't prepared for Joshua's next move. Instead of pocketing the cash and returning to Edinburgh, he spent it on a Norwegian exploration and service ship, changed the name of the family fishing company to Argo Energy, and borrowed what is widely believed to be several million pounds from his former employers at the Royal Bank. Critics thought him reckless, even insane.

"We thought he was mad," Jim Fairbairn told me as we stood in the harbour-side Balaclava Bar, "but offshore gas and oil were just a dream in them days. We weren't taking it seriously. We just thought the sea was for fishing, not drilling for oil in."

Argo's massive gamble paid off. Within months of his taking over the helm of the family firm, there were serious gas finds made in the UK sector of the North Sea and, the following year, BP's discovery of the massive Forties oil field 120 miles off Aberdeen. Argo Energy was quick to exploit the opportunities. Josh Argo predicted that the sector needed a wide range of new technologies to work in such a difficult environment. He began by investing heavily in specialist exploration vessels, pipe-laying barges, helicopters and even oil tankers. He then took his company into oil exploration, struck lucky off the Shetland Isles and made Argo Energy the most successful independent oil producer in the UK.

"It was like the gold rush," said Fairbairn. "They were making millions and millions but we never saw any of it here. At first he'd work eighteen hours a day in that old office of Zander's down on the harbour. You'd never see him in the town, but no matter when you went to sea or came home the light would be on in the office and his car would be parked outside. But then, after a couple of years, he upped and moved the whole shebang to Aberdeen."

Argo's early workaholic habits have lasted into his middle age and are said to be at the root of his two failed marriages. In recent years however he has developed a passion for sailing single-handed on the West Coast. "He may be a multi-millionaire," says Fairbairn, "but he is an Argo and the sea's in his blood. He's just doing for fun what his old man and his grandfather did for a living."

Donald Mitchell, head of maths at Fraserburgh Academy, was at school with Argo. "We were in the same year and both good at maths so I suppose I knew him as well as anybody. He was quite an introverted boy. We were all football daft, and because he had a gammy leg, he didn't mix much at playtime or after school. He was always very clever and he worked hard, I think he was quite driven even back then. He was usually top of the class in tests and exams, and I don't think he was best pleased on the one or two occasions that I beat him. I tell you, I really enjoyed that!"

Douglas Marr, chairman of the Fraserburgh Chamber of Commerce, is philosophical about Argo's decision to abandon the town. "Fraserburgh was never going to be the centre of the oil industry ... it was inevitable he'd move out. I just wish there was some reason for that huge company to get involved in some way here. Even a branch office would be a shot in the arm for the local economy. It would be nice to think that the Argo Group would do something for Fraserburgh. Josh's family were here for generations. The town was good to them, so it would be nice if he put something back in."

Argo Energy is just one component of the Argo Group, an empire that now encompasses oil and gas, shipping, helicopters, open-cast coal mining and Argo Aggregates. Today the group's dynamic founder makes time to sail his yacht on the West Coast, often berthing his yacht at Vallaig, just south of the beautiful Calltain peninsula he wants to destroy with his proposed super-quarry. If that happens, the vibrant artist colony that has grown up there will be dispersed. Many people believe that it's a heavy price to pay for a pile of rubble to build more motorways. The inhabitants of Calltain promise to fight the development, but Joshua Argo is a man used to getting his own way. As Douglas Marr of the Chamber of Commerce said about Fraserburgh, "I don't think Mr Argo is very sentimental about the place – or anything else when money is concerned."

The Herald, 27th September 2000

Dark energy – science fact not fiction for "hippy chick"
By Jonathan Armour

If Grizzel Gillespie looks serious as she walks the shore of Camas Calltain it's probably because she's contemplating the universe. But the self-confessed "hippy chick" child of 1960s influenced parents, who dropped out to "do their own thing", isn't chanting mantras or searching for ley lines. She's one of the leading young brains of the Clerk-Maxwell Astrophysicists Institute. The CMAI is at the forefront of the UK's research into Dark Energy – a mysterious force that many scientists believe is driving the expansion of the universe.

Gillespie is modest about her achievements – she has a first-class honours degree from Oxford – and simply claims she has a "knack" for science that even the most alternative of educations was unable to quell.

"My mother was a hippy, and still is I suppose," she told me. "I was brought up in a number of communes in England and Crete. My parents separated when I was very small and I grew up with my mum, who was heavily into meditation and astrology. It wasn't till I was eleven that my father, who I hardly knew, insisted that I was sent to a proper school."

That "proper" school was in fact a progressive boarding school in the Scottish Borders where the pupils decided what classes – if any – to attend. While she was there the young Grizzel discovered science.

Gillespie's "knack" for science is probably inherited from her father, Campbell Aaronson. Now known as a cult electronic composer, Aaronson – as revealed in *The Herald* earlier this year – was a brilliant young half-Scottish physicist who worked with Robert Oppenheimer on the Manhattan Project which built the first atom bombs. "I have no memory of Campbell until I was eleven," says Gillespie, who took her mother's surname. "When I flew in from Crete he was waiting for me at Edinburgh Airport to take me to school. He was very kind, and I remember that he just spoke to me as an equal as we drove there, and it wasn't really like having a dad. It was just as if I suddenly had a much older friend. He would come and visit me in school, but he wouldn't bring me sweets and stuff, like other parents. He always had a gyroscope or a magnifying glass or something like that for me, and he'd talk about the science of everyday things. I remember him telling me that a tree was one of the most powerful pumps on the planet. That somehow really struck me! He was completely unlike my mother's hippy friends. He used to tell me about a wooden tower house he was building, and I was desperate to see it. I always went home to Crete for the holidays until I was fourteen, but then I started going to Calltain and staying with Campbell instead. Of course, when I went to university, it became really useful to spend all my holidays with Campbell because he's got a really wide and deep understanding of science and he's a brilliant tutor."

In the aftermath of the bombing of Hiroshima and Nagasaki, Gillespie's father became disillusioned with science and studied electronic composition in France and Germany. I asked Gillespie why her father's experience hadn't deterred her from science. "Campbell never tried to stop me. His only advice was for me to strive to be all that I could be. But it was really quite weird, because I started exactly the way he started, studying nuclear physics at Oxford. Maybe all these years of Mum's hippy astrology finally got to me because I switched to astrophysics in my second year ... I mean if you go for physics you might as well go for the really big stuff."

The "big stuff" is of course the nature of the universe.

Gillespie was visiting her father at his home on the Calltain peninsula when I interviewed her. The New Age and arts-based community of Calltain seemed a highly inappropriate place to talk about her Dark Energy research at the Clerk-Maxwell Institute, and the fit 29-year-old insisted on taking me on a lengthy coastal walk. Perhaps she thought I'd need my cobwebs blown away if I was to understand her work, even though I'd begged her to keep it simple.

"If you're not confused, you probably haven't understood," she warned me. "Think science fiction, think anti-gravity – lots of spaceships in sci-fi have been powered that way. Well, that's what we think has been driving the universe ever since the Big Bang. We've known since 1929 that the universe was expanding as if it was being blown apart. But what we've just learned is that the rate of expansion is getting faster. It's the opposite of what you'd think would happen. You would think that the force of gravity would tend to pull the universe back together, but some much greater force is driving it apart. Because this force is mysterious we call it 'dark', and we call it 'energy' because we know that it's not matter because we can't see it."

I must have begun to look perplexed at this point, because she stopped to ask if I was following. "Don't worry," she said "Einstein didn't get it either. He basically believed the universe was static."

Gillespie – as simply as she could – explained her role at the CMAI. So here's the science bit. She specialises in the study of a phenomenon called red shift. As stars move through expanding space, their visible light gets stretched out into the longer wavelengths at the red end of the spectrum. By studying the "red shift" of light from distant supernovas, scientists have proved that the rate of the universe's expansion is speeding up. Understanding the rate of expansion has allowed boffins to date the Big Bang – the instant the universe was born – to 13.7 billions years ago.

We were standing on the pebble beach at Camas Calltain in the late afternoon by the time I had some dim insight into what Grizzel Gillespie did for a living. A yacht that had sailed into the bay was dropping its anchor and some gulls were squabbling over something someone had thrown overboard. I felt that this tiny speck of our expanding universe might be the most beautiful place in existence, but I couldn't help feeling that Gillespie was just waiting for the sun to go down and the stars to come out.

"In the past few years we've been making great discoveries about how the universe works," she said. "We know now a lot more about the composition of the universe and how it's expanding at a colossal rate, but it's really important to keep a grasp of some earthbound human reality too. A wise man once said that all truly great thoughts are conceived while walking. Coming to Calltain gives me the opportunity to really think about what's going on in the universe, while all the time keeping my feet firmly on the ground!"

The Summons

"So," said Harry Urquhart, "this hippy chick ... is she good looking, eh?" The *Herald's* features editor turned from his screen to Armour, a sly smile playing on his mouth. Armour sensed at once that his oldest friend was up to mischief.

"What makes you ask that?"

"Your copy ... long walks with a woman half your age ... a beautiful beach ... cute little nature notes ... it reads like you really fancy her."

"She's not half my age."

"Yeah, yeah. I'll really be glad when you are fifty, so that you can stop telling me that you aren't there yet."

"Unlike you, you old fart. What's wrong? Don't you like it?"

"Och, it's fine. I was just wondering if I should have sent a photographer."

"It's a long way. You can only get up and down in a day if you do a deal with the guy who runs the ferry."

"How many times have you been up?"

"That was my third. Hey, the last time was on Saturday ... it was my day off ... that article is above and beyond the call of duty."

"Much appreciated. It's really quite a good piece and she's certainly an interesting girl. I'll use it on Wednesday and tart it up with some science library illustration of the Big Bang or whatever. So when are you going back?"

"What makes you think I'm going back?"

"Jonno, I've known you for years ... through good and bad times ... but it's a long while since I've seen you look quite so shifty. I think you're being hauled back there by the gonads. I certainly fucking hope so. Time you got a bit of the big bang yourself."

Armour glanced round the open-plan office and wheeled his chair a little closer to Urquhart's to speak confidentially. "Actually, I was hoping to go back the weekend after next, and take the Friday off as well. It will mean bedding down the Saturday column a day early ... I was going to ask you if you'd cover that for me ... is that OK?"

“Yeah, sure. Staying over eh? So ... what’s she like, and where did she get the crazy name?”

“We’re just friendly, there’s nothing happening between us ... but she asked me back to stay over. I don’t really know why ... apparently we’re going to pick mushrooms. She’s very attractive ... bright as hell.”

“Mushrooms? I hope you have a magic time of it.”

“Very funny, Harry.”

“Look Jonno, joking apart, I hope you have a great time, and if you do get off with this wonder woman there’ll be nobody more pleased than me.” There was a brief embarrassed silence between them. Then Harry slouched back in his chair and began to laugh. Good old Harry. He always knew how to smooth over a painful situation. He’d once even removed the photo of himself with his wife and kids from his desktop, until Armour made him put it back.

“What?”

“I was just thinking ... if you hadn’t told me what you were up to, how surprised I’d have been when your article about mushroom picking landed in my inbox. Getting astrophysics from our arts correspondent was strange enough.”

“Harry, I promise. No articles about mushrooms.”

The first leaves fell from the trees, borne down by a light wind – not unusual for late September, except for the fact that this year Armour noticed them. An arty city boy, he normally got his nature second-hand from oil on canvas. The Pastoral was his least favourite of Beethoven’s symphonies. Now he closely watched autumn’s arrival as he walked in city parks, trying to imagine the scene in Campbell Aaronson’s hazel wood. He wrote about several new exhibitions of paintings, interviewed a set designer about her plans for a Christmas ballet, had dinner with Harry and Anne at their house, marvelling at how grown-up their kids were. But every time he wasn’t busy, every time he let his guard down, Grizzel came to him, striding through his mind towards him on Calltain jetty, her hair crazy in the wind. He tried to imagine her in his arms. She was quite skinny, not really his type at all. He cut back on the beer and the red wine, and plucked hairs from his nostrils. He longed to see her again, but fretted about potentially making a fool of himself over her. Calltain must be dull after Oxford, he reasoned. She just needs a new friend. Still, he could do with losing a few pounds.

Then, less than a week before he was due to travel, he received a letter from Caleb Burgess, summoning him back to his Hobbit hole beneath the hill. He read it several times to be sure that it didn't contain some coded denunciation of the article he had written and that it really was, as it appeared to be, an invitation to call again.

Camas Kilmailin
State of Altered Conscionsness
Artists' Republic of Calltain
28th September

Mr Jonathon Art Scribe Armour,

Congratulations! You turned out to be less of a fuckwit than most of your art kritic klan. I know these twisted failed-artist types – all stetson and no steers. All foreplay and no fucking.

However!

I broke my taboo and read your stuff. Put this on your web blog if you have one: Caleb Burgess don't wipe his ass on my stuff! AND - because Grizzel thinks you're OK. Now Grizz wants me to show you what I've really being doing for the last ten years. As you well know, I do the Cup & Ring Thing to make rich people happy and so that I can live without selling out or burning out. But it just happens that I'm also doing the biggest thing of my life. Site specific (to be specific!). It's what makes me tick – rather than just tick over. If you want to see it you'll have to be here.

I'll be straight. I may change my mind and tell you to fuck off. The runes are good for the coming weekend. Grizz tells me you'll be here. Don't write. If you don't come I will be consumed with indifference.

Yours,

Burgess

P.S. I admire your cahones. Nobody ever called Grizzly Gillespie a hippy chick before, and lived. Of course, you still may not!

"So ... it's you again." Matt Tyler seemed even more obnoxious than Armour had remembered, and the journalist was sorry to see that the small scab under his eye had gone. "What's it this time? Hippy chicks? Atom bombs?"

"Top-secret journalistic mission, Tyler. If I told you I'd have to kill you." Normally, Armour prefixed men's surnames with "Mister" until he knew them well enough to call them by their forenames. As far as he remembered, Tyler was the first person he had ever just called by his surname. It didn't sound to him at all Public School, but as in master to servant, or Highland laird to lowly ghillie. He hoped it sounded patronising, and decided to use the naked surname again.

"Look Tyler, this is my fourth visit, but you've never charged me for taking me across. What do I owe you?"

Something between an amused smile and a sneer played momentarily over Tyler's face until his grease-engrained hand moved to stroke his stubble. "Well, if ah charge your fat expense account fifty squid, I can let ma pals go for free." Armour thumbed crisp new notes from his wallet. They crackled in the wind momentarily before the boatman took them in his dangerous fist.

Tyler did seem to have pals that day, not just passengers. A few minutes later a woman with twin boys of about ten, and a younger daughter, clambered down onto the *Ran*. It seemed they had come to Vallaig on the same train as Armour. She carried two large plastic carrier bags emblazoned in red with "TK Max". The boys made for Tyler, calling him "Man" and engaging him in a complex ritual of high fives and hand-grips. The girl clung timidly to her mother. Tyler asked the woman, who seemed to be called Midge, how she'd got on. The boys were blurting out the plot of some all-action movie they'd seen in Glasgow, but Armour overheard fragments of the mother's tale about the girl being kept in overnight for tests at the city's Ear, Nose and Throat Hospital. A young couple with dreadlocks appeared and sat in the bow talking quietly, wrapped up in each other, and holding hands. The boy had a guitar case. Tyler greeted an intense, ascetic-looking middle-aged man who carried an apparently heavy bazooka-sized tube wrapped in brown paper under his arm. Armour surmised he must have been one of the two printers who lived in the upturned boat, Campbell or MacDonald. Whichever it was, he was anxious to talk to Tyler about a malfunctioning outboard motor. A homely middle-aged woman, who looked a bit like an older Ruth Sullivan, turned up towing a suitcase on wheels and smiled at everyone without speaking. She shyly returned Tyler's clenched fist salute. When she had settled herself, Tyler cast off and headed the *Ran* for Calltain. There was a heavy swell, and Armour's stomach churned as the vessel pitched and plunged across Loch Vallaig. He tried to find landmarks on the horizon to concentrate on, but found his attention being drawn to the rolling back of the ferryman in the tiny three-sided wheelhouse. Feet planted firmly on the deck, the man's knees and thighs absorbed the turbulence of the sea. He stood erect to get the best possible view ahead, and his powerful arms moved constantly, the wheel spinning though his hands to port and starboard as he laboured to keep the *Ran* on an even keel. He seemed to Armour so ... admirable. It disconcerted him to dislike and be disliked so much. He'd made professional enemies of course, mostly people in the arts and some politicians he'd criticised over funding squabbles, and he cherished their enmity like campaign medals of journalistic combat. But he couldn't fathom Tyler's hostility. The man was warm and affectionate with the kids of the woman called Midge, and he'd seen him relaxed and friendly with Doug and Ruth at their kitchen table. Grizzel certainly liked him well enough, although the man seemed taciturn, even surly in her company.

And then, it began to fit into place. Tyler, the young delinquent that Aaronson had taken under his wing, must have been in Calltain when Grizzel first came on her school holidays. He would only have been seven or eight years older than her. Tyler had seen her grow up to become a brilliant and attractive young woman, go to Oxford and graduate in astrophysics. That was it. Tyler wanted Grizzel. He worshipped the father, but he wanted the daughter. He was Calltain's Caliban. Armour recalled Tyler's angry outburst about being a "stupid fucking boatman" on the night they had fought. That was Tyler's problem: Grizzel was well out of his league. Tyler must have realised that Armour too desired her, and hated him for it. The thought pleased Armour, although he was no more in Grizzel Gillespie's league than the stupid fucking boatman, and had about as much chance of becoming her lover. Yet, all the same, as he rose to stand uncertainly on the deck of the wallowing *Ran* and prepared to cross a narrow gap over turbulent water onto the jetty, he felt a spiteful stab of satisfaction at the boatman's jealousy. Tyler had brought the boat alongside, jumped ashore to loop the bow rope once round a bollard, and stood holding it tight in one hand while fending off the side of the boat from the concrete with a foot. To Jonathan's surprise Tyler lent forward and took his arm with his free hand.

"Careful there, man."

The boat rose a foot or two on the swell and Armour stepped clumsily ashore. He muttered a "thank you", and made to move on. But Tyler held on to his arm, oblivious to the other passengers waiting to disembark.

"You mind Doug and Ruth?" He nodded in the direction of the woman with the suitcase. "That's Rachel, Ruth's sister. You might give her a hand with her bag. She's deaf and dumb, so don't expect a conversation." Tyler abruptly pushed him aside. "Now, I've got passengers to get aff."

"Jonathon!"

It was Grizzel. She was walking briskly along the jetty towards the two men, who stood together, watching her in silence.

Rachel, Grizzel and Armour walked the shore path to Doug and Ruth's A-frame. Grizzel and the deaf woman were deep in conversation, looking directly into each other's faces, silently mouthing words, their hands flickering in nimble sign language. Armour had no idea that Grizzel could sign, but she'd surprised him before, and he didn't doubt that she would do so again. He carried the woman's bag in their wake, the path being too rough to pull it on its tiny wheels. As he did so he was able to watch Grizzel closely. Excluded from the silent conversation, he was content to reacquaint himself with the physical presence of someone who had scarcely been out of his thoughts. She wasn't wearing her stockman's coat, but a short tan leather jacket zipped up to her throat. He thought she had a bum more like a boy's than a sexy woman's. A slight figure. Yes, not very tall and quite slim, although certainly not flat-chested. He tried to imagine what her breasts looked like. Ruth emerged from her house to embrace her sister, and then Grizzel and Armour in turn. She peered closely into his face, laughing mischievously, and said that he was looking much better than the last time she'd seen him. She turned to her sister and her hands began to relate the sinuous story of Armour and Tyler's fight.

"Come on," said Grizzel, "we've got lots to do." The pair left the sisters to their vigorous conversation.

"How did you learn sign language?"

"Oh just from Rachel. There are so few people here it's always nice to find someone new to talk to. I was about fifteen and Doug and Matt were just finishing building Ruth and Doug's house. I was up from school for Easter and I was bored and just hanging around. Rachel came up from Newcastle to help Ruth with the veg garden so I picked up signing during the holiday by just being around."

When they got to the tower house, Aaronson was nowhere to be seen. "I expect he's with his trees," she said. In the big circular room where he had first met the composer, a futon had been folded down and made up as a bed. "I'm afraid there's no curtains or blinds ... summer visitors get woken up by the sun very early I'm afraid, but you should be OK at this time of year. It's a lovely room to sleep in if it's a starry night. I sometimes drag my duvet up and sleep here myself. The bathroom's downstairs. You have to go through Campbell's recording studio. There's just the one loo I'm afraid. Campbell doesn't have many visitors."

"When am I expected at Burgess's place?"

"Tomorrow morning." She was standing quite close and gazed directly up into his face. "You're in for a big surprise."

"Will it be a nice surprise?" As he said it he realised how flirtatious it must sound to her, but she held his gaze.

"Oh yes, I think so."

"So what other plans do you have for me?"

"Mushrooms. I told you ... we're going to pick mushrooms."

"Magic," he said, recycling Harry Urquhart's joke.

"Probably not ... anyway I don't do hallucinogens any more. But with luck there'll be enough for a risotto and maybe some left over for breakfast. Anyway, re-discovering your hidden hunter–gatherer will set you up for what Caleb has in store for you tomorrow."

"Are you sure you won't poison us?"

"Absolutely. Campbell once gave me a book on fungi and I ..."

"Let me guess! You spent a school holiday here at Calltain studying it."

She laughed. "A university holiday actually ... and in those days I was looking for the magic type, but now I just like the idea of a free meal. We've never had decent television reception here, you know. That gives you a lot of time to get into other stuff."

"You're amazing."

"No Jon, I'm just curious about the world ... ever since I was little."

"You must have been a very annoying child."

"Well ... Campbell loved telling me all the science stuff I wanted to know, but my mother would see cumulus clouds and tell me that they were the souls of dead elephants. Even when I was eight I didn't think that was very plausible, so I had to find out what was really happening. When I explained to her that clouds were a mass of tiny water particles carried aloft by thermal convection currents she told me I had no soul. I think it was then that I knew I'd be a scientist." She rummaged in a kitchen drawer and handed him a sharp knife. "Fortunately fungi don't have souls, but they have a great taste."

He took the knife, pressing the fleshy part of his thumb on the steel as if to test the blade. "I think your mother may be on to something. I think clouds explain a lot."

"Oh God Jon, I hope you're not going all mystical on me."

"Oh no, it's just that I think clouds are a pretty good metaphor for what religion calls the soul and what scientists call human consciousness." The girl looked at him, her head tilted in curiosity. "I think our consciousness, or spirit or soul or whatever you want to call it, is an event in time and space. What is a cloud? Just water particles, as you said. But they're water particles that occupy a unique place in time and space. No cloud in the history of the planet will ever be the same as another one. I always think that's quite a useful way to explain what we are."

She stared at him in open curiosity.

"What?" he said, guardedly.

"It's just that ... that's almost exactly the comparison that Campbell makes. He describes music as just a transitory event in time and space, each note a unique vibration in the universe. He says that music is like what people call the soul, a unique and ephemeral event in creation."

That afternoon Grizzel taught him what fungi were good to eat and which to leave alone, and how to cut a mushroom cleanly at the stem. Together they filled a plastic bucket and, that night, she slow-cooked her risotto while he sat with Aaronson, who teased him about the initiation ceremony that Caleb Burgess would be sure to subject him to in the morning. The two men, artist and composer, were clearly still close friends. Over dinner, Aaronson expounded at length on the relationship between Kandinsky and Schoenberg, their influence on each other and their insistence that art belongs to the unconscious. Armour had studied art history at university before he worked in newspapers, and was quite up to such a conversation, but found it suddenly tedious after Grizzel announced that she was going to bed. At least she kissed them both on the cheek before she left. Why did she do that? Why kiss me, he wondered. Aaronson and he talked on for an hour or more, finishing off the bottle of wine that had been opened at dinner. Grizzel had drunk none of it, and her father only sparingly. At about eleven the old man went downstairs to his bedroom in the blackhouse.

Armour gave him ten minutes to do what had to be done, and then went down to use the bathroom himself, pausing at the foot of the spiral stair to glance around Aaronson's windowless studio. In the centre of the room a sleek blue Apple computer sat on a small,-battered desk. Across from the desk stood a long, solid and unpainted wooden table on which were arrayed a bank of expensive loudspeakers of different sizes. The speakers stood against the only part of the wall not covered from floor to ceiling with metal racks of recording equipment, records, CDs, tapes and an extensive collection of drums, wooden flutes and other ethnic instruments.

Armour used the bathroom. In the mirror he noticed a few persistent hairs sprouting from his nostrils again and plucked them, wincing at the pain. Upstairs, he stripped to his underpants and clambered into the folded-down futon. He felt Grizzel's kiss linger on his face, until at last he fell asleep.

In the morning, after scrambled eggs and the last of the mushrooms, Grizzel walked Armour briskly over the hill to Kilmailin Bay. The gusting light breeze that plucked at their clothes was from the south-west, and as they passed over the summit they found the air in the north corrie quiet and still.

"That's a relief," he said.

"It's disgusting!"

"What?"

"Can't you smell them? They stink to high heaven."

Armour stopped, sniffed suspiciously, then breathed in deeply through his nose. "I see what you mean, there's a sort of musty smell. Do you think something has died up here?"

"No such bloody luck!" She was standing with her back to him, staring long and hard along the ridge. "There they are, the smelly bastards, you often find them up there."

"What is it?" he said stepping beside her. "What do you see?"

"Look there ... he's just moving on the skyline ... the big one ... I can count eight of them."

"I see them! Fantastic ... I've never seen one before. I thought they were deer for a moment. But look how shaggy they are."

"I'd shoot the bloody lot of them."

"What?" He turned to her in surprise.

"I'm not joking. They're a complete menace ... they tear down fences, destroy gardens, eat Campbell's saplings ... you've no idea how destructive they are. They're not even a native species, they're just feral ... domesticated goats run wild. The crofters took their stupid sheep away with them thank God, but they left us these monsters. I'd shoot the fucking lot of them if I had a gun."

She raised a forefinger and squinted along it. "Bang! Bang ... bang, bang, bang."

He began a laugh which he had to stifle with a fake coughing fit when he realised she wasn't joking.

"You're really serious!"

“Haven’t you realised? I’m a serious sort of girl.” With that she blew imaginary smoke from the barrel of her forefinger, and thrust it into an invisible holster at her side. “Let’s vamoose pardner.”

They laughed their way down the hill.

As they approached the standing stone avenue leading to the grassy hillock that enclosed Burgess’s studio they fell silent. He was glad of the space to calm himself before the meeting in which he had invested so much anticipation, and she was content with her own thoughts. Stopping at last between the first two monoliths Grizzel turned to face him, taking both his hands in hers. “Enjoy,” she said simply, giving them a squeeze, and then without another word took off back up the hill.

Armour watched her go for a few moments, requiring a jolt of professional resolve to turn and face the parallel rows of monoliths. Burgess had constructed the entrance to his domain in a way that made it impossible just to walk or amble up it. Armour “progressed”, as if an initiate attending a solemn ritual. At the end he turned onto the shingle path that led round the green mound to the shore side.

Through the great windows that opened out to the sea he saw Burgess sitting hunched over a table. The artist was lost in concentration, painting something in myopic detail with a small brush. Armour paused, wondering whether to knock on the glass, until he noticed that one of the sliding panels was slightly open. He stuck his head in and said “Good afternoon.” Burgess’s eyes never left the paper in front of him.

“Come in, Jonathon Armour,” he commanded. “I’ll just finish up here. It’s as persnickety as hell.”

Armour squeezed through the gap, sliding it open a few more inches. In front of Burgess was a large sheet of thick paper on which were painted a score or more small images. He was working at one now. The brush was fine and he would deftly dip it in a cup of water before applying the tip of it to one of the coloured circles in a tin box of watercolours. Armour stood watching Burgess as he worked on in silence. The brush seemed puny in his powerful hands, yet he worked it deftly. Points of colour, reflections of the tiny images in front of him, danced on the surface of the round wire-framed spectacles he wore.

"Done!" He plopped the brush into the jar of dirty water and sat back in his chair, carefully removing the glasses and folding them. "So you've come?"

"Apparently so."

"Touché." Burgess gave a wizened smile. He didn't stand or invite his visitor to sit. "Yeah, it's quite obvious that you've come ... my senses, at least my ears and eyes tell me that you're here. I don't think it's necessary to shake your hand or sniff you. Of course ... I might have gone gaga and could be mistaking a complete stranger for the journalist who came here before."

"No, it's me. I haven't changed."

"Oh don't say that! I'm an artist ... it's my mission to change people. For all I know you could have had an epiphany since I last saw you. You could have fallen in love or had a vision ... or just a nervous breakdown."

"Touché," Armour quoted back at him.

Burgess frowned, picked up his glasses and used them to point at Armour. "You're not a Holy Fool are you, Jonathan? You don't speak in tongues or foam at the mouth and communicate with the dead? No visions or out-of-body experiences?"

The artist had thrust his craggy old head forward from its seemingly trim young body, his eyes wide and mischievous in his interrogation. His head moved slightly from side to side on a long neck, and Armour was reminded of a tortoise. He regarded the artist suspiciously, sensing imminent ridicule.

"Negative," he replied at last. "Unless you count the odd evening of alcohol-induced amnesia."

Burgess rose abruptly from his chair, which made a screeching noise on the flagstone floor. "Schizophrenia? Bad acid-trips? Near-death experiences?"

Armour shook his head.

"A pity ... but perhaps you've heard of the near-death phenomenon of the Vortex? People who have been revived after being to all intents and purposes clinically dead often describe plummeting through a vortex into another reality. Indian Shamans and people who take LSD and mescaline tell of the same thing ... being drawn through a swirling tunnel into the Spirit World. This is no coincidence, Jonathon, but a universal experience. Human beings are psycho-biologically hard-wired to experience altered states of consciousness. That ability is an essential part of being human, even though our society dismisses the visionary experience as being freakish, perverse ... the product of some pathologically sick mind. What they don't realise is that consciousness is like colour. It has a spectrum! No colour is more valid than another. But we've marginalised our experience of altered psychological states and consigned them to the funny farm, what you crazy Brits call the loony bin. We've forgotten that altered states are the foundation of every world religion. Ecstatic experience, trance, revelation. Look man!"

He held it up a fist, flicking out his thumb and fingers one at a time like switchblades as he chanted out his roll-call.

"Christ fasting in the wilderness. Buddha meditating under a tree. Shamans high on peyote. African Bushmen dancing their way into trance. William Blake's poetry. The differences are just cultural specificities. Shamanism, mysticism, religion, art – it's all the same thing, Jonathon."

His fingers snapped closed and he strode briskly towards Armour, theatrical and pugnacious, until his clenched fist was inches from Armour's face.

"We can have it all. We can re-connect with the full spectrum of our consciousness. We can play the whole goddamn piano, not just the notes in the middle! Our species evolved to do that, but Western rationalism and materialism have marginalised the extreme states of consciousness. They understand something of the brain, but they don't treasure the mind."

Armour regarded the clenched fist. He no longer had time for the fashionable sixties myth that mad people were just sane people in a mad world. He believed that mad people are just mad people in a mad world, but he was damned if he was going to speak before Burgess's fist was removed from the proximity of his face. Burgess seemed to catch the mood, switching his unblinking gaze to his own fingers as they uncurled. He looked at his hand with the wonder of one who had never seen it before.

"That's interesting," Armour now ventured, "but I don't believe that Western rationalism is all-conquering. I read somewhere that the majority of British people in their teens and twenties actually believe their horoscopes. That makes astrology the most widely accepted belief system in the country, even though it's just a load of mumbo-jumbo. Our brains can search the stars for the origins of the universe, but our minds still seek for some spiritual comfort blanket. People even think that Chinese crap about rearranging their furniture will change their luck. Look, I don't believe a word of it, but I'm still very pleased to read that Cancerians like myself are really very wonderful and creative people. Hey, there's a little of the mystic in even the most secular of us."

The artist snorted. "So people read crap in newspapers! They spend a whole ten seconds fantasising that they might hump a tall dark handsome stranger. So they go to their churches on Sundays and sing hymns and put their small change in a plate. That ain't exactly dancing with Dionysus! I'm talking about the urge to understand the chaos around us. I'm talking about the Palaeolithic mind-explosion that created us ... human fucking beings with a spectrum of consciousness vastly wider than any other species! It's at the ends of the spectrum that art and religion and mysticism and inspiration show up. We're not totally human unless we explore these ends."

"So, religious fundamentalism, whether it's in the Middle East or the Midwest ... are you saying that's OK? Suicide bombers? Banning Darwin in schools? Those seem pretty much the ends of the spectrum to me."

"I hate that crap, Jon. That's about power and materialism ... it's got jack-shit to do with what I'm talking about. Look, I'm the biggest atheist there is. Read my lips – Religion Is Nothing More Than The Attempt To Rationalise Sensations Caused By The Electro-Chemical Functioning Of The Brain. It's like dreams. They don't mean shit unless you think they do. They don't mean that you hated your old man and had the hots for your mom. They're just part of you, part of the great gift we've been given by just being human, the most wondrous goddamned creature on the planet."

"Sorry, I thought you were getting all religious on me. I really responded to the elements of ritual and paganism in your work, but at heart I've always believed that a secular society is more likely to be a liberal and democratic one, and one that I want to live in."

The artist gave a disturbing, choking laugh. "Sure ... even though the good old secularists Lenin and Stalin didn't do the cause much good ... but I know what you mean. Look ... just because we can finally begin to explain the spiritual or aesthetic experience scientifically, doesn't mean that Mozart and Michelangelo weren't geniuses. Because our geniuses aren't cut out from the herd for greatness by some Judeo-Christian deity doesn't mean to say that they aren't the most gifted creatures on the planet. What they are, are people who are able to live their lives at the edges of the spectrum. Artists are Shamans ... they travel to the boundaries of the human consciousness. They travel into Inner Space where most people never dare to ... or are never allowed. They have the vision, or they are compelled, to visit the places in their minds where society says, "Don't go! If you go there you're mad. Deviant! You'll be locked in an asylum. You'll be drugged out your skull. You'll be burnt at the stake. You'll live your life on the lunatic fringe. You won't be an artist ... you'll be an asshole sleeping in the street.

"Do you know your William Blake? 'Mind-forged manacles' he called them. It's the only way a hierarchical society can function. The vision of the many must be limited to preserve the authority of the few. Consumerist and Communist societies are as bad as each other. They just inherited the feudalism of the mind that makes them want to curb the experience of being really human. 'In every voice, in every ban, the mind-forged manacles I hear.'

"Artists have a duty to explore the human consciousness ... to be the foreign correspondents ... war correspondents reporting from the dangerous frontiers of the mind ... to lead people out of their thought ghettoes. A hundred years ago the communists wanted to save the masses. That's not good enough now. We need to save the whole planet. Christ, Jonathon, if I could make mankind disappear overnight I would, but that's not going to be possible. The only way to save Earth is for mankind to do it, and for that we need a psychic and aesthetic revolution. We need our Shamans to lead us through the Vortex into the Spirit World. We need to explore all the possibilities of being human so that we're back in harmony with creation, so that we see ourselves to be part of nature, not its slave-master."

Armour stood motionless and silent, spooked, and slightly scared. He watched Burgess's tightly wired body shrug down back into his chair as if suddenly exhausted. Tired and diminished. Weeks ago, while writing his article *Twilight of the Gods*, Armour had calculated Burgess's age. He'd been surprised, feeling that the man was younger than his years. It only struck him now that the sixty-seven-year-old artist was an old man, a slouched and exhausted old man.

"So, an artist works his ass off." Burgess shrugged. "Sometimes people see the point. Sometimes they don't. Sometimes they only get it decades after the artist has gone. Decades and decades and decades sometimes. Do you know when I finally got what the greatest artists in the world were all about? Thousands of years after they had died! Would you believe that? You look as if I'm talking in riddles. I'm not ... I'm not fucking you about ... I asked you here to tell you about the revelation I had and how it's changed me and my work. You know I've always been interested in primitive art. My dad had a thing about Indians. We lived in New Mexico. On weekends, when other dads took their kids to baseball matches, he'd take me to native gravesites. We'd look for arrowheads and pottery shards, and he'd label them and keep them in boxes. Look here ..."

Burgess rose and went to an old battered cabinet of small drawers that looked as if it belonged in a Victorian apothecary's shop. He slid a drawer out and placed it on the table, impatiently motioning Armour to come to him.

"Man, pick one of these up and see if you don't feel a vibe."

Armour carefully took a flint from the silk-lined drawer and held it between a nervous thumb and forefinger. The oil from his skin made it glisten.

"Sometimes the old man and I would get them out, and the two of us would look at them and touch them and try to imagine the people who made them. He spent his whole life in insurance, but he loved the way that the old Indians depended entirely on themselves, and that there were no safety nets for them, no security if someone got sick. It really tickled him when Native American motifs began to appear in my work at art school.

"I came to Europe ... it wasn't what clued-up American artists did in the sixties ... the smart ones went to New York, but shit, I was from New Mexico so what did I know? I hung out, I worked, I was poor ... I did all the right artist-in-Paris stuff. I knew this girl, a would-be writer with a rich daddy back in New Jersey. I was keen to get into her pants, but she had this French boyfriend who was a photographer. He showed me some of his stuff. He said he wasn't French, but a Breton ... you know, a Celt from Brittany. Anyway, he was crazy about what he called *dolmans*. That's standing stones to the rest of us. He had one photograph of a place called Carnac ... it was a Neolithic site with thousands of these stones. It blew my mind ... so he gave me the print ... I still have it. Anyway, I took off to Brittany, and there I got the bug. I was really inspired. I touched these things, I drew them, I photographed them, I read about them, I became a complete pain in the ass to anyone who knew anything about them. I went back to Paris and began to sculpt *le nouveau primitif*. Remember how the French loved Gauguin's primitivism? He got it from Tahiti ... Picasso got his from African art. Well man, it turned these French on to find a foreign artist who actually came to France to find that sort of inspiration. I had an exhibition that was pretty much a sell-out, and I used the money to come to England to see Stonehenge, then up to the Hebrides to see Callanish. I was born and raised in New Mexico, but I found that my soul really dug cold places. I spent a month on Lewis living in a tent on the beach and then I turned up in Edinburgh all ragged and grungy to find there was a famous arts festival going on that I'd never heard of. Shit, I'm from New Mexico. Well, because I looked like an artist I soon got in with a boho crowd and somebody offered me a share in a cheap studio. I was twenty-five and the juices were really flowing. I was never really much into dope and my mind was pretty clear. *Le nouveau primitif* seemed to do the trick with the Brits as well as the French ... after a couple of years my work began to get noticed, first in Edinburgh and then in New York and London. I then went and lived in Mexico for a while, but I often came back to Edinburgh because it was a cool place and I knew Demarco ... he dug what I was doing and he knew everyone in the arts scene ... anyway, one day I went to his gallery and he was with an old guy of about sixty, some weirdo composer he wanted me to meet.

"That, my friend, is how I met Campbell Aaronson. I was real lucky, because he'd become a bit of a recluse ... and anyway, I was mainly into jazz back then ... so I'd never heard of him, although he was big in the progressive scene. However, we all had some drinks and by the end of the night Campbell had agreed to provide the soundscape for an exhibition of mine that Demarco was putting on. Shit, we were drunk and I thought nothing would come of it, but Aaronson turned up the next morning wanting to see my work so that he could get started. That was the beginning of the *Liminal Landscapes.* My old man's arrowheads, the dolmans of Carnac and Campbell's music had led me to places that I could never have imagined. Campbell and I shared an interest in the evolution of the mind and the origins of art, and we soon discovered that we both recognised music in terms of colours. Even though we came from different backgrounds and disciplines we quickly became very close. We'd get drunk in my studio and play games. I'd splash paint onto something and he'd come up with a musical phrase on whatever primitive instrument he was into at the time. Sometimes it worked the other way. He'd play something and I'd dash around looking for my chrome yellow or scarlet madder to show him what I was hearing. He was like an older brother showing me stuff I'd never heard of before. I was on quite a high when I was working with him back then. I reckon I produced the best work of my career in the run-up to *Liminal Landscapes* because I had someone in my life with simpatico. But after the exhibition closed, everything dried up ... all inspiration, the ideas, the passion, the presence of the life force within me. I couldn't sculpt. I was haunted by the fear that my work had been some sort of gimmick, some fashionable fucking stunt. Demarco, the woman I was with at the time and even Campbell, all tried to get me working again, but I just hung out and started getting drunk and smoking dope. Campbell had just got the roof on his cottage here in Calltain and tried to get me to come up, but I felt so lifeless that I never did. Then one day I got a letter from a French guy who'd seen *Liminal Landscapes* in Edinburgh. He was an archaeologist working on the imagery of the Palaeolithic cave paintings in the Dordogne. He'd said he liked my work, but that he thought I should see the real thing and swung it for me to get into the caves. Lascaux has been closed to the public since the early sixties because of the micro-organisms people brought in with them ... all that farting and wheezing ... and Gabillou had never been open at all. Never in my wildest dreams did I expect to be so blown away by what I saw. I had a shelf full of books on primitive and cave art but nothing prepared me for descending into these tunnels and chambers."

Burgess began to prowl round his studio, his eyes wide, his step slow, his hands pointing to imagined images as his mind reconstructed his first subterranean journey. Armour watched in silence, astounded at the physical intensity of the man's remembering.

"The images weren't two-dimensional, they took their shapes from natural features in the surface of the rock. Sometimes just a few scratches or strokes of paint turned a lump on the wall into a creature. As I walked with a tiny light these creatures appeared and vanished in front of my eyes as if they were ghosts. Imagine what the experience must of been like if you were making that journey with just a tallow lamp! I fluttered my fingers over my torch to give the impression of flickering – and the creatures moved! Then I realised that when the creatures appeared from the rock there were never any landscape features around them. They weren't standing on grass ... there was never a tree or a bush or a hill ... because these aren't depictions of real creatures ... they're not real bison and horses, they're spirit animals! They're depictions of beings met in visions like the ones Native American Shamans describe ... animal spirit guides. By entering and penetrating deep into the caves I wasn't just making a physical journey but a psychic one into the Palaeolithic spirit world. I was experiencing the equivalent of a hallucinogenic trip. I was physically walking into the neurological vortex that Shamans describe!"

Burgess was now swaying his body, as if to some throbbing rhythm inside his head, and waving his arms in the direction of the invisible images conjured up by his mind's eye. "Imagine, entering the cave and leaving the light behind ... the darkness ... the flickering tallow lamp ... creatures appearing from the solid rock ... moving, vanishing ... perhaps the tribe chanting and drumming ... the air stale and the oxygen thin ... perhaps they had been fasting or dancing ... God knows what natural hallucinogenics they had ingested! Ergot? Hemp? Fungi? God knows! This is not a fucking art gallery, Jonathan. It's not even a temple. The people who made this were lifting the veil to reveal a realm of spirits that they had direct contact with. Sure, they scraped and they incised, they ground minerals into pigments and used them to make colour and shapes, but they weren't just artists. They weren't daubing on canvas for a few bucks and the chance of a retrospective in a hip gallery, they were explorers who used these caves to travel up and down the spectrum of human consciousness. Yeah, they had technique ... and they sure as hell weren't stoned or catatonic when they actually painted. What they did was to crawl into the depths of the earth to depict the world they experienced during their altered states of consciousness. This was hard, hard work. They must have built wooden scaffolding, they worked in semi-darkness ... they were the most committed artists the planet has ever produced and the most extraordinary human beings that ever existed. Although they lived thousands of years ago, they were much more complete human beings than we've ever been ... they explored the full potential of their consciousness! They hunted and gathered just what they needed and left time to explore the possibilities of their neurosystems. Imagine that, Jonathon, communities dedicated to the exploration of inner space! Human beings exploring their own minds, not side-tracked by all the glittering trash that we're fed with."

Uncomfortable at the sudden silence that followed Burgess's tirade, Armour shifted his weight uneasily from foot to foot, unconsciously shuffling away from the artist. Burgess did not take his eyes off him. Watching. Smiling at his discomfiture.

"It's more than words, Jonathon. I have a cave. It's my life's work. I have made it a cathedral dedicated to human consciousness. Come and join me in the Vortex."

Café Sarti (3)

I know now why I had been summoned to Caleb Burgess's Vortex by that extraordinary letter. He hadn't recognised in my writing any original insight into his art, but had nonetheless subtly flattered me into believing that I had critical qualities that merited his interest. Furthermore, Grizzel Gillespie had not cast any spell over him to get me that audience. I was just a useful idiot, brought there to serve a purpose. Of course I know now it was almost certainly Grizzel's idea. She was fighting to save Calltain from becoming the gravel-pit of Europe. It was the place where she had found stability after her mother's chaotic hippydom, where she'd re-connected with her father and realised that her fascination with the very matter of the universe was her inheritance, and where she had encountered her own first doubts about science and progress. She had used Burgess's years of work, scraping and painting the walls of a cavern in his quest to create his "Cathedral to Human Consciousness", simply to get me to write another article hostile to Argo Aggregates. She knew I'd be bowled over by the cave. She knew I would do everything I could to save it. Bringing me there served both Burgess's self-interest and Grizzel's campaign. It had been decided for me that I would pen an outraged article about how a unique work of art would be destroyed by the super-quarry. And that's what I did. I was a pushover, bending to her will without even realising it. I wrote so many articles about the place that my colleagues at *The Herald* began to call me "the Calltain correspondent", and all the time I thought that I was setting my own news agenda. "Get your own exclusives," I told them.

"Get your own exclusives." I have just said the words out loud as I wrote them in this scrawl-crammed notebook. The waiter is staring at me. Did I say that he was Mediterranean-good-looking, slim-hipped, smooth-skinned and that he must be about twenty? I supposed–I've confirmed myself in his dark young eyes as a loveless old loner who sits hunched and scribbling, eking out a coffee and a pension until my time runs out. He's turned away now, distracted by three thirty-something women in for an early lunch, all sharp suits and shapely legs. Successful young professionals from one of the Bath Street legal or accountancy offices. He greets them noisily with a bow and a flourish, and they exchange sly glances, shrugs and raised eyebrows of admiration as he leads them to a table, all snake-hips and attitude. I think of Grizzel, dancing naked in a cavern by lamplight. When the charming, good-looking European fucker comes back I will catch his eye, and I'll order brandy.

The Herald, 5th October 2000

Cave art for the 21st Century

A unique work of art will be destroyed if plans for a Highland super-quarry go ahead. Arts editor **Jonathan Armour** reports.

Twenty years ago artist Caleb Burgess turned his back on fame and critical acclaim to transform a cave in the remote West Highlands into a unique work of art. Until my visit, that work had only been seen by a handful of his close friends – but the wider public may now never see this masterpiece. It will be completely destroyed if Argo Aggregates is given the go-ahead to exploit the Calltain peninsula as a vast quarry supplying minerals to the construction industry.

Living as a near hermit on the fringe of the alternative and arts community that began in Calltain during the 1960s, Burgess has drawn inspiration for his new work from what he claims were "the Shamanistic cults that created the great Neolithic cave art of France and Spain". He describes the cave at Kilmalin Bay – the roof and sides of which he has richly carved and painted – as a "cathedral dedicated to human consciousness".

Burgess's 1979 exhibition *Twilight of the Gods* confirmed him as a major artist who was deeply influenced by primitive art and ritual. Since then, however, he has vanished from public view, releasing only small-scale works for private collectors and dedicating himself to his site-specific masterpiece.

The artist told me: "I discovered the cave when I was looking for a place to build a sculpture studio on Calltain, and I realised that everything I had done previously was just an apprenticeship for the work I would do there."

The cave consists of two wide chambers, connected by narrow passageways, that stretch 80 metres into the volcanic rock so highly prized by the motorway construction industry. The peninsula has deep-water fjords to its north and south that would make the quarried rock easy to ship all over Europe.

Over the past 20 years Burgess has carved and painted hundreds of abstract symbols and pictographs on the walls and ceiling of the cave, and likens the experience of travelling through it to entering the mystical vortex described by Siberian Shamans, Native American medicine men and people who have taken LSD or had "near-death" experiences.

"Mystics often talk of physically entering into another world," he said. "Alice did it when she fell down a rabbit hole into Wonderland, the kids that went to Narnia entered through a wardrobe, and all over Scotland and Ireland you have legends of barrows and hills where people have gone inside and discovered fairyland. These stories aren't just coincidences, they're the universal product of the way the mind of our species is wired. We've all been created with the ability to experience altered levels of consciousness – mystical experiences. Neolithic man knew this. His cave wasn't just art for art's sake. It was a tool with which to experience visions, a physical doorway into a world of the spirit."

In Burgess's cave he hasn't simply replicated the horses, bison and deer of Neolithic art. "While I'm neurologically identical to those Neolithic guys, I've got completely different cultural baggage from them. I've studied Picasso and Miró, I've seen movies and photographs. My dreams and visions and hallucinations are always going to be culturally specific to my time, not to ten thousand years BC. As I worked in the cave my images became less derivative of the cave art I'd seen and more and more abstract, more like the language of the twentieth century art that I grew up with. It's Picasso, Miró, Kandinsky and the structure of the atom and DNA that haunt my imagination, not mammoths and bison."

Entering Burgess's cave is an extraordinary experience. He forbids visitors to carry electric torches, and hands them old-fashioned crusie lamps with wicks floating in paraffin. He believes that a primitive light source held by a viewer passing through the chambers is as much part of the work as the paint and incisions on the rock surface. As you travel through the cave, hundreds of images appear and disappear in the flickering light. The passing of light makes many of the images appear to move. A bird flutters its wing, the back of an otter undulates, a giant spider vanishes into a crevice and odd marks in ochre reveal themselves to be parts of complex patterns. The effect is startling. There are hundreds of such images, and it would take many visits to the cave to view them all.

Burgess is still carving and painting on an almost daily basis, and says he has no idea when his work on the cave will be complete. Neither is it clear how such a site in so remote a place could be made accessible to the public, and the artist has so far refused permission to photograph his cave. However, there is no doubt in my mind that, with this work, Caleb Burgess has re-established his claim to be one of the most significant artists working in Britain today.

Burgess denies attempting to replicate or revive stone-age religion, and insists that he believes that all mystical experiences are purely the result of the electro-chemical functioning of the brain. "Just because these experiences don't come from God doesn't make them invalid. Understanding the brain doesn't undermine what it is to be human, it's part of the glory of being human. What science does is show that we all have the potential to fully explore our consciousness ... there is no great Jehovah up in the sky that bestows visions on the chosen few. We can all be there exploring inner space! If you want to enter the spirit world, get close to nature. Get close to art and music and dance and ritual."

Burgess claims that greed and consumerism have blunted our ability to fulfil our potential as individuals and to live in harmony with nature. He also passionately believes that art has the power to do nothing less than save mankind and the planet from social and environmental catastrophe. "I'm blessed with the gene of optimism," he says.

Burgess may also be blessed with the gene of artistic greatness. Unfortunately, his "cathedral dedicated to human consciousness" stands on the remote and sparsely populated corner of the Highlands that oil magnate Josh Argo dreams of blasting into oblivion. Argo, a self-made multi-millionaire, is one of Scotland's most successful entrepreneurs. Like Burgess, he is a visionary. Where others see a grey and misty humpbacked hill covered in bracken and heather, Argo sees millions of tons of raw materials, cargos for his mighty ships, and swathes of new motorways and frenetic bypasses. There is little room in that vision for the contemplation of art and nature. The world of commodities and high finance permits no time to question what it means to be a member of the species with the highest order of consciousness on the planet. No place for Caleb Burgess's great work of art.

The question is: which vision do the rest of us want to share?

The Vortex

The cave was, as it was intended to be, a disturbing revelation. For a start, it wasn't one of those coastal caverns ripe with the smell of rotting seaweed and echoing the screeches of cliff-nesting fulmars. Burgess had at first led him along the shore where such features might be expected, but the artist had then abruptly scrambled up what seemed to be a barely perceptible goat track that wiggled steeply into a chaos of broken rock that had tumbled from the living mountain. Neither was the cave limestone, like the painted caverns of France and Spain, but the result of some freakish bubble in the lava flow from the time Calltain was being thrust up in a firestorm from the earth's core. The entrance was a low, squat area of shadow beneath a lumpy outcrop on the mountain's flank. The cavern had been sealed for sixty billion years until the northern rock face had sheared from the mountain in another, much later, geological cataclysm. Had the narrow path worn by the artist not abruptly ended there, the opening would have been invisible. Burgess, with agility that belied his years, ducked in and disappeared.

Armour followed, crawling tentatively forward on hands and knees. The light dimmed until he could see nothing of Burgess in front of him. He thought he might be going uphill, but it was hard to tell. By the time he'd travelled twenty feet his knees ached and he'd scraped his scalp painfully on the rock above him. He could hear Burgess ahead shouting back at him but the words were muffled and unclear. He groped on, but found a void under his hand where the rock floor should have been, and cursed under his shortening breath.

"I said stop there. Wait till I light this goddamn lamp." Burgess's voice boomed, close and reverberating. Armour lay still, breathless and feeling foolish and afraid. Then there was a flicker of light below him. Four or five feet down in the void Burgess's face appeared, suffused in the warm glow of a Zippo. He was carefully lighting what appeared to be an old crusie, a shallow, crudely fashioned metal lamp shaped like a sauceboat in which a wick floated in oil. Its power was little more than a candle, but it was enough to reveal that Burgess was standing upright in a large chamber.

"There's a rope beside you to your right," he said, holding the lamp aloft. "You use it to swing down here. The floor is about ten feet beneath you."

Finding the rope, Armour wriggled forward till his head and shoulders were hanging over the chamber. He grasped the rope in both hands, and it scraped over his face as he pulled on it to drag his chest, his belly and then his groin and thighs from the narrow passage. He kicked hard with a foot and swung like a crazy pendulum for a few seconds before releasing his grip on the rope and landing heavily, jarring his back but keeping his balance. Burgess was grinning from ear to ear. It struck Armour that he might be incarcerated in a cave with a lunatic, but when the man reached out towards him it was to offer him a crusie that he then lit from the flame of the one he held. Burgess held his aloft in a dramatic gesture. The flame flickered frantically. Armour was shocked to see that a star-filled sky twinkled above him. He felt a stab of panic. Surely it was light outside! Burgess lowered the lamp and the sky darkened.

"I've closely observed the constellations, and with Grizzel's help I've recreated them to guide us here in the underworld. It's midsummer's day down here, the solstice, and we're going due west."

With that, the artist moved away. Armour thought he saw bats flitting above him. Burgess came to a halt, waving the flame before him and revealing a giant spider that vanished into a crevice.

"Do what I did Jonathon!"

Armour stepped forward and the creature appeared and disappeared in the fitful flame of his crusie.

"Look above you."

On the basalt sky an eagle soared, its wings beating in the tremulous light. As Armour's eyes grew more accustomed to the gloom, more and more figures appeared – otters, fish and deer. Burgess followed in silence as he discovered more and more animals. Some were painted in detail, while others had required only a few strokes to turn a natural protuberance or crack in the stone into the image of a recognisable creature. As he moved, the images came to life, like creatures in a hallucinogenic bestiary. Abstract shapes – dots, circles, spirals and zigzags – were interspersed amongst the animals. These were not painted, but carved into the hard surface, relying only on the movement of light to reveal them. Armour worked his way along the wall, swaying his lamp from side to side and up and down, and tracing the shapes with his fingertips. To his left, more stars appeared: the Southern sky. Above him, a human figure, rendered in white and red ochre, was falling head first from the black stone firmament. The figure was distinctly male, having greatly enlarged genitals. Armour gasped in astonishment. Before him lay revealed the entrance to another passage, surrounded by human figures that were falling or being sucked into a black hole. This, Armour realised, was Burgess' neurological vortex. His entrance. Without speaking, the artist stepped up and stood close to him to add the light of his lamp to the opening. Armour's shadow joined the images of humans plummeting into the underworld. There were about a dozen figures, men with giant penises and women with exaggerated buttocks and breasts.

Armour found himself light-headed and breathing heavily. Burgess heard or sensed his discomfort.

"Not much oxygen gets in here. If I've had lanterns burning all day I'm pretty high by the end of it." He put his hand firmly on Armour's back. "Go forward. A Shaman must enter the Spirit World alone."

Armour would never know what forces propelled him at that moment into the black depth of tunnel that led to the innermost chamber. In later years, drinking coffee in the Italian café he came to frequent, he would puzzle over the conflicting claims of the charisma of Caleb Burgess, his own curiosity, and the preternatural power of the gaping black hole of the vortex itself. Whatever forces were at work that afternoon, Jonathan Armour, an overweight arts correspondent approaching his fiftieth year, found himself pressing forward on all fours into the narrow darkness, into the depth of a six-billion-year-old mountain, a tremulous naked flame dancing before him.

Snakes and spiders, creatures that sometimes recalled those of a fairground's Ghost Train, and sometimes the paintings of Miró, scuttled in and out of Burgess's gigantic illusion. Armour was breathing hard, edging his body along the narrow passage on one elbow and his knees. Any chance of preserving the trousers of his suit had gone, and instead he concentrated on keeping the oil from spilling out the tiny lamp or from swamping the frail wick. He passed troupes of dancing figures, grotesquely masked faces, and half-human, half-animal creatures that seemed to be suspended or flying in the air. He was short of breath, and no longer knew if he was crawling up or downwards. His heartbeat thrummed in his ears. He dragged himself forward, and the flying creatures vanished. He pushed again with his elbow, found that the low ceiling no longer constricted his shoulders, and lurched ahead unexpectedly. The oil slopped in the crusie, immersing the flame and drowning him in darkness. He lay still, doggo as a hunted animal.

A surge of panic swept through him like a powerful chemical. He wanted to call out, but the thundering of his own pulse in his skull drowned out his cry before he could form it. He realised he'd dropped the crusie, and began to grope for it desperately, despite having neither matches nor lighter to re-ignite it. His arms flailed in a dark void. He felt a pounding on the soles of his feet, and somehow scrabbled forward down a steep slope to a place where his body was unconstricted by rock. From behind, a dim light.

"I thought you were stuck, Jonathon. I shouted for you to go on, but you didn't move." He turned to see Burgess crawling towards him, his grin sinister in the lamplight. The man drew up beside him. "Just a few more yards man, then we can stand up."

The artist wriggled past him, as sinuous as a snake, with his lamp thrust forward. Armour followed the light, shuffling along on his elbows. Ahead he could see Burgess rise and fumble about. By the time he'd caught up with him, the artist was putting the flame of his lamp to a wooden torch with a tar-impregnated rag tied to the end. He handed it to Armour with a rasping laugh. "Here's one I made earlier." Burgess took a second torch from what Armour could now see was a rough workbench, and held the blackened tarry end of it into Armour's flame until it too sprang into life. Standing with the burning brands in their hands, the entire second chamber was revealed to them.

They were in a cavern, perhaps the size of a small Highland church. Next to the workbench was a tower of tubular metal scaffolding. Armour's gaze was drawn up. A huge whorl of golden yellow dominated the cavern ceiling, thirty feet above them. Even from where he stood Armour could see that its luminous centre and spiral arms were composed of thousands of points of colour that danced in the light of their firebrands. The whole shape seemed to be turning, receding from them as they watched. Disorientated, Armour felt a wave of nausea and the ground beneath him sway. There was nothing to cling on to, so he sank to his knees, his head thrown back so as not to take his eyes off the spiral galaxy above him.

"The universe is exploding. Some galaxies are moving away from us at billions of miles an hour." Burgess spoke to the ceiling, but now turned to gaze down on Armour. "The Neolithics didn't have science as we know it but they had creation myths and cosmologies that they felt compelled to express on the walls of their caves. You'll find mine painted here ... astrophysics, the exploding universe, strands of DNA, single-cell creatures, and complex colonies of cells like ourselves that have grown skin and gut and cocks and pussies and brains."

Armour gave no sign that he was listening, but continued to stare at the rocky sky above him, his mouth opened wide as if to inhale as much as he could of the thin, smoky air. Undeterred, Burgess continued.

"We think of the cave painters as artists, but they were principally Shamans, exploring their universe from inside their minds and reaching out into the stars. They wore skins, they scavenged for carrion when they had to, they carved rock with stone tools, but they were rich, Armour. Rich and free. They lived at the edge of existence, in full knowledge of their physical and spiritual worlds.

"We spend our lives hypnotised by politicians and corporations who use television, advertising, and all that fashion and mass-produced pop-culture shit to turn us into good little corporate robots.

I wander through each chartered street
Near where the chartered Thames does flow,
And mark in every face I meet,

Marks of weakness, marks of woe.
In every cry of every man.
In every infant's cry of fear,
In every voice, in every ban,
The mind-forged manacles I hear ..."

The familiar words shook Armour from his fascination. He tore his eyes from the ceiling and rubbed his aching neck with his free hand.

"Our old friend Blake wrote that two hundred years ago, Jon, but try substituting 'Corporate' for 'Chartered' and you have an accurate description of where we are today. Think of it man ... mind-forged manacles!"

Armour stood and turned to the walls of the cavern. At first he could make little sense of what he saw, but as he worked his way round, slowly waving his smoky flame, he recognised the double helix of DNA spiralling up towards the nebula ceiling. Close to it were a complex series of marks, joined by straight lines, that seemed to Armour as if they might be either magical or scientific symbols (but would have been recognisable to a biochemist as accurate diagrams of amino acids). There was a scatter of carved cup marks, in-filled with red ochre and surrounded by irregular, organic shapes delineated in white. Amoebae. Armour recognised the single-cell organisms.

Holding his brand aloft and talking all the while, Burgess followed him round the chamber, an ovoid space perhaps twenty yards wide and forty long.

"These corporate guys aren't all-powerful, Jonathon, but they're smart. They've used the schools, the media, and consumerism to have us consent to their narrow definition of what it is to be human. We can consume anything we want, we can indulge every lust or whim we can imagine ... with the proviso that we live under their consensual dictatorship. But to be free, all we have to do is see through them. That's why artists need to be Shamans. We need to make people see clearly how lives are stunted and how we're condemned to extinction unless our minds and imaginations are big and wide enough to see what's really happening. We need to live on the edge of existence. We need to confront the realities of our physical and spiritual worlds!"

Some patches of the cave's walls were covered with incisions and paint, while others bore just a few rough charcoal sketches or were untouched. Although the cave was incomplete, it was clear that Burgess's intention was to create a subterranean cathedral to evolution and the cosmos, to creation itself.

Now Armour could see birds, fish and animals painted in meticulous detail and scattered over the living rock in a prelapsarian paradise. Then there were images of humans. Unlike the beasts, they were not painted in detail, but as stick people, crowded closely together and copulating, dancing, playing single-reed pipes, fighting with spears, and seemingly flying or floating in the air. To his right Armour could see a huge anatomically graphic phallus that rose as high as the cave's roof, thrusting towards the black hole at the centre of the spiral galaxy. Beyond the giant penis lay the spiralling DNA where he had first begun to explore. He had come full circle.

Burgess fell to his knees at the base of the double helix.

"This is where it began," he said, moving his flame along the surface of the wall, close to the cave's floor. Armour squatted beside him to stare at a patch of unpainted rough-grained rock, but could see nothing until the artist's light caught the rim of a narrow groove, causing a shadow in the indentation. As Burgess moved his arm, more shadows were revealed and Armour could see that they formed a rectangle, perhaps eight inches long and four wide. The shape contained two more grooves that trisected it into one narrow section and two larger ones of equal size.

"Now look at this." Burgess stood up, raising the burning torch briskly above his head. The flame flickered wildly for a few seconds casting a nightmarish gleam over his face. Just above the two men was another carved rectangle. It was the same size as the previous one, but divided into three equal areas. Armour stretched up to touch the shape, but it lay just beyond his reach.

"So far I've found four more throughout the cave. None of them are in obvious places, but hidden away in corners, or at least out of the line of vision of anyone making their way through the chambers. The lozenges are all the same size, but each one is divided into three sections of different proportions.

I don't know what they mean, but they must have been very powerful. Someone built a platform so that he could reach up to carve that one with stone tools. When I found the first one I tried to replicate it with just the materials that a Neolithic would have had – agates, flints, that kind of thing. It took me days, and my hands were raw by the time I'd finished. Whatever these shapes are, they're extremely potent magical or religious symbols. To the man who carved these, they were as real and as important as is our understanding of DNA or the Big Bang."

Armour felt himself dull, stupid, slow to take in what Burgess was saying. "You mean ... that these ... shapes ... are real?"

Burgess held his burning brand close to Armour's face, as if to regard his idiocy more closely. "Listen Mr Art Kritic," he gave the word a hard mock-German consonant, "I've spent twenty years on this work." He leaned close to Armour, their faces only inches apart now. "It's all fucking real, man. What you mean to ask is 'Are these lozenge carvings older than crazy old Caleb?'"

"Sorry ... that's what I meant ... I mean ... are these ancient carvings, or are they your work?"

"They're old. God knows how old ... probably thousands of years. I'd been working on the outer chamber and the Vortex for ten years before I discovered the first one. I kept shtoom about it, because I wasn't going to have some goddamn archaeologist taking over the place."

He stepped back to regard his work, thrusting his torch into a bracket welded onto the scaffolding. "It's funny you know, until I saw that first carving I'd never found any evidence of the cave ever having been occupied, no bone fragments or anything. Yet all the years I'd worked down here I felt that there was a vast amount of psychic energy imprinted on the walls. I was convinced that I wasn't the first person to work and create here. I've looked back at my diaries and there are several references to sensing a presence here. I'd no material evidence, but my inner core detected the spirit of a powerful Shaman. This is a place of great magic, a place you come to find meaning and understanding in a world that our everyday experience tells us is chaotic and barbaric. Here men of vision may resolve the struggle between reason and atavism. Are you a man of vision, Jonathon?"

Armour remained silent for a few moments before rolling with the artist's heavy-handed irony. "Oh you know me, Mr Burgess, I'm just an art critic. All stetson and no steers, all foreplay and no fucking."

Burgess grinned. "Yeah yeah, that's right. But you're perceptive ... at least, more so than most. I don't take daily newspapers, but I read your *artWORK* stuff ... and Grizzel thinks you're OK, which is pretty well good enough for me and everyone else on Calltain."

Grizzel. He had lost all sense of time in Burgess's caverns but it seemed to Armour that he had not thought of her for hours, even though Grizzel Gillespie had seldom been out his mind for days now. He looked into the dark, beyond the pool of light they now stood in. Above them dots of yellow ochre caught the flickering rays of their torches.

"Grizzel, has she ..."

"Been here? Sure she's been here. Nearly everyone on Calltain's been here. I kept the place secret when I first discovered it ... didn't tell a soul, except Campbell. That's the way it stayed for the first ten years or so while I worked on the outer chamber ... but when I was about to start on the vortex leading into the inner gallery, about a dozen of us came to consecrate it, to drink wine while I made the first marks. Campbell brought a bodhran and drummed while I used ochre and charcoal to accentuate natural markings on the wall that sort of looked like a long beaked bird. After that we came once or twice a year ... every time I completed a section or when we felt that the community needed to come together."

"It's some place for a party."

"Yeah, it's kind of grown into that. Parties that are rituals and rituals that are parties. Somehow the place inspires music and poetry so we celebrate that too ... and dancing! About twenty of us were here, three or four months back. You should have seen us, man! I'd made flaming torches and Campbell started drumming. Doug Fowlie has a bagpipe chanter and began on that. Trail came up with a wordless chant, and we all joined in clapping and stomping. Tyler and Grizzel began to dance, but the torches made it stiflingly hot so they stripped naked. Soon we were all bare-assed and dancing, even the old guys like Campbell and me. It was like a tribal gathering ... not a tribe ... a nexus of free spirits ... bound together by the need to be part of a community that's at one with nature ... where individuals are free to develop a personal relationship with creation and realise their full potential as creative and spiritual human beings."

A vivid, disturbing image suffused Armour's mind. It wasn't of old hippies prancing in their new age capers, but of Grizzel. Grizzel dancing, and naked. Naked and dancing, with Matt Tyler.

"That must have been quite a sight," he muttered, and was at once embarrassed by the double entendre, as if Burgess was a mind-reader who'd caught him in the act of erotic imagining. The artist was now watching him quizzically. "I mean, the cave, the paintings, the drumming ... it must have been quite something."

"It sure was. Campbell recorded it on a DAT machine. He may let you hear it one day." At that, Burgess inhaled deeply, threw his head back and emitted an ear-splitting bellow – half scream, half war cry – that reverberated ferociously in the stone chamber. Armour recoiled, clasping an ear with his free hand and striking the back of his head on the cavern wall. Burgess saw the pantomime and his bellow turned to a breathless, rasping laugh.

"Extraordinary acoustic, isn't it. Aaronson got very excited about it. When I first brought him here, he kept clapping his hands." Burgess now began to clap rhythmically in imitation, his body swaying as he did so. "He was amazed by the reverb. Right from the beginning he said it was the place for ritual, for ceremonies. It blew his mind when I found the ancient carvings! He knew the Greek myth about the nymph Echo, but then he discovered that all sorts of cultures have associated echoes with the spirit world. He brought his bodhran down there and played it all over the cave. In some places, it sounded like hoofbeats ... in others heartbeats. He now has a theory that there is a correlation between Neolithic petroglyphs and the echoes made in the part of the cave where they're found. Says that if he were twenty years younger he'd go round all the great cave paintings in the world with his bodhran testing his theory. He tried to get Grizzel to do it, but so far she's stuck to the astrophysics."

The back of Armour's head ached and he was now feeling nauseous as well as short of breath. He felt sick, lost and alone, and struggled to control the shuddering in his lower spine that manifested his panic.

"If you don't mind ... I think I'd like to get some fresh air."

"That's fine by me. I'm used to it ... the thin air, the fumes from the lamps, all the ancient vibes, but at first I found it pretty trippy down here after a few hours."

Burgess stood beneath the entrance to the narrow tunnel that led to the rest of the world, his back braced against the wall and his hands clasped in front of him. "Put your foot on my hands and I'll give you a shove up. Once you're in that passageway you're going slightly downhill so it's easier to get out of here than in."

"We'll see," thought Armour aloud.

The Celestial Sphere

The last shred of sunset was giving way to twilight when Jonathon Armour, the *Herald's* award-winning columnist and respected Arts and Culture correspondent, crawled into the early October afternoon from a hole in the ground. His face was smeared with soot and he coughed and retched in the chill salt-damp air, hacking up gobs of blackened phlegm. Leaning forward to spit, he saw that the knees of his trousers were in tatters and his grazed and stinging skin visible through the rips. The toes of his shoes were scuffed beyond redemption. The elbows of his Barbour were ripped through to the lining. It was in this bedraggled state that he saw Grizzel Gillespie again. He had returned to Burgess's home at the artist's insistence that he should collect a torch to see him safely up the *bealach* and over the hill to Aaronson's house. The woman was sitting behind the great glass studio doors, watching and waiting for them.

At first she could barely speak. Every time she began to ask Armour what he thought of Burgess's creation, she began to giggle, slightly hysterically, behind a raised hand. As he washed his face and regarded his reflection in Burgess's bathroom mirror he had to admit to himself that he cut a farcical figure. A mug of instant coffee laced with sugar and whisky was proffered, accepted and swiftly downed. He hadn't eaten since breakfast and the hot liquid and alcohol drove the chill from his body and replaced it with a glow of mild elation.

It was dark by the time Armour and Grizzel said their farewells to Burgess, passed through the avenue of monoliths, and began to climb the path over Calltain's rocky spine. Grizzel had refused Burgess's offer of a Maglite the size of a truncheon, saying that it was too wonderfully starry to spoil her night-vision with a torch.

They climbed in more or less silence until they reached the *bealach.* The air was cold but the wind was behind them, blowing her hair in twin tangles. To the south lay the darkness of Loch Calltain and, beyond, the lights of Vallaig.

"Don't look at Vallaig. Don't look at the lights, let your eyes become dark-adapted and just look up," she commanded urgently. "When I first came to Calltain, Campbell brought me up here on a night like this ... ever since then it's been my favourite spot on the entire planet." They stood quietly for a while, the stars gazing down on them. Occasionally Grizzel would murmur the name of a constellation to herself like a private mantra: Cassiopeia, Andromeda, Pisces. The longer they gazed up, the more accustomed their eyes became to the night sky. Gradually, layer after layer of smaller or more distant stars were revealed until Armour understood that he was not looking into a dark sky, but into a bowl of light. It seemed to him infinite and beautiful, but he felt there and then that he had never been lonelier in all his life.

"I've studied this for years," she said abruptly. "In all that time I've never got over the sense of wonder." She turned to him. "Were you a stargazer as a kid?"

"No, I'm afraid my lore doesn't cover the stars. I think I can recognise the Plough and Orion's belt, but that's it."

"You don't have to be an astrophysicist to navigate your way round the celestial sphere, you know."

"The what? The Celestial Sphere! I thought that was more in your loopy mother's line."

"Don't be deliberately thick, Jon. If you stand on a flat plain, or out in a boat on the sea, the sky is like a giant upturned bowl above and all around you ... except that it's not static, but moving, rotating round the earth."

"Really?"

"You're fucking joking? You're pulling my leg?"

He considered for a moment, not that he was thinking about the stars. He was pondering on the fact that he never really given stars much thought until that moment. "I know that the North Star is really important in navigation because it doesn't move ... so I suppose ... the others must. I've never really thought about it much."

"You city boys. Your minds are fogged with noise, electric light and petrol fumes. Don't you know the constellations? Look, it's easy. Pattern recognition is innate in our species, so humans have always recognised distinct groups of stars. Look at Pisces up there! It was first described by the Babylonians. The ancient cultures recognised the patterns and named them, and the Greeks and Romans wove myths around them ... at least the ones in the Northern Hemisphere. In Australia and New Zealand they had to wait till the eighteenth century to name constellations ... although I expect that the Aborigines had a pretty good idea about what was going on up there." She stood gazing up for what seemed an age before speaking again. "I'm afraid you can't see Cancer, but when you come here in December or January you'll see it as clear as anything over on the right there."

"What's so interesting about Cancer?"

"Your birth sign."

"How do you know that?"

She shrugged. "I don't know. You must have told me."

"Well, I wouldn't recognise it, but I know Orion's Belt and the Plough." He pointed to the low sky, just above the darkness of the sea. "There, that's the Plough, and the last two stars point to the North Star. It's up there somewhere."

"Yes, those are Merak and Dubhe, the pointers. Follow them up, about five times the distance that lies between them ... and that's Polaris, the Pole Star. All the stars in the northern sky appear to rotate round Polaris."

"True North? Not like a compass?"

"Actually just less than one degree off the true pole." She grinned, shaking her head, her shoulders juddering in silent laughter. "Sorry, I must sound like some terrible swot."

"Yeah, you've just won the Geek of the Week award."

Grizzel made to punch him on the arm, but he caught her wrist. She didn't pull away, but held him in a direct gaze with unblinking eyes that looked to Armour like beautiful dark planets. Her lips were half open as if she was about to say something, and never more desirable to him than at that moment. She inclined her head a fraction, her eyes widening as if questioning him. He leaned forward and kissed her.

It wasn't much of a kiss. A slight brush of the lips. A polite party kiss. He let go her arm, allowing her the freedom to draw back or recoil or even lash out at him, but she put her arms around him and rested the side of her face on his chest. He slipped one hand under her blowing hair and onto the cold nape of her long neck. His other hand found her coat open and the firm curve where her narrow waist met her hips beneath a layer of thick wool. He pulled her closer and they stood like that letting the celestial sphere whirl above them awhile, him amazed that he held her slim body in his arms, and neither of them daring to break the spell. When they kissed again it was with spontaneous clumsy hunger, teeth colliding, tongues urgent, their breath short and gasping, their mouths and chins wet with shared saliva.

That night, on the fold-down futon bed in the circular room of her father's tower house, Grizzel Gillespie and Jonathon Armour become lovers. She slipped in under his duvet sometime after midnight, peeling off a long floppy T-shirt in one effortless movement.

"I told you it was a great room to see the stars from," she whispered.

They made love, rested in an unbroken embrace and were passionately at each other again, with all the self-aware intensity that only human animals are capable of, when the sound of machine guns and bombs ripped through the room.

"What the hell ..." Armour sat bolt upright, his face almost colliding with Grizzel's. She lurched from her straddling position, pulling herself off his erect cock, and reached to the floor for her T-shirt.

"Shit! It's Campbell ... he sometimes does this."

"What?" Armour had a terrifying flash-image of himself being slaughtered by an outraged octogenarian father. Grizzel pulled her T-shirt over her head. The staccato gunfire had now taken on a complex but discernible rhythm.

"When he can't sleep, he gets up and works. He's below us in the studio working on a composition made up of snatches of gunfire and explosions that he's downloaded from the Channel 4 news."

"Jesus Christ, he almost gave me a heart attack."

"Yeah," she said, rising from the futon and pulling her T-shirt down as far as it would inadequately stretch. "It's been like living in Beirut recently." She crossed to the kitchen area and filled the kettle. They listened in silence to the percussion of a dozen or more digitally recorded wars.

"He's going to come up here to make tea in a little while. I'm afraid we've been caught out, the only way to my room is through the downstairs studio."

"How will he react?"

"Oh he'll be cool. He's an old hippy ... he just wants people to be happy."

"Well I certainly fit the bill then." He waited a moment before asking, "Are you ... happy?"

"Well, I'd have been happier if he'd left off for a minute or two, and let me finish what I was doing there ... but yeah ... I think so. I don't jump into bed with guys that I think will make me unhappy ... but I don't suppose anyone does. It's just ... hard to know."

"Would it make you happier if I asked to see you again soon ... perhaps when you're next in Glasgow ... on your way to wherever ... or just to stay with me at the flat?"

The music stopped. "I think you'd better put your pants on. Campbell will be up these stairs in thirty seconds."

The stealthily rising sun bleached out the stars from the sky as the two men watched from the big windows, drinking tea. Aaronson had behaved as if it was perfectly natural to find his daughter with a half naked man in his home. Grizzel had gone to shower and dress, and Armour was now wearing the wreck of a once smart black suit. The jacket, which had been covered by his Barbour, was fine but both knees had been torn out his trousers, which were also splattered with mud and soot. Aaronson regarded him with an amused and questioning arched eyebrow. Armour remained silent, watching the day dawning on the rest of his life. A faint but discernible feeling of what might be hope trickled through his veins.

After breakfast Grizzel walked him to the jetty. The wind was brisk, but the sun was shining and despite the imminence of separation, his spirits were high.

"I don't know anything about your ... circumstances," she said after a minute or so of silent hiking.

"Well, I'm not."

"Pardon? Not what?"

"Married. Isn't that what you were asking?"

She punched his arm playfully. "Am I so transparent?"

"Eh, 'fraid so. But after last night you've every right to know. Now, I'll answer your next question before you even have to ask it. Yes, I was married, but I'm not now. OK? Now, kindly change the subject."

She wanted to know next how he had got into journalism and he'd told her of his Art History degree – "the laziest degree in the world" – and of getting on to *The Herald's* graduate trainee scheme.

"How old are you, Jon?"

"Ah, I was afraid you'd ask that. I'm nearly fifty." He thought she looked fleetingly surprised, and wasn't sure if he was pleased about this or not.

"Have you worked for *The Herald* ... all that time since you were a graduate?"

"Yes ... you must think I'm stuck in a rut, but it's just that every time I got restless they gave me a better job ... you know, news reporter, then features writer, and then Arts and Culture Correspondent. I was always interested in the arts, so I reckon I've got the best job on the paper now, with no plans to move."

"And can you just write pretty well what you like?"

"Yeah, up to a point. There are obviously big exhibitions and events that I pretty well have to cover as diary jobs ... but I'm lucky, the features editor, Harry Urquhart, is a good mate of mine and gives me a lot of scope."

"I've an idea for an article," she said, stopping momentarily on the shore path.

"Let's hear it," he said, hoping that he sounded more enthusiastic than he felt.

"Why don't you interview Josh Argo?" She began to walk again and gestured towards the loch. "Invite him here to Calltain in his famous yacht. If he likes sailing as much as he's supposed to, he'll fall in love with this place ... everyone does."

"Yeah, but I think Argo's first love is money."

"But it would be great, Jon ... you get Argo here and get him talking about what he sees and feels. It would bring the whole super-quarry project down to a very human, personal level. Is he just a hard-hearted bastard? Or does he have a soul? Of course ... I hope he comes here, falls in love with the place and calls the whole thing off. But if he doesn't change his mind ... well, at least we'll have tried."

"And of course the Save Calltain Campaign can use my article as evidence that one of Scotland's most respected and successful businessmen is really just a hard-hearted bastard."

She punched his arm, and then took it in hers. "I am transparent, aren't I? But come on Jon, it would still be a good story for you, even if it didn't save Calltain."

"I'll think about it," he said guardedly, but he knew that Grizzel's naive attempt to manipulate him had a good idea at the core of it. Argo, the club-footed lone yachtsman, travelling to the very place he planned to destroy, to personally confront the environmental and economic issues of the age. He wasn't going to tell Grizzel, but he liked her idea a lot.

"I'm going to feel a right prat on the train ... dressed like this I mean," he said, glancing at the torn knees of his trousers. She laughed, covering her mouth with her hand.

"Well, if you will come to Calltain dressed for some trendy arts event what do you expect? At least your Barbour actually looks as if its been outdoors now. I bet you drive one of these 4X4s that never leave the city or get muddy."

"Me? A Chelsea tractor! No, you're wrong. I don't have a car."

"Lost your licence then?"

"That's what everyone says, including that lunatic Tyler. Actually, my ex-wife was pretty much teetotal ... a very focused and determined person. Well, I like my wine ... so she did most of the driving. I just lost the habit."

"Do you still see her?"

"She's not around anymore."

The woman with the witch name sensed she had reached a no-go area, and asked nothing more.

Passing the upturned boat that was Calltain Publishing Unlimited, they turned onto the shore road. Grizzel stopped in her tracks.

"Where the hell's Tyler?" She was staring towards the jetty. "He knew you were crossing. He should be here now. Where the hell's he gone?"

"Gone fish-ing," a voice sang out behind them. Armour turned to find a short stocky man in his thirties standing in the doorway of the boat house. He was dressed in a canvas fisherman's smock, baggy cargo shorts and sandals. His face was round and boyish, with a ready smile and merry eyes. Under a baseball cap that bore the logo "Wilson's Whisky" was a mop of darkish blond hair that appeared to have had highlights dyed into it some time in the not too recent past.

"Hi Andy! Do you know where the wandering boy's got too?"

"Yeah, he told me to look out for you. He got a call from Joe Phimster. Joe's desperate for lobsters, so Matt's checking out his creels. He's been gone a while now, so I expect he's caught some and will be taking them straight to Joe in Vallaig." The man turned to Armour. "You'll be the reporter then?"

"Oh I'm sorry, Andy. This is Jon Armour of *The Herald*." She turned to Armour. "Sorry ... when I come here I get into the habit of thinking that everyone knows everyone else. This is Andy Campbell, one half of Calltain Publishing Unlimited."

"Not the clever half, I'm afraid." A New Zealand accent, Armour decided. "Trail's got the talent, I'm just the muscle-man and gofer, but I also have a four-metre inflatable rib and an outboard motor that's actually behaving itself just now, so you're not stuck here, Jon ... as long as you don't mind giving me a hand to carry the bloody thing."

The inflatable dinghy was moored to the pier. Grizzel untied the line and pulled the boat ashore while Andy and Armour hefted the cumbersome engine down to the beach. There, Andy kicked off his sandals, took the full weight of the engine, and waded into the sea up to his thighs to clamp it onto the wooden transom. He held the boat firmly.

"Get in and sit in the middle, Jon."

Armour gingerly did what he was told, and sat facing the stubby bow. As he did so, Grizzel stepped in lightly, sat at the stern and tugged sharply at the motor's lanyard. It coughed into life on the second pull. Andy cheered and began to turn the rib's nose out to sea.

"Don't get frozen Andy, I can manage from here."

It just dawned on Armour at that moment that the capable Kiwi wasn't coming on this trip, and that it was up to Grizzel to get them over the choppy loch in the flimsy craft.

"Aren't you coming?" he blurted out.

"Hell no! It's too rough for me out there. I'm just a townie, you're far safer with Grizzel."

Andy gave the craft a shove. A twist of Grizzel's wrist and the outboard growled angrily, driving the inflatable swiftly out to sea as Andy waded ashore. Jon could see him standing there, waving and shaking dripping sea-water from his legs. Grizzel crouched in the stern, the tiller in her hand, wind in her hair and laughter on her face.

"Have you done this before?" he shouted.

"Loads of times ... I used to spend half my holidays here in boats. Tyler taught me lots. When you live on Calltain, being a boatman's a good skill to have ... and I love it!"

The surf was choppy where it broke on the jetty, but out on the loch the great mass of water undulated in a slow, relentless rhythm. Grizzel pointed the rib's bow at an angle to the swell, and the nerve-jangling din of the engine rose and fell in time to the pulse of the sea as the dinghy surged forward, pitching and yawing, as fast as the outboard would drive her.

Armour twisted round to look at her. Her head was thrown back and she was laughing with the sheer rush and exhilaration of powering a tiny boat at speed into the heavy swell. She caught him staring.

"I love this!" she shouted.

It was clear that Grizzel was more than competent, even skilled, at handling a small boat. Despite sea spray soakings, Armour found himself thrilled by the gusts of her enthusiasm and joy. The excitment of it even drove away his gnawing regret that a night stranded on Calltain might have meant another night with her. He realised that his trousers were now soaked, as well as ragged, and he didn't care.

They entered the calm water of Vallaig harbour. Grizzle throttled down and headed the rib for the slipway on the innermost wall. She called out, "Tyler," as they passed the moored *Ran*, and the man looked up from the basket of lobsters that he was selling to Joe Phimster in one of the discreet cash transactions that the old fish merchant preferred.

Tyler watched the couple motor past his vessel for a moment before half raising an arm in salutation. Armour thought he detected a tight-lipped, knowing look on the boatman's face, and it made him happy. If the bastard suspected that he and Grizzel were now lovers, well, tough luck!

On the shore Grizzel gently touched Armour's face with both hands and kissed him full on the mouth, a kiss just long enough, he thought, to be recognised as significant and sexual by anyone who cared to watch.

"I'll come to Glasgow soon, Jon. I promise."

"Yes, do ... soon."

She stepped back to regard his soaked and tattered trousers, her hand flew to cover her mouth and stifle a laugh. "Enjoy your journey!"

"Yeah, thanks a lot."

"Serves you right ... I haven't had a boyfriend who didn't have a car since I was at school."

Grizzel kissed him lightly again and he turned to go. She watched him stride for the train, drawing odd looks as he went.

The Boyfriend

So. It seemed that he was now A Boyfriend. He'd been a lover and a partner several times in his life. He'd been a husband once. But it was nearly thirty years, when he'd been at university, since he'd last been called A Boyfriend. The needle flickered and hovered at a pound or so over thirteen stone. A tiny improvement. He stepped back from the scales to view himself in the bathroom mirror. Front on, he thought, he didn't look bad, but in profile the pale arc of his belly made him look pregnant. He drew the blubber in for a few seconds to remind himself of the contour he aspired to. There was little fat round his face, which still carried a discernible trace of his youth, although his temples were rapidly turning grey. "Better grey hair than nae hair," he said out loud. His teeth were still showing the benefits of his recent visit to the dental hygienist, and the hairs in his nostrils had hardly grown back since the last painful plucking. He couldn't remember when these had first started to sprout, or at what point in his middle age he'd stopped noticing them. Embarking on a love affair, being A Boyfriend, had changed that. He'd spent his recent days off walking to, and around, Kelvingrove Art Gallery. He'd switched from pints of real ale to dry white wine and was being careful about what he ate. He was regularly doing sit-ups. In short, he was trying to acquire an acceptable Boyfriend look. It just wasn't happening fast enough. He had newly taken a shower, although he'd already had a bath that morning. He was trying to pass the time. She'd be on the train now, and arriving in just over an hour. He'd offered to meet her at the station, but she'd insisted on finding her own way.

When at last they embraced clumsily at his door he thought she smelled like an autumn morning.

"I brought you Calltain's finest," she said. She had a rucksack on her back, a laptop computer case in one hand and an old supermarket plastic bag in the other. She held the bag out for him to peer into. Mushrooms.

"I was just thinking that you smelled all outdoorsy."

"Doug and I picked these early this morning. I'll fry them for supper ... I hate mass-produced food."

She stood in his sitting room, taking it all in as if she was a prospective buyer. The developer had imposed a modish stripped-down style on the converted Merchant City warehouse. Armour had furnished it in black and stainless steel, but any attempt at fashionable minimalism he'd subverted with numerous paintings, ethnic rugs and walls of books.

"It's a great flat," she said at last.

"It's great to have you in it."

"You're lucky."

"Oh, I know."

She laughed and blew him a kiss. "No ... I mean it's lucky that I'm here at all, and not still stranded on Calltain. The police arrested Tyler last night."

"Tyler? Arrested? What for?"

"They didn't say, but it seems to be some sort of round-up of anyone they think might be an eco-warrior. All I know is that they grabbed him in Vallaig yesterday afternoon. Doug was with him. He says they came to Vallaig pier, told Tyler that he was wanted for questioning and huckled him off into the back of a van. Doug phoned Campbell and then took the *Ran* back over to Calltain. Andy and Trail are away just now, so it was Doug who brought me over to the mainland this morning, otherwise I might have been stuck there."

"So where's Tyler now?"

"Oh, he's out ... probably back in Vallaig by now. Campbell called a lawyer. They let him go this morning, but the poor guy had to spend the night in the cells."

"Did they charge him?"

"Charge him ... like money? For staying in a cell?"

"Christ no ... charge him with an offence. Is he having to go to court accused of something?"

"Oh no, it was nothing to do with him. Anyway he had lots of witnesses to say that he was on Calltain when it happened."

"What was nothing to do with him? ... what happened? ... what the hell did they think he had done?"

"You know he's a diver?"

"Yeah, I know he dives for scallops."

"Well, it seems that someone cut open the cages of a fish

farm somewhere and let hundreds of young halibut out. The police reckon it must have been a diver."

"So why pick on Tyler? There must be thousands of people who can dive."

"Oh I don't know," she said vaguely. "He used to be a tearaway when he was in his teens ... he like ...stole cars and stuff. They probably just don't like the look of him. He's no lover of authority. He'd just tell them to fuck off when they spoke to him."

Armour involuntarily brushed his left eyelid with his fingertips even though he knew the bruise left by Tyler's drunken fist had long faded. For a week now, he'd been desperately hoping that his lovemaking with Grizzel on the fold-down bed had been more to her than a one-night stand. Sure, she'd come to stay overnight with him on her way to Oxford, and – presumably – they'd sleep together, but it maddened him that she'd arrived so full of Matt Tyler and his doings.

"He's mad, bad and dangerous to know if you ask me," he blurted out, and then felt a stab of panic as Grizzel bristled.

"He's a decent man," she said forcefully. "You may have got off to a bad start with him, but there's a lot of people in Calltain who love and respect him."

He suppressed the urge to ask if there were also people on Calltain who'd lie for Tyler, who'd back up a fabricated alibi for him. Grizzel was clearly angry with him, still wearing her stockman's coat, the rucksack on her back and holding the laptop case and the bag of mushrooms in her hands. Earlier, he'd planned to show her round, point out the bathroom, get her to dump her rucksack in the bedroom, settle her down with a glass of wine. All that afternoon he'd pondered long and hard about whether he'd have to wait until evening before he'd get her into bed, or whether he should bring the subject up as soon as she arrived. Perhaps she would suggest it ... after all, she'd initiated their lovemaking in Calltain. He desperately wanted to say something to defuse the bloody Tyler situation.

"They should have locked the arsehole up," was what he wanted to say. What he did say was, "Well Grizzel, if you think he's a good guy I suppose he must be OK."

She stared at him, seeing through his deception. "You can't stand him, can you?"

"Well ... as you said yourself ... we got off to a bad start."

"You stabbed him in the eye!"

"Christ, Grizzel! That was an accident. You know that."

"Do I?"

He couldn't believe she'd said that. "You know what happened! Tyler was prancing about like a drunken lunatic. He stumbled and my pencil scratched his face."

"We've only got your word for that. Tyler told me he was too drunk to remember what happened."

"He was pissed out his mind. That's why he got hurt. What is it with you and him?"

"What do you mean exactly?"

"How come you've got it into your head that I stabbed Tyler in the eye? I thought you came here because we were having some sort of relationship ... not to accuse me of kebabing Tyler."

Grizzel let the plastic bag fall to her feet and pressed the fingertips of her hand to her forehead as if suddenly in pain.

"No ... of course you didn't. I'm sorry ... it's just that Tyler and I go back a long way. I'm sorry I lost the rag. Look, if it's alright with you I'd like a bath. It's been ... a difficult day." She smiled, her eyes fixed on his, and she moved towards him and kissed him lightly. "After my bath I'd like us to make love ... we'll have a great time ... I promise."

Later, in between the clean white sheets that Armour had put on his bed that morning, Grizzel spoke to her new lover of her mother, her father and her first love. When she turned fourteen, she said, she'd suddenly baulked at the thought of another long summer at her mother's Greek commune and decided to get to know the man who was paying the fees of her progressive school in the Scottish Borders, and who occasionally turned up to visit her there or drive her to or from an airport.

"Did you not get on with your mother?"

She chewed her lower lip in thought for a few moments. "It's not that, but I don't have much to do with her now. She's pretty self-absorbed, and I suppose I am too, so we don't really miss each other. What I really hated were all these creeps she hung out with."

"The hippies?"

"Well, them too. What was worse were some of the sleazy ex-pats living off the piles of cash they'd made during the housing boom in England. A few of them gravitated towards a sort of alternative lifestyle, probably to eke out their ill-gotten gains, and my mother attracted people like that. They were always hanging round our place drinking cheap brandy and smoking dope. Over the years Mum took up with a succession of these guys. She's always been very beautiful and ... well ... highly sexed, so there was always a guy about."

Grizzel stopped suddenly, clearly in the grip of vivid memory. "I don't know why I'm telling you this – I've never told anyone – but the first hard-on I ever encountered was sitting on my so-called Uncle Nigel's knee. I felt something really funny going on down there in his shorts, and although I was only twelve I thought, Uh-oh! I don't like this at all! After that I started avoiding him and all his creepy mates. I guess I got kind of suspicious and withdrawn, so it came as a relief to my mother when I stopped going home to her in the holidays. I let her think it was a teenage thing. Haven't seen her since. Well, anyway I told Dad I was unhappy seeing Mum's friends ... although I never told him about the hard-on."

Her father, she went on, had responded by inviting her to Calltain for the summer. By 1985 the once transient collection of drop-outs and blow-ins had slowly evolved into a stable community of about eighty people. Some had been there for years and, while most of the old croft buildings had already been restored by then, fanciful new eco-friendly houses, unfettered by planning permission, were being built. At the heart of all this activity was the ever-inventive and resourceful Matt Tyler. Timber, cement mixers, generators, entire kit-houses were somehow loaded onto the *Ran* and miraculously shipped over Loch Vallaig and unloaded onto the jetty. Tyler had the knack of picking up skills as he, or more commonly someone else in the community, needed them. He laid foundations, assembled timber frames, roofed entire buildings, bored for water, erected windmills and installed solar panels. Everything old and mechanical or electrical on Calltain had at some time been coaxed back to life by Tyler. He was still young and wild, but several years of living around Aaronson and his succession of arty women had smoothed some of his rough edges. Grizzel lay with her head on

Armour's chest as she told him this.

"I was surrounded by all these interesting people, artists and revolutionaries and whatnot, but to me Tyler was the main man. He just seemed so cool. He was always on the go, always busy making or fixing something. Everyone liked and respected him. Even Campbell and Burgess would defer to him when it came to anything at all practical. He'd built our tower and Caleb's earth house by then. I thought he was gorgeous. I just followed him around over a couple of summers. I told everyone, including myself, that I was his assistant, but I suppose I was just getting in his way. Well, eventually he deigned to notice me and we sort of became an item."

"How old was he?"

She paused a moment, frowning. "He'd be twenty-six ... yes, he's ten years older than me."

"For Christ sake! Did you screw him?"

"Screw?"

"Screw ... fuck ... shag him I suppose to your generation."

"My generation? Oh, let me get this right ... when we do it, I'm shagging but you're screwing?"

"I thought we'd just made love."

"O...K? So if I do it with you it's making love ... but if I do it with someone else it's just screwing ... or is it shagging? You've got a problem, Jon. First you think I'm fucking my father, now you're obsessing about Tyler and me. Isn't what we've got enough? Do you need to get turned on by thinking about me with other guys ... or was it just that you expected me to remain a virgin until I was twenty-nine in the happenstance that you might come along?"

"Look Grizzel, I don't want to pry, but you know how it is with Tyler and me ... I just want to know where he and I stand ... when it comes to you. Are Tyler and I going to punch each other's lights out again?"

She sat up in bed now, clutching her knees, her right breast so close to his face that he could have leaned forward and kissed it. "Look Jon, my past is just that ... mine and past. It's got nothing to do with anyone else. I am who I am today because of what I was before ... good and bad. As it happens, Tyler and I did have a thing going for a year or two ... I'm not letting you into a big secret, everyone in Calltain knows. There are folk like Ruth around who are still pissed off that I dumped Tyler when I went to university ... they think I got stuck-up at Oxford. It wasn't that ... I simply grew up and changed a little. I was just lucky that the first guy I fancied wasn't some pop star in *Jackie* magazine but a real guy ... and a decent guy like Tyler."

"What did your father think?"

"My father?" She shook her head, smiling. "It's still weird to hear him called that! I love him a lot, but when I first came to Calltain ... he came to Vallaig to meet me off the train ... he told me that we were going to be best friends. It was as if being his daughter was just nothing ... what mattered to him was that we'd be friends. Well, we did become best friends. He's the most wonderful person I've ever met and I know he loves me and will always be there for me, but he's never done the stern father routine. One of his girlfriends back then had a long talk with me about not getting pregnant ... I don't know if that was Campbell's idea ... he just seemed to be happy that I had a boyfriend I really liked. And of course, he loves Tyler ... he's a sort of adopted son to him I suppose. Anyway, Campbell's not exactly the person to take a high moral tone about matters sexual. It seemed for a while that every time I came home to Calltain from school, or at least every summer, Campbell had a different woman in tow. When I went to university in the early nineties a couple of girlfriends and I would sometimes spend weekends protesting against the Cruise missiles at Greenham Common ... and I'd keep bumping into Campbell's exes." She laughed. "They remembered me from Calltain and it gave me great street-cred with my mates that I knew all these heavy earth-mothers and peace protesters, although it appalled some of my more right-on feminist friends when they found out that they were all my dad's ex-girlfriends."

"So, you were protesting at Greenham Common ... and Tyler joined the Army ... strange."

"Yeah, that was my fault. In the middle of my second term I'd decided that Matt and I weren't an item any more, and I was really crass and wrote him a letter. I don't think Matt had ever had a letter written to him before ... well, anyway, he took it pretty bad. I knew of course that he was a complex guy, but I didn't expect him to join the bloody Army! Still, I don't know what else I could have done. You see, I'd only been at university a month or so when he hitched down from Calltain. He'd just started building the primary school and came to me with the idea that I should go back with him and start breeding babies to fill it! Well, I made it clear that at seventeen I had no desire to be barefoot and pregnant. Then the bastard caught a dose of the clap and gave it to me. So there I was at Oxford signing on at the VD clinic! I was really angry with him and even wondered if he did it deliberately to spite me. Then I wrote the letter. Apparently he didn't tell anyone anything ... the silly idiot just packed a rucksack and stomped off to join up. It was really weird ... Calltain was his home, and he loved it there ... it was just as if he was trying to piss everyone off. Well, I was young and crass enough to make out that I didn't care, but Campbell took it very badly. Matt had become like a son to him, especially in the years before I made contact with him again. It was about that time that he decided that he couldn't be bothered with any more of his younger lovers, so, with Tyler and me both away, he felt pretty lonely and down. I was worried about him for a bit ... and then I realised that I was pretty lonely and down too. I just buried myself in work and promised myself that I'd get a first class degree. Campbell did the same ... only with his music. Of course Matt came back from the army after the Gulf War, as if nothing had happened. Campbell was overjoyed to see him. So was I, but we sure as hell weren't an item any more." She hesitated for a moment. "You're the first for ages you know." Her seriousness gave way to a giggle that she tried to stifle with her hand. "I inherited Campbell's scientific genes but not quite all of his promiscuity ones!"

His jealousy, her touchiness, had brought him close to losing her. At that moment he knew he hadn't. He laid his cheek on her breast.

"That's nice", she said.

He kissed the firm dark pink knot of her nipple lingeringly before he spoke. "Apparently, years ago, when Campbell was a star of the Edinburgh Festival Fringe, they used to say that he was hornier than *The Monarch of the Glen.*"

She laughed, slipping her hand under the duvet and gently taking his tumescence in her hand.

"Look who's talking."

Free Radicals

"Free Radicals," intoned Harry Urquhart. "Oxygen molecules with one, two or three additional electrons produced by an oxidative process within the body ... blah, blah ... thought to be responsible for tissue damage and disease ... blah, blah ... including Alzheimer's ... so, now we know."

He slouched back from the screen. The editor, arms folded, was perched, one buttock, on his features editor's desk.

"So Harry, we're in contact with a militant animal rights group who choose to go by the name of something that gives you dementia. Fucking lovely."

"Well, strictly speaking, they're in contact with us, we've got no way of contacting them."

The editor picked up the sheet of plain white A4 and read it to himself again. Harry clicked out of Google.

"Are you sure you've no idea who this might have come from?"

"Not a clue. I can't imagine why it was sent to me. If I were claiming responsibility for some direct action I'd carried out, I'd send it to a reporter whose by-line I'd read, or to 'the editor' or 'the newsdesk'. I wouldn't send it to the features editor ... I mean, how do they even know my name?"

"It's on the website, but you're right ... you're a strange choice to send it to ... no offence and all that."

"I keep racking my brains to see if I can come up with somebody I've met in the past who's into animal rights, but everyone I've ever known seems to have been an unreconstructed carnivore."

"Terrible waste of halibut."

"I didn't even know they farmed halibut. I take it you're going to tell the cops?"

"Yes ... editorial responsibility, public interest and all that. Anyway," the editor waved the mysterious communication, "we can use this to run the story under a '*Herald* exclusive' tag tomorrow." He held the paper up to the light, as if looking for traces of invisible ink. "We're clearly not just dealing with animal rights here. Look at their slogan ... and there's nothing about the cruelty of keeping little fish in cages ... this is more the rhetoric of the anti-capitalist or the environmental movement. I'll call my contact in Special Branch rather than just go to the plods, then we can use a 'Special Branch follow up a *Herald* lead' tag on the story. We'll run that on page one and then print a scan of ..." he looked again at the word processor printed page "... eh, 'Free Radicals – Communiqué No 11' on page three."

"I like their slogan."

"Oh yes," said the editor glancing down to the foot of the page. "'Stop being an eco-worrier. Be an eco-warrior!' Rather good, Harry. If the person who wrote that wasn't a complete loony, he might make a very good headline writer."

"Same thing in my book."

"Very funny. Right ..." he stood up. "I'll get a scan of this done and then I'll call Dalgety. If you get Communiqué No 12 from your Free Radical Friends let me know at once."

The Herald, 17th October 2000

Fish firms on alert after eco-warriors release thousands of halibut

A *Herald* exclusive

Fish farms across Scotland are on high security alert today after hard-line eco-activists claimed responsibility for an attack on a halibut farm in which thousands of fish were released into the wild.

Hundreds of thousands of pounds worth of damage was caused at the farm near Kilkentra in Argyll. Marine experts said that it was highly unlikely that the escaped fish could survive in the open sea.

Police originally believed that the ALF (Animal Liberation Front) was responsible, but *The Herald* can reveal that a shadowy eco-terrorist group called "Free Radicals" has claimed responsibility for the attack. The group's communication to this newspaper stated: "All the pens were destroyed and sunk and we saw hundreds, if not thousands, of fish swimming free. Real food for real people! Another blow against globalisation and the capitalist destruction of the planet!"

A Special Branch spokesman has confirmed that a group calling itself Free Radicals has previously claimed responsibility for attacks on earth-moving machinery on two motorway construction sites in the Midlands. Commenting on the slogan "Stop being an eco-worrier. Be an eco-warrior!" contained in the group's communiqué to this newspaper, a Special Branch spokesman said: "It is unlikely that this is just an animal rights protest. This new group seems to have wide ranging environmental and anti-capitalist issues. We take the threat of such groups very seriously."

The environmental impact of such a large-scale escape of farmed fish is unclear. A spokesman for the Scottish Executive said: "We are extremely concerned that the escaped fish may drive out wild fish from their natural habitat, interbreed with wild fish, and become a disease threat by lowering the natural immunity of native species."

Willie MacLaurin, manager of the Kilkentra fish farm said: "We're devastated. Months of work have gone for nothing. These fish were reared in captivity, and out in the wild they'll just starve to death. Releasing them was completely irresponsible. There were no animal experiments or anything like that going on here, our halibut were being raised to provide high quality food. We're just farmers. It's just the same as raising cows or pigs."

Police are following several leads throughout Scotland and south of the border.

Departure

In the morning he walked her to the station, already anticipating the sense of loss that her departure would bring, but with the euphoric glow of love and sex still coursing through his bloodstream. They'd made love again shortly after waking, and nothing that she had said or done that new day suggested that she had any regrets about their relationship. Armour felt, though, that Grizzel seemed a little distracted, as if she was already preoccupied with the somewhere or something else she was now heading for. He hoped it wasn't someone else.

He wanted to ask her: "Look Grizzel, are we lovers, or are you just fucking me for the exercise?" What he said was: "When are you next coming up?" It was the best he could do. She regarded him quizzically. "I mean, either to Glasgow or Calltain ... even if you were just passing through town ... we could have dinner or something."

"I won't be back for ages."

"Oh."

"Wait there. I'll get my ticket."

"Fuck, fuck, fuck," Armour muttered as he watched her stride away. They'd slept together twice now and their lovemaking had been great, but they'd never talked about their relationship. Armour was afraid to ask, afraid to be told that he was just her distraction on her duty visits north, and that her real life and love were in Oxford.

An old woman in a faded orange anorak caught his eye. She'd stopped suddenly to stare at a young beggar who sat hunched and oblivious, his arms drawn inside his T-shirt and clasped around himself. The old woman gave the youth a vigorous V-sign and moved on, muttering to herself. Armour stood, pondering on whether to give the beggar a couple of pounds, but somehow he couldn't muster the energy. It was all so depressing.

"Sorry Jon," Grizzel said as she ran up to him clutching her ticket. "I've got a frantic schedule for the next two weeks ... then I'm off to the States."

"The US?"

"Yeah, there's an academic conference in Albuquerque. I've been invited to give a paper by the department of physics and astronomy there." He held her gaze until Grizzel cast her eyes down. She thrust the ticket into her coat pocket and took his hand in hers.

"It's quite an honour to be asked before I've even got my PhD, so I really have to go."

"Albuquerque?" It was one of those beguiling American names that people all over the world know, without really thinking that people might actually live there, far less study physics and astronomy. He vaguely remembered a poem about falling in love with American names and wondered if Albuquerque was in it, and where exactly it was.

"It's in New Mexico."

"So ... your paper, is it about ... Dark Energy?"

"Well, yeah. If you really want to know, I'll be suggesting that Dark Energy might be a system of neutral leptons interacting with a scalar. You following?"

"Oh yes, absolutely. It's the way you tell them. It's all just fallen into place now."

She shook her head. "I'm sorry, I told you I was a geek. It's just what I know about ... just the way my brain's wired, nothing special. I've got a knack for it, something inherited from Campbell. Why don't you come along?"

"To Albuquerque?" He felt a rush of confused excitement. His mind raced for a reason to say yes. "Astrophysics? What do I know about it? It *is* rocket science to me."

"The conference is just on for a couple of days, but I'm going for a whole week." Her eyes widened in excitement as she spoke now. "It's New Mexico, Jon ... where Campbell was with Oppenheimer. They worked right out in the desert. There's still a log cabin there that was the Los Alamos dining room. It's a National Monument now. It's where the guys relaxed with a beer after a hard day building the atom bomb. It would be amazing to see that! Maybe we could hire a car and go up to the Grand Canyon or something. I've never been to the States before. It'll be great!"

He knew he had an excuse now, a reason to go. He could tell her he'd find it really interesting, tell her he'd write a feature for *The Herald*, tell her anything except that what he wanted more than life itself was to be naked with her in a motel bedroom. She poked him in the stomach with her finger.

"Hey man, it's on Route 66, where's your sense of adventure?"

"I suppose I could ... *The Herald* owes me weeks of leave ... I just never get round to taking them."

"I'm flying out on the third of November ... I'll send you my flight numbers. If you book quickly we could fly together. I'm staying somewhere called the Hiway House Motel ... I can e-mail them to make it a double room."

He felt a jolt of excitement. She eyed him, a slight look of amusement playing on her face.

"Is that alright with you? Tell me I'm reading this situation correctly ... I'm not just an occasional screw ... or fuck, or whatever you call it?" She was laughing – laughing off their argument and his jealousy, and he loved her for it.

"Yes. It's a lot better than alright ... just a bit sudden, that's all."

"Look Jonathan, I don't just sleep with guys for the fun of it. If I seem a bit full-on to you it's because I'm following a hunch. Scientists do that you know. As I see it, we're attracted to each other and we might even be good together, and in that situation I just don't see the point of hanging around waiting for the man to make the first move."

Surprised and confused, he had no words for her, but leaned forward and kissed her lovely open mouth. She let his lips linger, then stepped back.

"I could now bore your pants off with some contemporary theory about the nature of time, but the plain fact is that time is running out." She kissed him back, longer and hard, then turned and ran towards the waiting train.

Schedule

I have her e-mail still, or at least a printout of it. Grizzel's schedule looked as if it would work like clockwork. A scientist's attention to detail, I suppose. I desperately wanted to be with her, but I was also glad of the chance to get away from *The Herald.* My article "Cave Art for the Twenty-First Century" had created quite a stir. Apparently, poor old Burgess had to spend a week fending off magazines and TV companies who wanted to photograph or film his cave. Meanwhile, a number of unnamed but seemingly important people saw the article as a bit of a pro-Calltain, anti-developer rant, and the editor called me to his office to tell me so. I defended it by saying that I thought Burgess's cave to be a major work of art. I showed him a copy of the letter that I'd just sent to Joshua Argo, asking for an exclusive interview so that he could put his case for the super-quarry directly to *The Herald's* discerning readers. I pointed out that I'd asked Argo to meet me in Calltain for the interview. The editor snorted, sceptically. It's a rare talent – disbelief and disdain combined succinctly in a sharp nasal ingress. I then told him that I was planning to take some time off. He said that was a good idea, and I left his office with the distinct impression that he was glad to be shot of me for a while.

Grizzel and I met in Heathrow Airport. I did my usual travelling trick and drank all the in-flight alcohol that was offered to me, plus a couple of little bottles of white wine that they gave to her. We made the Phoenix–Albuquerque connection, and touched down into a hot dry evening that smelled nowhere like home. There was a Hertz car at the airport for us. Grizzel had driven on the right-hand side before, in Europe she said. I was relieved because, although completely sober, she was now tired, yet at the same time excited and distracted by highway America, and the half-familiar images garnered unconsciously from a thousand songs, movies and TV shows. We checked in at the Hiway House and then walked to a little restaurant a few hundred yards away for tequila cocktails and Mexican food. I was tired and got quite drunk, and after the meal Grizzel hit the exhaustion wall. I put my arm round her and she rested her head on my shoulder as we walked back. Without unpacking her case she undressed in the bathroom and showered. Our lovemaking that night was brief, and clumsy. I think we both just wanted to get it over and done with. In the morning it was different. Slow and horny as hell. The second time she was on top of me, her pelvis thrusting, her eyes closed. "Don't come yet! Don't you dare come yet," she spat out through clenched teeth as she brought herself to a climax. It was after midday when we stepped out into the blinding southern light.

"No time for lunch," she said, "we have to get to Los Alamos." We stopped once at a roadside store to buy iced water. I was hungry, but content to sit in post-coital contentment watching the broken, arid scenery drift past as she drove, complaining occasionally how American cars, being automatic, didn't give drivers enough to do. I told her she drove well. She said she'd learned years ago in an ancient Land Rover of Tyler's.

We cruised a rugged plateau up to Los Alamos. I somehow expected it to be frozen in time, unchanged since Oppenheimer's days. I thought that the hastily built laboratory complex would still be there, preserved as an atomic ghost town where tumbleweed blew. I was surprised and a little disappointed that a sprawling modern city had grown up around the remote ranch that the US military had taken over and shrouded in secrecy nearly sixty years before.

The Bradbury Science Museum on Central Avenue, with its exhibits on the Manhattan Project, was well signposted. She wasn't interested, but drove on till we saw the sign for Fuller Lodge. The rough-hewn log building was startlingly out of place in the modern street. Once it had been a refectory for the sons of the well-heeled who attended the Los Alamos Ranch School way back before the nuclear age. Later it became the dining and recreation room for Oppenheimer's geniuses. Bodies and minds were nourished here that would change the world forever. A historic building. The gang hut of the Mighty Atom Crew.

I told her that before the boffins arrived William Burroughs had been at school there. She looked at me blankly, and I said: "You know ... *The Naked Lunch.*" She seemed to think I was talking about a TV chef, and when I told her about the experimental novel she looked back at me strangely and said: "You should know me by now Jon. I'm well into experiments, but I don't do novels. What's the fucking point? People just make things up."

Fuller Lodge had become some sort of community centre, and there were signs pointing to the local Historical Society and Arts Centre that were housed within its spacious grounds. The garden was carefully tended, and people stopped to greet and gossip there. The birthplace of the atomic bomb was a relaxed and cheerful place. Inside, handbills pinned on a board gave notice of evening classes, craft fairs, club events and public meetings. Grizzel said she wanted to poke about for a bit. I sensed that she wanted to do it alone, so I pretended to read the notices as she walked off. As she entered a large hall where piles of chairs were stacked, she paused to touch the timber of the doorframe. I knew she was thinking of a very young Campbell Aaronson, entering that very same space sixty years back along the time continuum. I went over to the Arts Centre – I reckoned she'd work out for herself that's where I'd head for – and drifted for a dull hour through a hodgepodge local talent exhibition that ranged from crap to competent. I didn't buy anything.

When I went outside she was sitting on the veranda. I watched her for a moment as she stared into space. I laughed to myself when I remembered that staring into space was what she did, and approached her cheerfully.

"Hi Grizz." I'd never called her "Grizz" before. "Pick up any good vibrations from your dad?"

She handed me the keys, which were warm and moist from being clutched in her fist. "Would you please drive," was all she said. We got into the car. As the engine started into life my hand momentarily fluttered over the non-existent gear stick. I cursed out loud, but I was glad it was an automatic. I hadn't driven for years, but by the time we'd crossed a few busy junctions and reached the edge of the town I was beginning to feel comfortable behind the wheel. We drove on till the sprawling city fringes petered out, heading south for Albuquerque.

We were soon cruising through a tortured red landscape that looked as if it had been cauterised by a sun with the power of a million atom bombs. It came to me suddenly in that air-conditioned bubble that I loved the sad, sulky girl who sat beside me. We'd had comfortable silences together before – on the plane, in between making love, and in the car on our way to Los Alamos – but Grizzel's muteness was now morose and stifling. At first I ignored it, concentrating on getting to grips with the gorgeous, terrifying experience of being in love again.

I wanted to give her space, but the undemanding drive on a straight blacktop and the drone of the engine on cruise control conspired against me. Her silence was oppressive, and I gave in to the chatter compulsion.

"It must have been strange ... being where your dad was all these years ago. I mean ... these guys changed history. It's weird thinking of them eating hamburgers and playing pool in that building back there while they thought about nuclear fission."

"I don't want to talk about it," she said abruptly. I glanced round at her. She had tears in her eyes. After a while she turned on the radio and found some country music station. If there's one kind of music I hate, it's country. Good God! They even played a song called "She Thinks My Tractor's Sexy." But it filled the silence. It was early evening when we reached the motel. "I want to go out for a really nice dinner tonight," she said, slamming the passenger door shut with decisive force. "But before that I need to fuck my brains out."

Argo

Joshua Argo had been working diligently and uninterrupted at his desk for an hour. "Set sail before dawn if you want to fill the net," he once used to tell colleagues. They sometimes mocked him behind his back for his seafaring homilies, delivered not from the wheelhouse of a storm-tossed trawler but from behind the comfort of an executive desk, but nobody had ever doubted his ability to fill the net. Now fifty-three years old, he had been a multi-millionaire for nearly half his life. Argo was a habitual early riser. Even when he and the business were young, back in the days when he sought his pleasure into the wee small hours in the company of footballers and beautiful and impossibly blonde young women, he had made it a point of honour to be in the office by seven a.m.

The smoked-glass door facing his desk opened.

"Morning, boss."

He couldn't remember when Isabel Downie had dropped the formal "Mr Argo" in favour of "Boss". The Americanism had always sounded incongruous in her refined Edinburgh accent, but he enjoyed the faintly ironic familiarity of the term, although he often wondered why in nearly thirteen years she'd never taken him up on his repeated invitation to call him Josh. He pushed himself back on the castors of his chair with his good leg, to make room for her to plonk the brown paper bag down in front of him.

"Orange juice ... black coffee ... Danish," she intoned, producing his breakfast from the bag, and revealing each item with a flourish as though they were surprises. She had performed the same rite, with the same offerings and to the same mantra, every working day she'd been his PA.

"Isabel. You're a star." It was what he always said, part of the ritual. He saw she had an opened letter tucked under her arm. "Anything in the snail-mail?"

"Nothing I can't handle, apart from this. Do you want me to send the usual mind-your-own-business reply?"

Argo was struck by the unconscious irony of her phrase "Nothing I can't handle," because for the past month Isabel had physically handled very little mail. His company now employed a security guard, who had been trained in spotting and dealing with potentially suspicious packages, after a miniature malt whisky bottle containing alcohol mixed with concentrated caustic soda had been sent to him. The cocktail would have to have been knocked back in a single gulp to prove fatal, not something that he was likely to do, but it was a development that Argo took seriously, although he had never reported it to the police.

"Let's see it."

"Let me know what you think. I can fob him off. Oh, by the way, the Press Office say there are some Calltain cuttings this morning, one written by the so-called gentleman of the press who's written you that letter. They'll send them up as soon as they've finished perusing all the papers." In Isobel's world, Argo's team of press officers always "perused" the papers, never read them.

He murmured a perfunctory "thanks" as she turned to leave. The single sheet he held in his hand bore the letterhead of *The Herald*. He looked at the signature. Indecipherable. But neatly printed beneath it was: "Jonathon Armour, Arts and Culture Correspondent".

"We know him," said Isabel, framed in the open door. "He's that jumped-up little man that went to Fraserburgh and wrote all that rubbish about you. If you take my advice you'll throw his letter in the bin."

"Thank you Isabel." He looked up and found she hadn't moved. "I'll ring when I need you."

When she'd gone he placed the letter down on the slab of polished oak before him, carefully smoothed it out, and read it closely. He had received written requests for interviews before, usually from business and financial journalists, but never one from an arts correspondent. He had also never had a request that specified exactly where the interview should take place, and pretentiously citing the *genius loci* as the reason. The writer had actually used that phrase! The notion was crazy of course; he was far too busy for such a madcap ploy – to sail out to Calltain on a precious weekend to meet a hostile hack. Nevertheless, the proposed escapade intrigued him. When he had read the letter a second time, he sat back and swivelled to face the energetic, expressive seascape on the wall. *A View from Catterline.* Catterline was a tiny village on the north-east coast where the famous painter of the picture had once lived and worked. It had cost him a pretty penny, and he had two more oils by her in his study at home. He thought of the collection of art that he and his money had gathered: Eardlys, MacTaggarts, Houstons, Robertsons, Bellanys. All of his considerable collection was modern-Scottish, figurative, and almost all seascapes. As a yachtsman he responded particularly to Eardly's paintings because he recognised that they were not just beautiful, but had been painted with a mariner's profound understanding of the sea as a mass of water in perpetual, unpredictable motion, capable of pounding and crushing as well as bearing aloft.

Argo had always enjoyed – even cultivated – his reputation as a hard-nosed businessman, and never had any qualms about the huge amounts of money he had made for himself and others. Throughout his career he had found that even people who recognised that creating wealth was essential to a healthy society, somehow didn't expect the wealth creators to have artistic sensibilities, finer feelings, even what they called "souls". In all the years he had been a public figure, whether because of his wealth or lifestyle, no reporter had ever mentioned his superb collection of paintings in an article about him. He was damned sure that this Jonathon Armour character didn't know that he had a fine Joan Eardly in his office and two more at home. The painting he now considered showed the cliffs near Catterline in a storm. He had often wondered what it would be like to be caught in such a tempest while sailing *The Argonaut.* For all his experience as a yachtsman, he knew that the sea, which had claimed his oldest brother, his uncle and his grandfather, had never really tested him.

The handful of press cuttings that Isabel returned with came mostly, as usual, from the financial pages, but the largest clipping was of an arts feature:

> Cave art for the 21st Century
> A unique work of art will be destroyed if plans for a
> Highland super-quarry go ahead.

Arts editor Jonathon Armour reports.

He read it once, carefully, while Isabel hovered.

"Send a polite note to Mr Armour and tell him I'll see him."

She looked at him sceptically. "You know of course where he's coming from, don't you, boss?"

"Oh aye, I do that. And I know where he's going if he wants his interview."

"Goodness gracious! You must realise what his agenda is," she replied sharply. "He's just going to do another knocking piece."

"Right enough ... but there may be something to be gained. I don't want to be seen as secretive or running scared of the press. Write to him. He says he's out the country until the twelth, so let's put the pressure on him and offer him ... hey, the thirteenth."

"Right then ... here on the thirteenth." She frowned, consulting the diary that she always carried in her employer's presence. Oh ... it's a Sunday, I've got you down as sailing that weekend, but if you ask me it's far too late in the year for you to be off sailing on your own."

"Isabel, don't start! I'm not taking *The Argonaut* out of the water until I've had a decent weekend sailing. I've been up to my eyes all this year and I've hardly seen her. Remember, fishing's in my blood. I'll be fine. Look, I promise you, after this weekend she'll go to the marina for the winter and have her bottom scraped."

Years of working for Argo had inured Isabel Downie to her boss's buccaneering tendencies in the matter of business and, in his younger days, sex, but never to what she considered his reckless and regrettable habit of sailing solo. "Well, if that's what you want to do, it's your funeral," she said huffily. "Do you not want to make your meeting with this pest of a *Herald* chappie later in the week?"

"No. I'll do it on the Sunday. Tell him to be at Camas Calltain in the late afternoon. I'll be moored in the bay. Tell him to bring his sea legs as well as his toothbrush. He can stay on board overnight and we'll go for a sail in the morning. If he wants an interview we'll make the bugger work for it."

Her face puckered up, as if she'd detected a bad smell. "You're actually meeting him at Calltain on *The Argonaut*?"

“Exactly.”

“Well, if you’re sure ...”

He handed her the cutting and the letter. “Don’t you worry Isabel, if I don’t like the way things are going ... I can chuck him over the side.”

She shrugged. “That’s up to you I suppose ... you’re the boss. But frankly, I’d never trust a reporter. Not even someone who calls himself a culture correspondent, whatever that is. Cave art for the twenty-first century! I’ve never heard so much rubbish in my life. I daresay that Yank will be looking for a fat grant of British taxpayers’ money.”

“Oh, Isabel,” she turned as she was about to exit, “be sure to also phone and leave a message for Mr Armour at the *Herald* office. I don’t want him missing the letter and trying to rearrange the time and place.”

“I know, if you can’t control the agenda, at least control the timetable,” she said, quoting one of his well-worn maxims back at him.

“Precisely!”

When she’d gone, he stood up and went to the picture on the wall, kicking out with his lame leg, making it lead rather than drag. Up close he could see that the paint had been laid onto the canvas in thick, bold splodges. He had owned it for years but it still amazed him that such marks, such seemingly haphazard globules of colour, the result of hundreds of tiny actions by the painter, could combine together to make a work of art that had continued to fascinate him for years. He loved such paintings, and if anything had made him happy about earning the many millions he possessed, it was the fact that he could afford to indulge his passion. He had long given up on the hope that a successful businessman could ever be perceived by the mass of his countrymen as having a “soul”. Single-minded obsession with doing things absolutely in accordance with your own vision was lauded as evidence of true creativity in painters and other artists, but decried as psychopathic in the entrepreneur. His life in business had given him satisfaction, personal freedom and power, but surely his striving had also been a virtuous mission that had brought decent jobs and progress too? The lesson of the century that had just closed was, to Argo’s mind, that it was the virulently anti-business regimes like Russia and China that crushed freedom, democracy and self-expression. It was people like himself who made liberty possible – and people like him could be just as thrilled by a great painting, or the sight from the cockpit of *The Argonaut* of the sun dissolving into an Atlantic Ocean the colour of molten copper, as they were by a healthy balance sheet that signified profit and prosperity. It was not the spirit of this age to recognise that. He knew that Jonathon Armour, Arts and Culture correspondent of *The Herald*, hadn't asked for a meeting to discuss contemporary art and aesthetics. Armour would already have made his mind up that he, Josh Argo, captain of industry, captain of *The Argonaut*, had no "soul" to be captain of.

"I just hope the bugger outlives me," he said aloud.

Grizzel's body entranced him. Although they had slept together before coming to America, his new intimacy with her nakedness in the Hiway Motel was a gorgeous, unfolding revelation. Her breasts were firm and well developed for a skinny girl, although her body was slight enough to show her ribs. He wondered if she had ever had an eating disorder. He caught her regarding her body in the mirror, touching her belly with the palm of her hand as if the sight saddened her. Once he would have said that she was too scrawny for his tastes. He supposed that she was what the tabloids had begun to call "heroin chic".

"You're gorgeous," he told her.

"You're biased," she replied.

"Two bottomed."

She cast him a quizzical glance.

"Bi ... assed," he intonated slowly ... "two bottomed."

"I've put on weight."

"You're as skinny as hell. You could do with feeding up."

Throughout their time in America they made love every night, even when Grizzel had come back exhausted from the strain of giving her paper and making whatever stands for formal dinner small talk among astrophysicists. There was urgency to her nightly passion, as if they had been newly reunited after a long separation.

They left Albuquerque the morning after the conference ended and drove all day, stopping only to eat burgers in a diner and take photographs of each other posing beside Route 66 signs. They found a hotel in Flagstaff and, in the evening, drove up Mars Hill to gaze at the stars through the Clark telescope at the Lowell Observatory, Grizzel reeling off their names with authority and delight. He was touched that she was so thrilled, but embarrassed by her reluctance to give up her place at the historic instrument to a family with three tired pre-teens who clearly didn't share their father's astronomical interest. Grizzel bent menacingly towards the youngest child as he waited his turn to view: “Remember kid, when you stare into the universe, the universe stares right back at you.” Armour saw the boy’s face turn from bemusement to fear as his mother shot a spiteful glance at the pair of them and steered the child away with a protective arm.

“Little bastards! That’s the telescope that first led to our discovery that the universe is expanding,” she muttered far too loudly. “What the fuck do these drongos care about that?”

Armour manoeuvred her away.

The following day they struck north from Flagstaff, driving eighty miles to stand, holding hands, and look down in silent awe from the south rim of the Grand Canyon. Armour, his feet a few inches from the edge, his body held back from the abyss only by a metal railing, was surer of his footing there and at that moment than at any other place or time in his life before. That night in their hotel, as he lay on the bed sated with sex, he told her that he loved her.

“Do you?” She closed her eyes and smiled. “I’m glad.”

In the morning they trekked a steeply descending mile or two, marvelling at the view. He’d carried his camera and insisted on taking her photograph even though she was reluctant.

“I have to,” he insisted. “I’ve carried the bloody thing for miles.”

“Why don’t you photograph the canyon then? You haven’t taken a single shot of it yet.”

“It’s pointless. There’s no way I can capture how extraordinary the place is. I’d be better buying a postcard. A picture of you will have to do.”

“Talk about being condemned by faint praise!”

“Don’t be daft now, you know I love you.”

She struck a pose and he took her picture. Neither of them had mentioned Jon’s use of the world “love” the night before, and now she let it pass again. They sat in silence for a time before beginning the steep climb back up to the canyon’s rim. When they got there she kissed him lightly on the lips.

“Jon, I’d like to go to that big touristy shop we passed. Being here’s made me feel terribly ignorant. I want to get a book on Grand Canyon geology.”

“Ah, you can take the girl out the science lab, but not the...”

“Science lab out the girl.” she echoed, rolling her eyes in affected boredom. “Yeah, yeah, but you knew I was a sad geek before you signed up to come out here.”

In the shop Grizzel went straight to the hardback book counter and began leafing through anything she could find on geology. Jonathon found an illustrated account of the first white men ever to travel down the Colorado River by boat. He read that the party had split up somewhere in the canyon when three men rebelled and decided to walk out, rather than face more rapids in their flimsy boats. The three had never been seen again while the others, led by a one-armed Civil War veteran, paddled to safety and into the history books. He read a few passages, enough for him to get hooked, and went to pay for it. It seemed to him a good tale with a severe moral lesson for the fainthearted. He tucked the book, wrapped in a paper bag, under his arm and browsed some more.

Then he saw the little dancing man. Recognition struck him instantly – although his mind was in flux as he tried to remember just where he had previously seen the matchstick figure with the triangular body, preposterously long neck, great antlers sprouting from a tiny head, and expressive hand gestures like the Mudras of Hindu ritual.

“Jesus bloody Christ,” he muttered. An elderly couple standing nearby gave him a strange look and edged away. He pulled the slim paperback from the revolving rack. It was richly illustrated with photographs and drawings, and under its title, *Prehistoric Indian Rock Art*, was a photograph of a carving of a little dancing Shaman, identical to the one he’d seen in Caleb Burgess’s drawings. Burgess had included the figure in his sketchbook because he had a crackpot notion that it had been carved to warn future generations of some unknowable catastrophe. $9.99. When he’d paid he wandered over to Grizzel’s side. He wanted to show her the dancing Shaman, but she was intent on a thin volume, and her lips seemed to be silently mouthing what she read.

“Interesting?”

“I don’t believe it, Jon. This is just such crap.”

He leaned to look at the cover. *The Grand Canyon: A Different View.* "What's wrong with it?"

"I don't fucking believe it. This is just such pure crap, such medieval bollocks." She spoke too loudly, and Armour saw the elderly couple he'd previously embarrassed turn to look at her disapprovingly.

"So don't buy it," he said gently, "there are plenty of others."

"But this is a creationist book. Some tour guide who actually works here has written it. The fuckwit believes that the Grand Canyon was created by Noah's flood. This guy takes Genesis seriously, and they're selling his ravings in a National Park! Listen to this. 'For years as a Colorado river guide, I told people how the Grand Canyon was formed over the evolutionary timescale of years. Then I met the Lord. Now, I have a different view of the canyon, which according to a biblical timescale, can't be more than a few thousand years old.' This is insane, Jon! We're in the most scientifically advanced country in the world, and they're passing off this fundamentalist Christian stuff in a geological National Park. This is the country that put a man on the fucking moon ... and it produces this crap!"

She snapped it closed and strode for the counter.

"You're not going to buy it, are you?" He trailed behind, confused.

"You bet I am. I'm having this. Whenever I get disillusioned with science, I'll be able to read this to remind me what the alternative is. Welcome to the new Dark Age!"

They travelled for three hours, and as he drove she sat stiffly, reading *A Different View*, occasionally cursing under her breath. Sometimes she grimaced in a way that made her look as if she was in sudden pain. He observed her carefully in sly, unnoticed glances. She wore a pretty flower-patterned blouse with a scalloped neckline and boot-cut blue jeans worn raggedy at the ankles from being trailed on the ground. It was her style, something frilly and feminine worn with combat pants or jeans. One bare foot was raised and resting on her knee, its sole dirtied with red dust. She'd tied her hair back and her face was tanned by desert sun. Her Ray-Bans were pushed back onto the top of her head. It occurred to him then that if he'd just set eyes on her for the first time he'd have assumed she was American. The thought brought home to him how little he knew of her. He'd slept with her every night for a week, holding her naked, gazing at her in post-sex intimacy, yet as she sat beside him now he hardly recognised her. He tried to remember her as he'd first seen her from Tyler's boat. He even tried to imagine her wearing a white coat in some physics laboratory. He struggled to define Grizzel Gillespie. In the past few days his confused thoughts about the human condition called love had become more insistent, but he felt further than ever from knowing who she was. Her sustained anger had taken him by surprise. He couldn't understand how someone about to complete their PhD, a soon-to-be doctor of astrophysics, could give over a precious afternoon to fury about a twelve-dollar paperback written by some Bible-basher.

"You're missing some amazing scenery."

"Sorry?"

"The landscape, you're missing it. We're flying home soon. It's a pity not to see it. There was a pile of Joshua trees back there."

She threw *A Different View* over her shoulder onto the rear seat.

"Sorry, I'm being a bore." She stared out her side window in silence for a few moments. "Yeah, it is a great view." She turned to look at him and brushed his cheek with the back of her hand. "So what day did God make this on? Was it in the morning, or the afternoon? Or was he working nightshift?"

"Sometime on day two I think ... that would be a Tuesday. The Book of Genesis doesn't specify morning or afternoon ... and doesn't mention tea-breaks. I think all creation theories are a little woolly on the fine detail."

"I wonder what the Indians thought created all this", she said. "Of course, they had a bit of an advantage over mere Westerners, because they had peyote which has powerful psychoactive properties. They must have been really tripped out when they wrote their Book of Genesis."

"I'd forgotten you were a magic mushroom expert."

She shot a patronising glance his way.

"Peyote is a cactus, not a fungus."

"You scientists! You're so literal!"

"I like to get the facts right. I'm not a fucking journalist."

"Okay, so not literal ... just ... obsessive."

"Yeah, yeah, I guess I'm just a little obsessive." She sat for a few moments, and then spoke without turning to even glance at him. "When I first got to school in the borders it was just newly springtime. There was this cherry tree that you could see from the head teacher's window. There were no formal competitive games or anything like that at the school, but one day the head got asked to referee a football match that the kids had organised. I hated games ... and anyway I didn't really know anyone then, so I went off this day on my own and climbed the cherry tree. It wasn't very big. Anyway ... I started picking the flowers ... I don't know ... time just passed. When the head got back to his office, every blossom was on the ground ... I'd picked off every one. I was at the school for four more years after that... in all that time the tree never blossomed again."

They sat in silence for a while, the engine unchanging in its pitch as it droned on through the flatlands. At last he asked her what she was thinking.

"I was thinking about you."

"Yeah?"

"I was thinking that you're a writer, and that you could come up with a decent creation myth."

"You think?"

She turned to smile at him, her first in nearly two hundred miles.

"Yeah, why not? They say everybody has a book in them. Have you ever written ... creative stuff?"

"You mean, as opposed to all the journalistic shite I churn out."

She punched his shoulder. "It's not shite you write ... well, not all the time! But have you never wanted to write a novel, or poetry?"

"I wrote embarrassingly bad poetry at university ... which was quite a good thing, because it was so bad it made me realise that if I was ever to make a living from writing it would have to be in journalism."

"Well, I reckon you could write a novel or something ... I think my idea about you writing a new creation myth is brilliant."

He thought for a second.

"It's hard ... you know, to beat, "In the beginning ...", a straightforward but classy line."

"Huh?"

"In the beginning ...", he intoned. She continued to look at him quizzically. "It's the opening line of the Bible, the first words of Genesis. "In the beginning God created the heavens and the earth. The earth was without form and void, and darkness was upon the face of the deep." Surely you know that?"

"Yeah, I've heard it. It creeps me out. How come people can quote that and not Darwin?"

"The Bible is ingrained in our culture ... even today I think you need to know something about religion, if you really want to understand western music and art and literature. What's Campbell's view? I mean, I know he was a scientist ... but Calltain's pretty New Age, and his following is rather cultish."

"Oh Campbell may seem all arty-farty and into saving the planet, but he's no mystic. All the old hippies love him, but he's still the same hard-nosed, half-Scottish, half-Jewish scientific atheist he's always been ... but I'm not entirely sure about Caleb."

"You mean Caleb actually believes he's a Shaman?"

"Well, of course he would deny it. Intellectually he understands that so-called mystical experiences are just what happens sometimes when neurons press buttons in our brains, but with Caleb ... well, I always feel that he's somehow capable of making that leap into faith. How about you, Jon? Are you a closet holy roller?"

"No, not at all. I'm still an atheist, thank God." He paused momentarily. "I've got a theory," he went on. She shot him a sceptical glance. "It's just a joke theory, but it goes like this. God does exist, and he's all-powerful ... but he's got a sick sense of humour."

"O...K."

"And I've got proof."

"Proof of the existence of God?"

"Oh no, just proof that if he does exist he's a sick bastard."

"You're weird," she said, laughing.

"Back at my flat I've got an envelope half full of press cuttings about people who've died because of their daft devotion to religion." He saw her eyes widen in curiosity, and went on. "I've got ones about a man who carried an enormous wooden cross on a marathon and died of a heart attack, and another about New Age types playing the bongos and dancing round a guy they thought was astral travelling, when in fact he'd spent so long in a sweat lodge that he was dying of dehydration. My favourite is about a Thai businessman who got a prayer flag from a Buddhist priest to bring luck to his failing factory, and then fell and was killed when he tried to hang it from the roof. Then there's one about a guy in Taiwan who jumped into the lion enclosure of the zoo in an attempt to convert the lions to Christianity. He doesn't really count, because the zookeepers managed to pull him out before the lions had actually killed him."

"Are these for real?"

"Absolutely! I've got the cuttings at home. Honest, I'll show you them."

"I love it! And here's me thinking that we atheists were an endangered species, while all the time natural selection is weeding out the religious loonies." She was laughing out loud, and it made him giddy with happiness. "We'll show these Bible bashers! You'll write that creation myth for me, Jon. I know you will! I may be a sour scientific rationalist but I do have a witch's name." She pointed a finger at him and inscribed circles in the air with it. "Wooo ... you're under my spell."

THE SHAMAN (2)

He sensed them on the wind after the noise that sounded like distant thunder. He smelt the bitter dust. The Shaman left the desert and entered the scrubland that surrounded the sacred Black Mountain. Using its meagre cover he closed in swiftly on the strangers, an iron-tipped arrow notched on his bowstring. He heard voices, raucous unintelligible cries, echoing off the cliff. He could smell meat on a fire. The white men had a camp in the mouth of a small canyon. Dogs barked. These he feared. The whites were often blind to what surrounded them, but their dogs were sharp-eared and dangerous. He moved silently to skirt their camp and encountered a steep slope of broken rock shards where nothing grew. If he could get up this unseen he would reach the foot of a ridge that ran up the side of the canyon. Keeping on the far side of the rim, he could climb unseen high enough to look down on the white men. The noise from the whites increased. Several were now shouting, some close by, and others echoing from deeper in the canyon. Their cries seemed urgent and full of menace. He breathed deeply and slowly several times, thrust the arrow into the quiver on his back, murmured a prayer to the God of the mountain, and sprinted forward as fast as his sixty-four cycles of the seasons and the surface of broken rock would allow. The effort of a few seconds passed like an age. Although exhausted from three sun's journeying in the desert with little water, his will was strong and his limbs moved as they had done when he was half his age. But his step was unsure. A rock, which had looked firm, gave way beneath him and clattered down the slope. His stride broken, he stumbled forward using both hands, running like a bear not a warrior. He should have been over the ridge now. Three, perhaps four, strides to go. A final last leap to the rim, and then a bruising roll down the other side. If they saw him they would hunt him down. He knew that he could not outrun the white men now, or kill them all with his bow, or hide from their dogs.

Down on the canyon floor Davy Thomas turned at the sound of the falling rock and raised his hand to shield his eyes from the searing light. Dazzled for a second, he screwed his eyes shut. When he opened them the mountainside was bare. He hated this land of desert, rattlesnakes and Indians. His nerves were constantly on edge. He should never have left the valleys. He'd seldom been hungry in America, but at home he had slept without fear. When he dreamed in America he dreamed of being home.

Clinging to the rocky slope, the Shaman strove to control his heaving breath and hammering heart, seeking quietness to strain for the sound of voices, dogs and gunshots. When none came he began to pick his way up the side of the ridge, crouching and placing each footstep with care. He climbed slowly, following the ridge to a point where he reckoned he'd be directly above the whites' camp. He removed the bow and quiver from his shoulder and crawled forward inch by inch, finally pressing down on the solid rock with the palms of his hands to slowly raise his head and shoulders.

Below him was a small horseshoe canyon that stretched a bowshot into the mountain. It was said that his people had once trapped the wild horses that came to drink in the shallow pool that formed here when the rains came. Now the bottom of the canyon was filled with jagged rubble. Six white men were making their way back across the broken rock from the cliff at the canyon end to its mouth, stumbling and shouting excitedly. In the clearing among the scrub perhaps another ten whites were standing. They were shouting at the six running towards them, waving their arms and cheering. The dogs, catching the mood of their masters, ran among them yowling. One of the men was waving a piece of cloth, the colour of fresh blood, on what looked like a lance.

When Davy saw that the men were safe he dropped the flag and took the watch from the waistcoat he wore unfastened over his sweat-stained vest. He nodded in approval, slipped the watch back into his pocket, and put his fingers in his ears. Some of the others saw him and did the same.

The Shaman watched. What strange ritual was this? Did not the white men have their Jesus? Why were they here at the mountain of the great dancing Sky God whose power they denied? Surely this was defilement!

The mountain answered him. He felt the first tremor through his fingers, and then heard the earth give a great sigh. The walls of the canyon began to shimmer and the mountain's moan became a terrible roar of anguish. A torrent of rock began to pour down the cliff face like water at the great fall in the river. A cloud of dust billowed into the sky, turning the low sun into a pale ghost. The shockwave filled his eyes with grit and, as the cry of the mountain pierced his ears, he recoiled clutching his hands to his head. He fell backwards down the ridge, slipping and rolling down its steep side to the bottom of a gully. Sharp fragments of rock rained down on him as he cowered on the ground, grievously wounded in the spirit.

"Stay back, boys. Stay back!" Davy Thomas knew that if he let them, the men would rush forward into the dust to hack away at the broken rocks with their picks searching for the mother lode. "Wait till the dust clears!" There was no reason to believe that a charge had not exploded, but he'd seen men killed in coalmines for making that mistake. It had taken days to bore the holes and lay the charges. A few minutes more would make no difference.

The Editor

The two men entered the spacious bar in the fashionable Merchant City watering hole that had once been a Victorian bank. It was one of those glitzy places that stayed open late because it was the only way the developers could ever get their investment back. The Glasgow city fathers were happy to extend licensing hours to the right sort of bars, in repayment for turning the run-down old commercial centre of the city into a high-spending playground for the smart, salaried twenties and thirties. Both men were older than that, but comfortable in their surroundings and looking forward to their first drink of the night. Harry went to the bar while his editor sat on a leather couch, unfolded a copy of the first edition that he'd brought with him, drew a pair of half-moon glasses from his shirt pocket and placed them carefully on the bridge of his long nose. In all, it had been a good night. There was a strong political lead story with more than a whiff of scandal about it, a powerful colour photograph of a bemused and terrified child in a war zone, and rumours of management purges in not one, but two Premier League football teams. The elements had come together under *The Herald* masthead to make a strong, clean front page that would stand out clearly on the news-stands in a very few hours' time. There was only one element in the composition that niggled away at the editor's professional satisfaction. It lay at the bottom right-hand corner of the page – two stubby columns capped by the headline: **Blaze at GM Lab**. The story beneath started with a bare factual account of firemen in East Lothian, called to the research laboratory of a company that developed genetically modified crops, and a witness who had described the premises as "well alight". It then went on to retell stories of previous protests by environmentalists at the laboratory, with the word "controversial" sloppily used three times in the copy. It was a decent enough stab at late-breaking news, but the editor had a sour feeling that by the time the morning radio and TV bulletins went on air the story would be all "suspicious circumstances" and "suspected arson".

“What’s wrong? Found a spelling mistake already, or are we still fighting a losing battle on the apostrophe front?” Harry put the editor’s large glass of wine on the table and sat to take a swallow of lager.

“Hell no, Harry, I’ve beaten that out of them. It’s this GM laboratory fire. I just know it’s going to turn out to have been arson. I think we should have gone heavier on it ... taken a flyer ... called it ‘suspected eco-terrorism’ or something. The way it stands it looks pretty lame on page one.”

“So is that the word ... that it’s some sort of Attack of the Tree Huggers?”

“No, nothing certain. It came from a stringer at short notice so we weren’t able to work it up ourselves, but it looks to me like another of those eco-attacks. There was the Free Radicals business last week, and it turns out that a Norwegian-owned salmon farm on Skye had two outboard motors dropped into the loch and a Portacabin set on fire only a couple of days before. Last month some loony attacked earth-moving plant on a motorway construction site with Molotov cocktails and in the same week a new Tesco was firebombed just two days before it opened.”

“Co-ordinated campaign ... or coincidence?”

“We don’t know for sure, or at least the plods aren’t saying. We haven’t heard from our Free Radical friends again, but it seems to be too much of a coincidence for all these to be unrelated. They could be copy-cat actions, but my bet is on some loose coalition of eco-nutters somehow connected on the internet. We’ve had a peace camp at the Faslane submarine base and sit-down protests outside nuclear power plants for years, but now we’ve got these opportunist attacks on completely different kinds of targets, soft targets in isolated areas. Individually they could pass for random acts of vandalism, if it wasn’t that there’s been such a spate of them. Inevitably the plods are saying that it’s only a matter of time before someone gets hurt.”

The feature editor, who had taken a long draught of his lager, wiped his mouth with the back of his hand. “Sounds like there’s an authored piece to be done drawing all these stories together and making the argument that there actually may be some new eco-warrior or anarchist group at work here

... Free Radicals or whoever. Would you like me to get someone onto it tomorrow?"

"Yeah Harry, that's a good idea. Cheers." The editor took a mouthful of wine and washed it appreciatively round his mouth. "Who do you have in mind?"

"I was thinking about Jon Armour. He's got interested in environmental stuff and it would stretch him a bit, but he's not due back from the States for a couple of days. I'll give it to one of the young 'uns, but I'll keep an eye on whoever it is."

"That reminds me Harry, when did Armour get this eco-bug? Every time I look at the culture pages he's raving on about some threatened artist colony in the Highlands. What is it with him ... hanging out with all these oddballs, geeks and freaks? I asked him about it before he went on leave, but he was pretty evasive. There's me expecting to read descriptions of Tracey Emin's grotty underwear, and instead all I get from him are prophecies of ecological doom."

"Jon's a good writer and he's well connected. He really knows the arts scene, and he's right, there's some interesting stuff happening at Calltain. Also ..." Harry hesitated. The editor peered like an inquisitor over the rims of his lenses. "If Jon's suddenly developed new interests, it just might be because he's found himself a woman."

"Yeah? Not another of his flaky artists I hope."

"No ... I think she may be an astrophysicist ... the one with the Calltain connections he wrote about recently."

"Is she very plain? I noticed you didn't use a photograph of this wonder woman."

"Actually, she might be young and rather attractive. I'm not sure, but I think she's the girl I saw him with in Sarti's recently. I'd just dropped in for a carry-out cappuccino and they were having lunch. He certainly seemed very taken with her. You know what he's like, when you're out with him ... it's like when he's at some arty reception ... always scanning the room over your shoulder to see if anyone more interesting has just walked in. But he didn't even see me that time. He just sat talking to this girl ... couldn't take his eyes off her. Also, he's been on a diet. I think he's lost a few pounds.'

'Sounds serious.'

'Yeah ... I've noticed that he's taken to having hush-hush phone calls. Usually I can hear every word he says, but sometimes now he cups his hand round the mouthpiece and speaks really quietly. He seems pretty happy. Christ, he's even gone on holiday! Usually I can't get him out the office. It must be a woman, and if it's the one I saw him with, he's damn right to be happy."

"How long has it been?"

"About three years. The four of us were pretty close ... I was his best man. It came as a bit of a shock to Anne and I, but Jonno took it really hard. Suzanne had put off having kids for years because of her work at the Art School ... then comes back from a sabbatical in the States, pregnant to some Japanese American architect."

"I never met the lady. She still with the guy?"

"Yes, Anne gets the occasional card or e-mail from her ... successful husband, cute baby, paintings selling like mad, lovely home in Seattle ... that sort of thing. Jonno's never really got over it. He was really proud of Suzanne ... good looking, lots of talent ... and he'd really have liked to have had kids with her. Just wasn't part of her plan."

The pair sat for a few bleak moments with their drinks. The editor was getting to his feet to fetch another round when his mobile rang. He sank into the couch, listening intently, and sometimes cursing as much to himself as to the caller. "I'm on my way back," he said abruptly. He pocketed the phone.

"Shit, you're not going to believe this. Some nutter has just fire-bombed Josh Argo's BMW."

Games with the Faces

Jon had limbo time at Heathrow before his connecting flight to Glasgow, and she had insisted on waiting with him. He said he needed a news junkie's fix of print, and bought an armful of papers. As he paid he realised that he'd hardly missed the British press at all. The thought prompted a guilt buzz, and he decided to call his office. He ordered two coffees at a kiosk and left Grizzel, perched on a stool, while he looked for a public phone. He dialled and was put through to the Features Desk.

"Hey stranger, where are you? We've been trying to call you on your mobile." It was Harry Urquhart, stalwartly at his post on a Saturday afternoon, working on a supplement for the Monday edition.

"It doesn't work in the States, so I left it at home. I'm at Heathrow waiting for the Glasgow flight. What's been happening, Harry?"

"Nothing we couldn't handle, but Josh Argo's secretary has been on the phone every other bloody day asking if you'd got her message."

"Yeah? Before I left I wrote to Argo to see if he'd speak about his plans for Calltain. I never thought there was any chance of him getting back to me."

"Well, you thought wrong. He wants to meet. I've left the message on your desk ... let me get it." The phone thundered down. Armour recognised the buzz of the open-plan office – Sunday's paper scurrying towards its deadline – and distinctly heard Harry say, "It's Jonno back from his nookie trip to the States." Somebody laughed.

How the hell did he know? Armour had just said he was going on holiday. He'd deliberately not mentioned that he was going with a woman. He'd told no one about Grizzel, not even his oldest and best friend. He heard the phone being picked up.

"The message is from Isabel Downie, Argo's PA. She's left her office number, but I doubt she'll be there at the weekend. She's quite a nippy sweetie by the way ... that's if her telephone manner is anything to go by. Anyway, she says that Argo will meet you tomorrow evening. I told her you were due back by then and would probably be able to make it."

"Great, Harry. Where?"

"Ah well, it's really weird. She says that her boss is sailing up the west coast this weekend and that on Sunday afternoon he'll be anchoring his yacht overnight at a place called ... Camas Calltain ... she said you'd know where it is. You've to be there about six o'clock, shout from the shore and he'll row in and take you back in his dinghy. Apparently you've to spend the night there and go sailing with him in the morning. Sounds as if he wants a captive audience to work his fast-talking corporate spell on."

"Christ, he's gone for it!"

"Huh?"

"It's what I asked him to do ... meet me at Calltain ... the place he plans to blow to buggery. I never in a million years thought he'd do it. I just expected that if he ever did talk to me it would be in his office with a gang of press officers hanging over him." Armour thought fast. "Look Harry, this is going to be big. Argo is a pretty reclusive guy and I don't want to lose him. I'll head up to Calltain first thing in the morning."

"Sounds good, Jonno. We could run your piece in Wednesday's paper. I'll ring Isabel Downie's number now, and leave a message saying you're definitely coming. You never know, she may pick up her voicemail over the weekend and tell Argo you're on your way. I think it's amazing he's talking to you. Some nutter firebombed his BMW last night."

"You're joking! Was he in it?"

"Oh no, it was about midnight and the car was in his drive ... seems to have been an old fashioned Molotov cocktail, but the car was burned out."

"Any idea who did it?"

"Well the police aren't saying, but he's got lots of enemies. We're running a piece tomorrow suggesting that there might be a new extremist environmental group operating in Scotland. Argo seems neither up nor down about it, and has apparently already left on his yacht. By the way ... how was your holiday?" There was more than a hint of slyness in the tone of his old friend's question.

"Great, Harry, great. Be sure to tell everyone I had lots of nookie." And with that, Armour hung up.

He went back to the coffee kiosk. For a moment he had been puzzled by his colleagues' interest in his sex life. Then he realised that after bitter years of singledom there was no one more amazed than himself to find that he was now in a relationship with someone young and lovely. Why hadn't he told Harry, he wondered. Probably because he hardly believed it himself.

"Hey, you're looking pleased with yourself. Good news?"

He sat on the high stool next to Grizzel, close enough for their knees to touch, and told her about Argo. She hugged him, almost spilling his coffee.

"That's wonderful. When will you see him?"

"At six tomorrow evening ... at Camas Calltain. I'll drive up in the morning." He grinned at her. "You won." She looked at him blankly. "Remember ... this was your idea."

She stroked his face, smiling just for an instant. "Look, tomorrow's Sunday. It's quite usual for some Calltain folk to get cabin fever and go to a pub in Vallaig on a Saturday and stay overnight. Trooper does it himself usually ... anyway, he always sails from Vallaig at noon on a Sunday to bring folk home. He calls it the hangover cure ... it's one of his regular runs."

"Good, I'll leave in plenty of time to catch him."

"I could sit here and fill your head with statistics about projected figures of car ownership and how the motorways are wrecking the countryside, but it would be a crap way to end a holiday," she said.

"No, that's OK ... I put a lot of stats together myself before I wrote to him, they're in a file at home. I'll read them tonight. Don't worry, Argo won't get an easy ride."

"I know you'll be brilliant, darling. I know we'll stop Argo in his tracks. He can't get off with destroying Calltain."

They spent half an hour perched at the kiosk. Mostly they sat in silence watching the ebb and flow of humanity.

"Playing games with the faces," he sang out of tune. "I said the man in the gabardine suit was a spy. She said, 'Be careful, his bow tie is really a camera!'"

"What?"

"Simon and Garfunkel song ... before your time."

For a little while they invented preposterous motives for the journeys of people that caught their attention.

"Drug runner!"

"Dirty weekend, there's no way that lady's his wife!"

"Arms dealer!"

"On route to a sex change clinic."

"Joining the Foreign Legion."

"Off to Lourdes to cure his sta ... sta... stammer!"

After a while she told him that it was time for him to catch his connection. She said that she envied him going to Calltain because he'd see the geese arrive.

"They come in October, bringing the winter with them from the Arctic. Mostly they're heading for Islay, but some stay with us in Calltain. Caleb usually manages to shoot one every year, with a bow and arrow. He says he's getting in touch with his inner hunter-gatherer, but he always gets Campbell to gut it and cook it."

At last they hugged in final parting. Over her shoulder he thought he caught a few curious glances. A middle-aged man in fashionable, if rumpled, linen. A slim young woman in jeans and tight T-shirt. Classic sugar daddy stuff. Draw your own conclusions, suckers. Make up your own stories. It felt so damn good. His heart leapt when he saw moisture in her dark eyes. They forced themselves apart – she on her way into London and then on to Oxford, he for the plane that would take him to Glasgow, and to Argo. She gave him the phone number of the flat she shared, and carefully wrote down his. Over her shoulder she promised to call him often. It was strange. They'd been lovers for ... what? ...three weeks ... and intimate every night for days now ... and they were only just exchanging home numbers. He'd asked her a couple of days before if there was anyone waiting for her in Oxford. She said there wasn't, and he wanted to believe her. He told her he'd imagined there would be a handsome young astrophysicist. She just laughed and said she wasn't starry eyed about astrophysicists.

As soon as she was gone he felt his happiness leach away, and began to have a nagging feeling that the whole trip had been some sort of dream. He put it down to jet lag, and perhaps the gin and wine he'd downed somewhere over the Atlantic. When he found that his Glasgow connection had been delayed, he bought a beer and settled down to sift through his pile of newsprint. Usually he opened papers with a sense of anticipation, but somehow these seemed scant and lifeless.

Armour took a greedy glug of his pint and tried to recall what he'd said in his letter to Argo. After a second draught he dug deep into his jacket, pulled out his notebook and propelling pencil, and set himself to write up the list of questions that would draw Argo out, and expose the greed and selfishness of his schemes and scams. Whenever he could, Armour carefully planned his interviews, memorising detailed questions and designing little digressions that would make his inquiries sound spontaneous, free-flowing, even a little chaotic. Once his interviewees were put at ease by his seemingly genial blandness, Armour would use a number of techniques designed to lead them inadvertently into revealing thoughts that they would have preferred to have kept to themselves. He called it the Innocent Flower/Serpent Routine. Then there was the Long Silence Technique. Armour was good at long silences. If an interviewee was reticent, he'd put down his notebook and pencil, cross his arms and stare into the middle distance. People hate silences in conversation, and he had frequently been surprised by what they would blurt out when confronted with a minute or even two of interrogator muteness. And then there was the Know-All Tactic of mugging up on everything in the public domain there was to know about a person before you met them. You could use that information in any number of ways – to flatter, to rattle, to bully, to point out inconsistencies and to embarrass. Armour knew the power of a carefully digested folder of yellowing press cuttings, and what it could unleash. That night he'd plough again through the file of notes and cuttings that he had on Joshua Argo. He was tired and sighed out loud at the prospect. Then he remembered that for the first time in more than a week he'd go to bed without her. Hell, he might as well sit up and work all night. He finished the beer, and rose to buy another.

The Pink Telephone Box (2)

Tyler stood slouched inside, listening to the tattoo of rain that beat on the streaked windowpanes. It didn't smell good in there, but the salt-spray-bleached telephone box sheltered him from the wind that was whipping up outside. He didn't want to be already wet and chilled when he took the *Ran* back over the loch to Calltain. She phoned, as usual, on time, but the first harsh ring startled him nonetheless. He let it ring twice more until he had recaptured his calm, then picked up the receiver with an oily hand.

"Howdy pardner."

"Tyler. We're back."

"Aye, I guessed. How was the US of A?"

"It was good. I think my paper went down really well, and... like... we were in the Lowell Observatory and we saw the Grand Canyon. It was amazing."

"So... how was... the nightlife?"

"Piss off, Tyler."

"Where are you?"

"I'm in Heathrow. I've just left Jon... he's flying up to Glasgow tonight. Things are really moving. Argo has agreed to see him at Calltain tomorrow evening. He's agreed to the interview and everything!"

"In Calltain?"

"Yes, he's insisted on meeting Jon on his yacht and taking him sailing. Jon's even staying on board overnight."

"Fuck me. The eejit fell for it?"

"Absolutely. Apparently Argo had planned to be away on his boat all this weekend anyway, but now he's going to anchor at Camas Calltain specially to meet Jon. He'll be heading there now."

"Is he on his ownsome?"

"I don't know, Tyler! It's you that says he always sails alone. You even spent a night concocting a daft theory that he was seeking an atavistic connection to his fisher-folk roots ... to show he's as good as them ... while you know perfectly well that he's just a sad lame fuck with no mates."

“That couldnae have been me Grizz ... I got nae clue what atavistic means ... but sad fuck or not, he’s got some balls to be sailing the West Coast on his tod in November. Either that or he’s aff his fuckin heid. The forecast is for a storm tomorrow. What about Armour?”

“I told you, he’s flying up to Glasgow just now. He’s driving to Vallaig tomorrow morning.”

“I thought the bastard didn’t drive.”

“He’s got no choice ... you know what the trains are like. Look, I’ve told him that you’ll be sailing from Vallaig at twelve tomorrow.”

“Nae probs, a’ll sort something out. So Grizz ... what was it like ... with him and that?”

“Tyler, you’ve got a knack of asking highly inappropriate questions.”

“Aye I know. That’s what makes me so loveable.”

“Goodnight Tyler.”

“Yeah, I love you too Grizz.”

There was silence on the line before he heard her say “Take care Tyler,” and hang up.

“Aye ... and you too, babes.”

Terror Incognita

The hired car was parked in the street below. He had collected it on touchdown at the airport, hoping that the man behind the rental desk wouldn't smell the beer and in-flight wine on his breath. Swallowing three aspirins for his dull headache, he had gone to bed and lain listening to a brisk wind thrumming on his window as he waited for the pain to subside. Without the soothing exhaustion of sex he didn't sleep, but rose at three and worked at his desk, hunched over his laptop, worrying away again at the questions he had prepared for Argo. At seven he showered, drank half a mug of milkless tea, and stuffed some overnight things into his shoulder bag. He remembered to close the living room windows, having opened them the previous evening believing that the room had a stale, unpleasant smell. For all his warm and spacious flat's comforts, for all his tasteful possessions, he'd somehow been unable to feel at home that night. He shivered as he pulled the door behind him and turned the key in the heavy mortise lock.

A blood-orange dawn had turned morose grey by the time he reached the city limits and, as he drove north, the weather worsened as an ocean of rain tumbled in from the west. The small, light car, the cheapest he could hire, was battered by rainy squalls, and by the time he reached Vallaig the wind was fierce. There was no sign of the *Ran* or Tyler at the end of the pier. He asked at the Harbour Office but the youth behind the counter had seen neither boat nor man since the day before. Armour checked again after eating lunch in a dreary pub. It was a different official in the Harbour Office now, an older man with a greying beard and red face.

"There's no way Tyler would bring the *Ran* over in these conditions," the man said forcefully, "just look at the sea out there." He shook his head, waved the intruder away with his hand and bent to his paperwork. As Armour left, a sullen rumble of thunder confirmed the greybeard's opinion.

Armour returned to the pub where he'd eaten the thickly battered haddock and chips that now lay stolidly in his stomach. A mumble club of old men eyed him in suspicious silence as he ordered and drank another pint of beer and considered his options. Of course, he only had one. He would walk the rough coastal path round Loch Calltain.

He went to the toilet, on his way overtaking an elderly man dressed in a flat cap, dark trousers and a threadbare brown tweed jacket, shuffling along the corridor on arthritic legs. A classic West Highland *bodach*. By the time he had pissed and washed his hands the old man was frailly pushing at the lavatory door. Armour pulled the metal handle and held the door open for him.

"Thank you," the man wheezed.

"It's terrible weather we're having," commented Armour, for the want of anything else to say.

"Och, it's better than nothing," croaked the *bodach*.

Better than nothing! Better than being dead ... than non-existence? My God! He'd met an existentialist *bodach*!

He hurried from pub to car and drove a few hundred yards beyond Vallaig. The road ended in a semicircle of mud and gravel where the hillside had been hacked and blasted for stone by the Victorian navvies who built the town's harbour. The old quarry faced west down the sea loch and had, at some time, been turned into a car park for summer walkers. Armour was the only person to park there this grim afternoon. He clambered out. At once the damp cold air made him shudder, zip up the Barbour jacket with the tattered elbows and wish that he'd brought hat and gloves. He shrugged the strap of his bag onto his shoulder, and pushed through the low gate that led to the coastal path. The rough track meandered up the shoreline to the head of the loch before hairpinning back on itself along the south coast of Calltain. He reckoned it was ten miles to the bay where Argo was anchored. Although the path was rough he should get there in less than four hours, and easily by Argo's appointed time.

He set off at a good pace with a thunderous sky above, and the wind behind him. The sea-scented air and the exercise quickened his mind, and the solitude gave him the space to feel a thrill of anticipation about the carefully planned interrogation he was about to conduct. There would be no press officers to impose limits to his questioning, no security guards to huckle him off the premises. He'd be utterly alone with Argo, and nothing would be off limits. The multi-millions made, the women bedded, the solitary seafaring, the club foot, and the driving ambition of the one who had been the runt of Zander Argo's litter of fisher boys – all of the great man's past would be fair game once he stepped aboard *The Argonaut.*

An hour of hard walking warmed him and brought him to the head of the sea loch. He followed the curve of the bay to the northern shore, with the wind now whipping salt spray into his face. Although he had made good time, pewter-grey clouds had smothered the last glimpses of sun and turned the afternoon into dusk. Rain drummed down. The change of direction had him walking straight into the blast of an unrelenting wind that stung his eyes and numbed his ears. The path now climbed steeply from sea level along the rising edge of a cliff to about four hundred feet. Rain pouring off the hillside had turned the rock-strewn track into a fast- flowing burn. He squelched along as fast as he dared. Twice he stumbled in the gloom, the second time grazing his wrist as his arms flailed out to break his fall. As he trudged on, blood leaked out from beneath his right cuff onto his hand and was washed away by the rain. His shoes were soaked through, and the thick moleskin jeans that he'd put on for warmth that morning were now sodden and freezing and clung to his legs. His jacket was waterproof, but closed so tightly round his neck that it restricted his breathing, and rain trickled down inside where he'd had to leave it open.

His pace slowed on the uphill, his breathing heavy and his temperature dropping. The back of his shirt was damp with sweat that now chilled his skin. Walkers had built cairns along the path, and he crouched down on the lee side of one to catch his breath, but the wind still gusted about him, sucking the heat from his body and making him shiver. He remembered news stories about ill-equipped hill walkers dying of exhaustion and exposure on the Scottish mountains because they were unprepared for sudden turns in the weather, and struggled to his feet to press on. The wind was now much stronger, blustering gale force as he neared the path's summit, and he found himself leaning into it and walking almost doubled up. He thought he heard a low rumble of distant thunder. He stopped and straightened, shielding his eyes from the gale with his aching, bloodied hand. A large marker cairn, where people picnicked to enjoy the view on sunny days, loomed ahead. After that, he reckoned, the path would go downhill. He would still be walking straight into the wind and rain, but it at least it was downhill, and he didn't want to be near the summit if there was lightning. He tried to remember how to calculate the closeness of lightning from the delay between the flash and the clap of thunder, but he couldn't concentrate. The storm had immersed him, bludgeoning his mind and senses. There was a dull ringing in his ears. Something kept him mechanically plodding on. Doug and Ruth's house lay only a couple of miles beyond this godforsaken place. He could stop there and warm up for a bit.

A sudden gust caught him off balance. He knew he had to get below the summit and out of the worst of the wind, or become another mountain fatalities statistic, a small sad paragraph at the foot of an inside page in a newspaper. He stumbled forward a few yards, and for an instant thought he saw a figure approaching. He shielded his face with both hands to see better. Yes, there was someone else, someone standing to one side of the summit cairn. He waved, moving forward, his shout of "hello" torn away by the wind. There were two figures now, one on either side of the path. They weren't moving. They towered above the cairn. He heard the noise again, not thunder but a sound like a cracked church bell being rung by a madman, and he knew at that moment that the figures were not human. A surge of terror coursed through him. For an instant he knew to the core of his being that the giant, spectral Grey Man that haunted a mountain in Scottish legend was no myth.

Fear turned quickly to humiliation. His thighs were warmed by the flow of hot urine just as he realised that he was gazing on two enormous sculptures. Armour sobbed out loud, in relief and shame. He could see now that the spectres were spear and shield bearing warriors, fantastical nine-foot giants constructed by Caleb Burgess. He struggled towards them until he could make out that they were roughly built from un-dressed timber. Their coarsely carved faces were painted black and white and ochre. Their armour breastplates were of flattened food cans nailed to wood, the tattered capes around their shoulders, rough sacking. Their shields were not solid, but made of several plates of steel, wired together so that they rang and clanged in the storm. They were Campbell Aaronson wind chimes.

Armour stood beneath the swaying figures. He knew now what they were. They were guardians, magical figures to protect Calltain from evil, from Joshua Argo and all the greedy forces of Argo Aggregates and the industrial world. It was as if the two artists were summoning supernatural powers to defend their realm. These giants were Burgess and Aaronson's outlandish declaration of war. Had they conducted some weird ritual here? Did they believe that their sorcery would save Calltain from those who would blast and plunder it for profit? Were they that mad, or desperate, or were they just masters of the elaborate publicity stunt? These uncanny warriors were exactly what a picture editor would grab to sex up a news page, an arresting photograph to illustrate some worthy but dull environmental story. The thought gave him strength and resolve. His journey through the storm had spiralled down into a struggle for survival, but now he remembered its purpose. He must keep his appointment with Argo. He recalled Grizzel on a sunny day that seemed an age ago, dreaming up the scheme to interview Argo on Calltain and make the man confront what he wanted to destroy. He had promised he would do that for her. He looked at his watch. There was just enough light to show that he was well behind schedule. At best he was going to be more than an hour late, perhaps two if he couldn't make up time on the downhill. At least, he thought, Argo wouldn't leave the anchorage in weather like this. He'd just have to make a grovelling apology to the man, and hope that the rain had soaked his jeans enough to hide the fact that he had pissed his pants. He turned from the sculptures to plod on downhill, into the wind for miles, past the warm glowing windows of Doug and Ruth's home, past Tyler's unlit cottage and the pier, and on to Camas Calltain with its hazel wood, safe anchorage, the yacht *Argonaut* and Joshua Argo.

THE SHAMAN (3)

Fire and peyote. He would have to chant and dance the ceremony alone, but a Shaman had the power to enter the Otherworld with only fire, peyote and understanding. The God would surely recognise that the ritual could not be as it should.

The bleeding stopped two days after he had killed the white man who had waved the red banner. He had singled out and stalked him because he was the one who had given the sign to defile the mountain. War to the knife, he had vowed, knife to the hilt. When he slew the man he hadn't turned to run until he had seen him fall with the arrow in his throat, and the hesitation had cost him a bullet under his left arm. The whites, perhaps thinking that they were being attacked by a war party, had been slow to pursue him but, when they did, they came with horses and dogs. It had taken all his strength and guile to escape. Only on the second night did he believe they would not find him. He had plugged the wound with boiled and mashed bark, eaten a leathery dried top of peyote, and passed out. When he awoke the bleeding had stopped and his path was clear.

Slowly, and bearing a great pain that threatened to rob him of his mindfulness, the old Shaman made his last journey to the Sheltering Boulder. As he travelled he struggled to keep his mind on the ritual, looking out as he was for signs of the white men, and for sticks and dried bison dung with which to build a fire. The messenger that the peyote had brought guided his eyes.

When he reached the sacred place he cleared an area of stones in the shadow of the great rock and built a small fire with the dried husks of plants and pellets of dung. He placed four arrows on the ground with their feathers so close to the flames that they withered in the heat. Their iron heads radiated out – south, west, north, east.

Back at the settlement by the river lay the crescent-shaped altar of baked clay that had been fashioned when his grandfather was a child. The ceremonial wooden round house had been rebuilt over it many times. It would have been crowded tonight. Men would have chanted, shaken deer-hoof rattles, and danced from midday to sunset. Women would have pounded the cactus in stone bowls and tended the fire. Many voices would have been raised in hymns of praise to the peyote for its protection of the tribe, its beautiful intoxication, and the insight it bestowed into the nature of the Otherworld and the purpose of their lives. Broken in his body, he knew that he could not travel to his people's village by the river.

The fire he built was small, too insignificant under the great expanse of stars for the white men to see from their camp. He put his trust in the Sky God to protect his mortal husk. His body would remain here for many hours while his spirit travelled to the Otherworld.

Gently, he took from his pouch the bulbous green nodules of spineless cactus – more of them than fingers on both his hands – and pounded the flesh in the stone bowl, using a rough lump of black rock from the mountain. Carefully, so as not to spill a morsel, he emptied the mush into a gourd and mixed it with water squeezed from the skin bag. When the mountain's shadow enveloped him as the sun slid down behind the hallowed place, he raised the gourd to his lips and swallowed the sweet and sacred pulp.

Facing south, towards the blue black mountain, and shaking the deer-hoof rattle, he began to chant.

"Bless me, Father, God of the Sky.
Reveal to me your desire.
Bless me, Father, God of the Sky.
Reveal to me your will.
Guide me, Great Spirit,
Ancestor of all things.
Bless me, Father ..."

He began to move his feet in a clumsy shuffle, and danced and chanted as much as the searing pain in his side would allow. Slowly he followed the journey of the sun round the fire at the centre of the world. He moved in a painful parody of the young Shaman who first led his people in the sacred ritual on the day his uncle died and the tribe had called upon him to be the one amongst them who talked to the spirits. His own father had no gift of visions, but from when he was a child his uncle recognised him as his heir and declared him to be his successor. From then on he had two fathers, the hunter and warrior, and the healer and seer. His life had been such that he had been all of these things. Now it was ending, and there was but one more role to fill.

"Bless me my father, God of the Sky.
Guide me in the Otherworld, Great Spirit.
Heal my wounds. Give me understanding."

A wave of nausea overtook him, doubling him up as he struggled to keep the potion down. He began to feel weak and disorientated. He sat by the fire, instinctively seeking to pull around his shoulders the blanket that lay abandoned two painful sun's walk away.

"Bless me, Father, God of the Sky.
Guide me in the Otherworld.
Bless me, Father ... "

Fixing his gaze on the heart of the flames, he chanted the words over and over again until they had no meaning other than their own sound. The sickness in his belly passed. His fear and pain ebbed away and he rolled back comfortably on the earth still intoning the invocation. As he waited for the divine messenger, the night sky grew both familiar and mysterious to him. Away from the fire's tiny circle of light the stars grew brighter, and he felt that he was travelling towards them. The sound of his chanting now had modulated into the thin, insistent song of a reed pipe. The light from the stars began to merge into an intense canopy of radiant white. It blinded him, but he found himself paralysed, unable to raise his hands against its brightness or even close his eyelids. The light seared his retinas but as he heard himself scream, the luminance began to change. As his body accelerated towards it, he could see that it was not white, but made up of tiny shimmering particles of every colour he knew. All the colours of the world were there, shapeless and scintillating – the blues of the sky, the reds of blood and the earth, the greens of the valley where the river ran and the hues of all living things. Silence. He knew this place. It was what existed before the God had danced and turned chaos into the world. It was beautiful and terrifying, and he involuntarily recoiled from it, tumbling back and plummeting into darkness.

He woke abruptly, not in alarm, but full of vitality and wellbeing. His weariness and pain and long winters had gone. He rose and supped the last drops of water from the skin bag. It tasted as if he was drinking from a cool spring. He recognised the mesquite and the low straggly creosote around him and the far-off yucca, but perceived them as he had never done before. Shapes, details, colours entranced him. He could smell all the plants of the plain, even the forest of saguaro cactus in the far distance, and he could distinguish their scent one from another. He heard the cry of a red-tailed hunting bird high on the mountain, and the march of ants at his feet. He found that he could pick out the sound of an individual insect from the living murmur of the land. For the first time he could see the hummingbird's wings. This is how the first Shaman felt when the spirit piped him into the newly made world and the great God had danced. He wandered through the land in ecstasy among the eagle, the turkey and the quail, the bear, the elk and the deer, the wolf, the beaver and the prairie dog.

For three days and nights he walked in the new-made tracks of the Dancing God. The beauty of all he saw, felt, smelled and touched transfixed him. He killed a deer with a single arrow from his bow, caught fish in his hands and drank water from clear springs that bubbled up fresh from the earth. There was no ache in his side, or his heart. His limbs were strong and his hair as black as a raven's wing. At night, his sleep was untroubled.

On the fourth day, he was wakened by the sound of children. They were washing and splashing on the far side of a fast-flowing river that he had never seen before. The children were from a village, and he saw tepees, a corral for horses, and the first thin smoke of morning fires. The people may have been a band of his own tribe, maybe the first ever band of his tribe, but the river was too deep and ran too fast for him to cross. The children waved and shouted, but he could not hear their words above the clamour of the torrent. His heart was heavy when he left the river, but he fixed his eyes on the sacred Black Mountain and ran for an entire day towards it without tiring.

The next morning he woke with a hunger and a thirst. He had no food and he hadn't filled the water skin from the sweet river. He took a pebble from his pouch, put it in his mouth, shouldered his bow and strode south without stopping until the sun was high. The Black Mountain called to him, but in the clear morning light it seemed no closer than it had been on the dawn of the previous day, although he reckoned he must have travelled half the distance. His eyes did not deceive him. They were clear and sharp and he recognised the wheeling flock of carrion birds when they were tiny dots in the sky. He had not seen or heard any other birds or animals that morning. The vultures signified a dead or dying creature. If the meat wasn't spoiled, he'd eat.

He was tiring and eased his pace, breathing in a deep rhythm that conserved his power. He could see the birds clearly now. Whatever they had found must have rotted. The smell of death and putrefaction hung in the hot air. They swooped and squabbled near the ground. He could see that their flight was heavy from the meat they had gorged on. They landed on pale mounds and picked half-heartedly with their black beaks. He stopped short of the plain of slaughter. Before him were the carcasses of more bison than he had ever seen alive. The animals had been skinned but the unconsumed flesh lay rotting in the sun. His own people killed the great creatures when they could, but the bison were powerful. If they smelt or heard a hunter they would charge and could outrun any man and all but the fleetest of horses. His tribe had never taken more animals in a year than the fingers of his hands. They had eaten the flesh till the bones were white. They had cured the hide, fashioned the bones into tools, dried sinews to sew garments and used the horns in their ceremonial headdress. His people respected the brother bison. Why would the God send them another until they had consumed the one they had slain?

The birds squawked angrily at him as he passed, flopping off the skinned bodies clumsily into the air or onto the blood-dark soil. Some had feasted until they were too bloated to fly, and hopped away. He saw that a few of the carcasses had their tongues cut out. Whoever had destroyed the herd had taken only the hides and the choicest meat. He followed the trail of slaughter. The hoofmarks of horses mingled with those of the bison. The horses had been iron-shod. None of the bison had been killed with an arrow. He hunkered down by a year-old female. He reckoned it had been dead for four or five days. When it spoke to him, it did so in the voice of a girl of thirteen or fourteen cycles of the seasons.

"We are destroyed, brother. You and I."

The tongue of the creature had been gouged out, and the rotting head made no movement, but it spoke to him in the soft voice of his woman in the days when he first took her from her father's tepee to be his wife.

"I live," he replied out loud. "My people live. I have seen them on the far shore of a great river."

"Your people will be consumed like my kind. The white men will come and destroy us all. They will unmake the world the God created in ancient times. The sound of the Piping Spirit will be heard no more."

"The white men? They too live in God's creation."

A great sigh came from the dead creature. "They have killed the bison. They will destroy your kind. They will end the world. They will leave nowhere for even their own children to live. They too will die, and all will be silent as in the time before the God began to dance."

He remembered the soundless chaos of the shimmering light beyond the stars. What had seemed beautiful now filled him with terror. He felt a great claw grasp and crush his heart as he rose to his feet. He staggered, the blackness overtook him, and he fell to the blood-caked ground.

The Herald, Monday 13th November 2000
Multi-millionaire dies in mystery yacht blaze
A *Herald* exclusive

Multi-millionaire Joshua Argo died yesterday when fire swept through the cabin of his yacht as it lay anchored in a remote bay off the west coast of Scotland. Police investigating the tragedy have refused to reveal the cause of death, or to confirm that a murder investigation is under way.

A spokesman for the Argo Group of Companies said last night that Mr Argo had been sailing alone on his yacht, *The Argonaut*, and had died as the result of an accident.

However, *The Herald* can reveal that his death is being treated as "suspicious", and that Mr Argo died at Camas Calltain, a bay on the Calltain peninsula that one of his companies, Argo Aggregates, has controversial plans to turn into a giant super-quarry. The Argo Aggregates scheme to blast seven million~~-of~~ tons of rock a year from Calltain to supply the construction industry has been condemned by the local community, which includes a number of prominent artists.

Herald journalist Jonathon Armour discovered the tragedy and alerted the authorities. He had travelled to Calltain, at Joshua Argo's invitation, to interview the tycoon about the plans for the £60 million super-quarry, and discovered the cabin of *The Argonaut* burning at Camas Calltain. Unable to reach the yacht from the shore, Armour ran more than a mile to raise the alarm. After alerting the police and other emergency services, he returned to the bay with two local men and a rubber dinghy.

"The yacht was still floating, but by the time we rowed out to it the cabin was completely gutted. There was a body there, it was unrecognisable but I'm certain it was Argo," said Armour last night. "I had arranged to meet him on *The Argonaut*, stay on board with him overnight, and interview him about his plans for the Calltain super-quarry. There was nobody else on or near the yacht." Mr Armour has given a full statement to officers of the Northern Constabulary.

Joshua (Josh) Argo inherited his family fishing business after the death of his father and brothers. He was one of the first native

Scots entrepreneurs to grasp the opportunity of North Sea oil exploration, and quickly turned his small fishing concern into a fleet of support vessels for the oil industry. He later expanded into oil exploration and production, and then into shipping and aggregates, making himself a multi-millionaire. While Argo was briefly associated with a playboy lifestyle in the eighties, he was a renowned workaholic. In recent years his only known recreation was sailing solo in his yacht *The Argonaut.* Mr Argo was divorced from his second wife, Yvonne, in 1983. He had no children.

- Jonathon Armour writes about his tragic discovery on Page 8.
- Malcolm Eagles considers the future of the Argo group on Page 3 of the Business Section.

Café Sarti (4)

I have often sat, here at my usual table by the window, with my notebook in front of me, trying to dredge up memories and sensations from that terrible night and sort them into some sort of comprehensible account. Comprehensible, if only to me. I write, seeking to understand what has happened to our lives.

Of course, as soon as I got to a rare spot on Calltain with mobile phone reception, I dictated an article about Argo's death to *The Herald*, although I spared readers some of the grisly details. I never mentioned that Argo's head had been blown off above the jaw line in a spout of boiling blood, or that remnants of scorched flesh and shattered bone had been splattered throughout the cabin. I never tried to describe the smell in the place, the acrid chemical stink with a waft of burnt barbecue.

When I arrived at Camas Calltain, *The Argonaut* was bucking and straining at her mooring, its inflatable tender frantically bobbing from a rope at the stern. I realised that it would only be a very bold and experienced sailor that would put out to pick me up in these conditions. I shouted, but my cries were overwhelmed by the storm, and I stared intently through the rain and spume that stung my eyes for some sign that Argo had seen me. Then, between squalls, I saw that the yacht's cabin was blackened and perhaps even smoking. I was confused, unable to imagine what might have happened, but I sensed that something was dreadfully wrong and instinctively sought help. I turned and struggled back along the coast towards Doug's place. Ruth made me drink sweet tea as her man clambered into his waterproofs. Heading back to Camas Calltain, Doug threw open the door of Tyler's place, but he wasn't there. Then the pair of us ran to the house with the boat hull roof to raise Andy and Trail. Trail rushed off to find somewhere with a mobile phone signal. I don't know if it was the sugar or adrenaline that had kicked in, but I helped Andy half-carry, half-drag, his inflatable back to Camas Calltain, while Doug staggered along behind us, bowed down by the dead weight of the outboard engine over his shoulder. Andy proved both bold and experienced, wading into the waves to push us out, then clambering into the dinghy to start the engine while Doug fended us off from the shore with an oar. I'd thought myself done for, but I felt a surge of energy as we approached what I could now clearly see was the badly burned *Argonaut.* As soon as Doug had grabbed its anchor chain I seized the side rail and heaved myself on board.

When I told the police my story, over and over again to satisfy their desire to glean every scrap of information, I didn't tell them everything. Naturally, I described the scene – how the fire damage to the cabin was quite superficial although the smoke was thick, about the more or less headless body slumped on the bunk, about the whisky bottle and the position on the floor of the pistol which had fired the emergency flare that had decapitated Argo. No, I had not touched anything. Yes, I had been the first person to scramble on board and enter the cabin. I told the detectives that as a young reporter I'd attended the scene of many fatalities and that I knew the score. I had stopped Doug Fowlie at the cabin door so that he wouldn't disturb any evidence. The police were, of course, grateful for my assistance, but I could sense that they felt something was missing from my testimony. Whether they thought that I hadn't noticed a vital clue, or that I had forgotten to tell them about it, or that I was deliberately holding something back, I do not know. I only know that no one could have seen me lift from the table the second stubby whisky glass, with what may have been a smear of liquid still in it, and put it in my pocket, and that no one saw me slip it over the side of the dinghy into the sea when Andy Campbell took us back ashore.

Of course I realise now that the second glass has – or had, for it will have been smashed to pieces on the rocky seabed by now – a significant bearing on the case. Solitary drinking and its stable mate, depression, have driven many a talented man to suicide, but the post mortem showed that Argo had consumed only a moderate amount of whisky. He turned out to have been an abstemious soul who, for the past decade or more, only occasionally drank, and then only socially. The glass that I dropped into the sea was the only evidence that there might have been anyone else on board *The Argonaut* that evening. I had destroyed evidence, and I continued in the fiction that there was nothing else I could recall about what I saw or did that night.

Why did I take the glass? Why did I maintain my deception in the face of such detailed cross-examination? I have no idea. It was an inexplicable action. I was of course exhausted, and probably hypothermic. I was certainly in shock. I had even pissed myself. I had to be half-dragged back to Andy's place, my arms around the shoulders of the two strong men. In the warm room where we found Trail hand-setting type, they stripped me and dressed me in a coarse woollen sweater and dry jeans. I remember insisting that I call the *Herald*. Trail helped me into an oilskin and took me by the arm, shaking and stumbling, to the rocky hillock behind the house where he'd been able to phone the police and coastguard. I must have been functioning on instinct and experience, for when I read the article two days later I had no memory of dictating it. After they had got me to drink something hot, they left me. I could hear Andy talking loudly and excitedly to his partner in the adjoining kitchen, but I had retreated somewhere into myself and couldn't understand his words. The room and all that it contained, including myself, were vague and insubstantial. It was if I was not there, but simply recalling some distant dream. I have a faint memory of seeing myself, hunched in a chair among the wooden racks of type, between the stove and the old American printing press of black cast iron, adorned with a gold painted eagle mounted on the frame. Trapped in a waking dream, my mind seemed to be watching my physical self from a floating position about nine feet from the ground under the hull of the roof. When my perception returned to somewhere inside my head, I looked up to gaze at the metal eagle, which I could have sworn I hadn't noticed before. I'd had such out-of-body experiences while drifting in and out of sleep in my early teens, and now knew them to have been robbed of their mystery by science. Delusion, once caused by the chaotic hormones of puberty, had been turned on once more by exhaustion, exposure and horror.

I must have slept, for when I looked up Campbell Aaronson sat on a chair facing me. At first I did not react, believing him to have been just conjured up in the tumult of my mind.

Rainwater from his stockman's coat had dripped onto the floor around him. He sat quite still, with his hands resting on his knees and his eyes on me, as if I was a portrait photographer about to take his picture. There was no pity in his eyes, although I must have seemed a pitiful sight. To me he looked like some great genius, a Darwin or a Newton, painted for grateful posterity to revere; aloof, preoccupied, wrestling with the great issues of the age.

"I need to know."

I said nothing. I was still trying to figure out if the figure before me was real or a hallucination.

He leaned forward, as if to incarnate himself to me. "Was Argo ... assassinated?"

"Yes."

I said it without any evidence that it was true, but I said it without hesitation.

He slouched to one side so hard I thought he would fall to the floor. After a moment he spoke, quietly but distinctly, to the puddle at his feet. "I'm an old man. It would be but a small matter for me to die for this place ... dying is easy, it's just a question of the world as only you have experienced it coming to an end ... but this isn't any kind of end." His body didn't move, but his neck twisted slowly until he looked me in the eyes. "We built a bomb, Armour ... a bomb of such cataclysmic power that we thought it would make future war impossible. We wanted freedom from fear. What we failed to understand was that as long as one person can kill another, even with a stone or a sharp stick, fear will always be with us. We knew the science. We knew the politics. We just didn't understand our own hearts."

His voice, once so confident and commanding, now came in a whisper. "He who fights with monsters ..." Then he stood up and shuffled slowly across the storm- puddled floor and left the room.

It was only the next day that I recalled that final meeting with Campbell Aaronson. Sometimes I wonder if it really occurred.

To the police, I was the one with the answers. To myself, I was wracked by doubt and uncertainty. Was my action in the cabin of *The Argonaut* just an aberrant symptom of mental confusion brought on by exhaustion and hypothermia, or could it be that some intuitive force was at work within me? Had I somehow reached a higher level of consciousness through physical privation and the experience of sheer terror when I encountered Burgess's giant supernatural beings and Argo's headless corpse? To this day I can't understand my behaviour on that evening any better than I could then.

An early outcome of my lie was the attention of William Dalgety. I had been ordered a fortnight of complete rest by the doctor who examined me after the police had supposedly finished their interrogation, but three days after I found Argo's body he appeared at my flat to, as he put it, "clear up some ... tiddling details". I'd only got home the night before and was still pretty ill and worn out. The doctor had written "exhaustion and exposure" on a sick-note to present to *The Herald*, not that I needed it, as my physical state was well known to my colleagues, and in any case I'd just presented them with a genuine old-fashioned scoop. I am normally a bad patient who hates being ill, but I'd decided to take a few days off – not, if I'm completely honest, to recuperate, but to track down Grizzel. When I'd finally got a chance to phone her, she wasn't at her Oxford flat. I'd called several times before I got an answer. A rather vague- sounding young man – I remembered she'd mentioned having flatmates – thought he recalled seeing her a couple of days before. I called the Clerk-Maxwell Astrophysics Institute and finally spoke to someone who'd seen her around "sometime recently", but didn't know where she was now. I cursed Calltain's lack of phones and the reluctance of its inhabitants to carry mobiles, and although I knew Aaronson had a broadband connection, I never felt it right to phone and worry someone so old. Eventually I called the Vallaig Harbour Office to see if anyone had seen Tyler. His boat wasn't there, and he hadn't been seen around. By the time Dalgety got to me I was frantic.

William Dalgety was a large man with pale blue eyes that seemed too big even for his broad pasty face. He was clearly balding, but disguised it by keeping his soft grey-blond hair closely cropped. It made him look like an enormous fat baby. On reflection, I doubt if he was forty but he seemed older, a bit of an old buffer. In all the times I met him he was on his own, and he never took notes or even produced a notebook.

Instead, he would sit quite still, except that he would occasionally knead the knuckles of his left hand with the podgy fingers of his right. He hardly ever blinked, and he peppered his sentences with odd pauses, like a man on some powerful sedative. The effect was most disconcerting, and I expect that, even if I had been entirely truthful with him, his demeanour would still have instilled in me a feeling of nervousness and guilt. His voice was soft and high, and I found myself speculating that he might be gay.

"I see you're still not yet well. I'll not keep you long ... it's just a few ... tiddling details I'd like to clear up," he said sitting down heavily on the couch. "I could come back ... if you'd prefer ... it must have been a shock ... nasty business." He looked at me with an expression that might have passed for sympathy. I told him I was fine, and going back to work in a couple of days. He waved aside the offer of coffee. "Could you just tell me ... Mr Armour, why exactly you were going to Calltain that night?" And so I again told the entire story – well, not the entire story, but at least everything I'd told before. Dalgety asked few questions, but nodded slightly at any pause in my well-practised narrative, encouraging me to continue. When I got to the part about being handed over to detectives in Vallaig after being interviewed by uniformed police in Calltain, he interrupted. "I expect, Mr Armour, that as a journalist ... you have already worked out that I represent the Special Branch, and for me ... this case has wider implications than simply the ... nasty business of Mr Argo's death."

Of course, I realised it the moment he said it. Suddenly it was crashingly obvious that Dalgety was no ordinary plainclothes plod trying to sort out a case of mysterious death. He took no notes because he already knew everything I was going to say before I'd said it. He was just there to watch me tell my story. It was my performance, not tiddling details that I might dredge from my memory, that Dalgety was interested in. It was at that instant I realised that, to him, I was more suspect than witness. Somehow the notion seemed quite exciting, a bit of a game. My weakness was that I was guilty of destroying a piece of evidence. My strength was that I had nothing to do with Argo's death. Dalgety could have his suspicions, but the only evidence that could ever be brought against me was now smashed to pieces on the stormy, rocky shore of Calltain.

"I read your articles," he said suddenly. "I expect you think I just read crime stories and the court cases, but my wife and I ... we're quite regular visitors to art galleries." I made some fatuous comment about how everybody should enjoy art, but he interrupted. "I was interested when you started writing about ... environmental matters. My wife even mentioned it to me one morning, quite unprompted ... how surprised she was. How did you get interested in ... that sort of thing?"

Under his lugubrious stare I bumbled on a bit about discovering Aaronson and meeting Caleb Burgess, and how that had got me interested in the super-quarry plans for Calltain, yet all the time my mind was seething with memories of Grizzel. I didn't mention her.

"So it's artists you're still interested in ... rather than saving the planet ... the wife will be happy about that." I must have looked confused, because he concluded, "She often says, 'We must go and see that!' after she's read one of your reviews. But one more thing ... if you really think that these ... cave paintings by the American gentleman are as good as you said in your article ... you can't have been ... well, very ... sympathetic to Mr Argo."

"I didn't much like his plans for Calltain," I heard myself say, "but I never met the man."

"Of course you didn't. By the time you saw him he was ... decapitated ... nasty business. A Very pistol ... of all things ... one that fires a whopping big distress flare. Him so experienced a yachtsman too." He shook his head as if in disbelief. "One more thing, Mr Armour ... I'm sorry, it's another one more thing ... you know Mr Aaronson's daughter ... Grizzel Gillespie."

Not a question, but a statement.

It was then I knew, absolutely knew with certainty, that Grizzel was somehow connected to Argo's death. I didn't know how I knew. I had no facts or insights or even a theory, but I knew nonetheless. What's more, I realised that, deep within a dark territory of my mind I didn't care to visit, I had known this all along. My mind; chaotic.

I suppose only a second or so passed before I got my reeling imagination under control, for Dalgety didn't have to repeat the question. It occurred to me to tell him that it was none of his fucking business and that I was tired and sick and would he now please leave. Somehow it came out as: "We're friends. In fact I'm just back from visiting the States with her."

"The United States? Well you'll be good ... friends then. And Miss Gillespie's ... friend ... Matthew Tyler ... do you know him?"

"Hardly at all," I told him. "I've crossed over on his boat a few times, but he's not exactly what I'd call communicative."

"Someone told me that you were supposed to stay in his cottage but you'd had an argument and ... an altercation. I don't think you mentioned this to my uniformed colleagues, but never mind. What I'd like to know is ... if Mr Tyler was ... uncommunicative ... how did the two of you manage to get into a fight without ... communicating in the first place?"

I'd fallen straight into his trap. I burbled on about how, with all the stress of the past three days, I'd entirely forgotten my punch-up with Tyler, and that anyway we'd been drunk and that I didn't think it was relevant.

"Well, now you see Mr Armour, that's my point. People often forget things ... sometimes ... as no doubt in this case, just tiddling little things that hardly matter, but now and again people know things that are material to an inquiry, even if they don't think them to be ... relevant. You see, the newspapers and the police dramas on TV are all mad keen on DNA testing and psychological profiling, but you still get the best results by ... asking the right person the right ... question. That's where I come in ... encouraging people to remember little things ... they've ... ah ... forgotten, or things they don't think ... are relevant. For instance, did Tyler ever mention to you any places he visited ... to see friends or that sort of thing?"

"No, as far as I know he didn't travel much, not even back to wherever he came from. Most of his fishing and scallop diving was done just in the loch, and he always sold what he caught at Vallaig pier to a local guy called Joe Phimster."

"Ahhh," he sighed. "That's a pity. We've been unable to ... locate Mr Tyler. He seems to have ... vanished."

"Really?"

"Vanished most certainly. We've found his boat, tied up safe and sound, but no trace of its ... skipper. Interesting chap, you know. Brief Army career ... dishonourable discharge for substance abuse, but apparently ... heroic ... destroyed an Iraqi tank single-handed. Our man sauntered up to it, cool as you like, and tossed a couple of hand grenades down the hatch. Quite an ... unusual chap I'd say ... wouldn't you?" His gaze swept over me, missing nothing, hunting the faintest twitch or tremor. "You won't hesitate to call me if you have any inkling of where he might be, or if you remember ... anything at all?"

"Of course."

"Ahh, good." He took out a card from the breast pocket of his jacket and handed it to me as he bestowed what he may have believed was a kindly smile.

"Did Tyler kill Argo?" I blurted out.

"Oh Mr Armour! A gentleman of the press like yourself must be more circumspect! Nobody's accusing Mr Tyler of anything. We're just anxious to talk to him ... we want to talk to everyone who was around Calltain at that time. As far as we're concerned ... at the moment ... no crime has been committed. Unless ... you have any information that might cast a ... different light on things?"

"No!" I almost shouted, "I've told you everything I know."

"I hope you have Mr Armour ...and now, unless there's anything else you've remembered, I'll leave you to ... recuperate."

I saw him to the door. As he left he asked if I had any plans to go abroad again. I told him I didn't. He smiled. "I bet you thought policemen only said that on TV ... cop shows. But it really is part of ... the routine." He smiled, and I swear he winked a bulbous blue eye at me as he turned to descend the stairs.

Return

That night, Armour slept fitfully, his consciousness drifting in and out of the nightmarish corporeal world where Joshua Argo's killer roamed at large. Awake, he thought of Tyler – a man who was deadly with a hand grenade. Asleep, he dreamed of Tyler – thrusting a flare pistol into Argo's screaming mouth.

Armour woke in a sweat. The first thing that entered his mind was not the absence of Grizzel beside him – how quickly he had got used to waking beside her! – but Tyler, the murderer, still on the loose. He rose, and resolved to go back to work at *The Herald* that morning. Harry Urquhart had told him to take all the time he needed to get well, but Armour now craved the routine, needed the undemanding companionship of the workplace. He could continue his search for Grizzel from the office. He would phone her Oxford flat and the Clerk-Maxwell Institute again. He would contact Aaronson in Calltain. Could she have gone to Calltain? If so, why would she pass through Glasgow without seeing him? Should he go to Calltain? The *Ran* had been discovered. Had it been impounded by the police? If not, Doug Fowlie or Andy MacDonald were more than capable of running the ferry service. He could travel there easily. Armour was on automatic pilot now, heading for the office.

"Christ, Jon, you arts hacks will do anything to get onto the front page!" Mike, the senior guy on the News Desk turned to his colleagues. "Imagine! Blowing some poor bastard's head off!"

Armour raised two fingers as he passed the laughing newsmen. "Come and talk to me once you've read a book, you fucking old fire-engine chaser." The reporters laughed louder. He was making a good impersonation of being there. His body responded to the command to walk. His wit and tongue gave the appearance of being in control. To his taxi-driver, the receptionist behind the front desk and the journalists on the third floor, Jonathon Armour was back at work.

Harry Urquhart was already at the Features Desk and rose to throw an arm round Jonathon.

"Great to have you back, Jonno. Such an amazing story! You must have been totally knackered, but you did a brilliant job of writing it up. I thought we'd go for lunch, you, me and the boss. I'll tell him you're back. Don't worry, a welcome back lunch was his idea and he's paying. Twelve thirty? OK?"

He heard himself agree and spent the morning half-reading e-mails, opening mail and accepting compliments about his exclusive, and sympathetic enquiries about his health. Grizzel did not phone. He wanted to scream out to the world: "Grizzel! Where the fuck are you?" He had not heard a word from her since they had parted at Heathrow five days before. He sat for an hour or more, deleting e-mails and binning press releases after he had scanned them with his eyes, a process that allowed almost none of their content to register in his brain. The morning passed in a weird agony of disassociation, longing and fear. He tried to recall every conversation, every gesture, every iota of information he knew about Grizzel, seeking a clue as to where she was, and why she hadn't phoned. The violent death of a multi-millionaire was national news that even an unworldly astrophysicist must have noticed. Where had she gone? Not Oxford. Not Calltain. Where the hell did her mother live now? He was descending fast into a dark glen of loss and misery from which only she could guide him. He had to be with her if he wasn't to remain forever in that realm of despair, and he knew too that somehow only Grizzel could make sense of what he'd seen and done in the cabin of *The Argonaut.*

He phoned her flat. No answer. He phoned the Clerk-Maxwell Institute. She wasn't there, and no, the person he spoke to didn't know where she was. He opened "Contacts" on his computer, typed in "Aaronson" and dialled the number as soon as it appeared on the screen. The old man took nearly three minutes to answer. He seemed distant, distracted, diminished. Perhaps he didn't know who Armour was. Anyway, Grizzel wasn't there. He hadn't heard from her, but he hadn't been expecting to, he explained. He sounded guarded, suspicious, or possibly wandered. Yes, it was a terrible business about Argo, even though he had been an utter bastard. "I wonder," the old man mused, "what it's like ... the sound of a distress rocket exploding in your brain."

In the glass box that served as the editor's office, powerful digestive juices were beginning to flow. The editor rose late, never breakfasted and liked to lunch early. He fancied Italian. He spoke briefly to his PA and strode over to Armour's desk in the Features area, collecting Harry Urquhart on the way.

"Great to have you back, Jon. You did a terrific job for us there. Thought we'd have lunch to welcome you home. Sarti's is good. Do you know it?"

Sarti's? In years of eating and drinking at Sarti's he'd never once seen the editor there. He felt he was living in the pages of some novel whose author played fast and loose with coincidence. The three men stepped out briskly into the sharp November afternoon.

Lunch at Café Sarti

The three of us sat comfortably at a round table for four. It only struck me then that I'd hardly eaten anything for the past two days and that I was extremely hungry and a bit light-headed. Harry and the editor at once lapsed into silence, the way people do when first confronted with an unfamiliar menu. The table was deep in the back basement and I was sitting with my back to the table Grizzel and I had shared only two months before. I turned once to glance back at it, and saw what looked like a retired couple, in town for a day's shopping, having lunch, a clutter of plastic bags at their feet. As I turned back, a waving figure caught my eye – a solitary diner, strangely familiar. He raised a glass of sparking water in my direction and I stupidly returned the greeting, miming a toast with an empty hand, before it dawned on me who it was.

"Who's that, Jonno?" asked Harry, one of the most curious and gossipy people around.

"He's a policeman. His name is Dalgety."

"Dalgety?" The editor looked up from his antipasti deliberations. "Bill Dalgety?"

"I suppose so, he introduced himself as William."

The editor squirmed round uncomfortably in his chair and clocked the fat detective, who was now grinning over in our direction. "Hi Bill," he whispered with exaggerated facial movements as he raised his hand in greeting. William Dalgety repeated his watery toast and beamed at us.

"Interesting guy," said the editor in a low voice. "I've known him forever. He's always at the sharp end of something. He's been with Special Branch for years now and we've done each other a few favours. How do you know him, Jon?" The editor emphasised the word "you" and looked at me with unconcealed suspicion. He was known to have one of the best contact books in the business, and he kept his connections close and hated people muscling in on them.

"He thinks I killed Josh Argo," I heard myself say.

The editor theatrically raised his eyebrows. "Goodness, Jon, I hope you didn't. I admire ambition in my staff, but the

Press Complaints Commission is going to take it very badly if my journos start murdering people just for a front page splash." His jovial mood swung abruptly. "Fuck it! It was Dalgety I gave the Free Radicals stuff to ... I didn't know that he was in on this Argo business. You know what this means?"

I looked at him stupidly.

"It means that Argo was murdered ... even if it wasn't by you. Officially, the police are putting it about that Argo killed himself, but if Bill Dalgety's on the case, then Argo's head being blown off wasn't an accident or suicide. If he's investigating Argo's death, and at the same time running with the Free Radicals business, it means he thinks they're linked and that Argo was killed by some eco-terrorist!"

He swivelled round in his chair, waving to Dalgety. "Bill!" he bellowed so that all the restaurant could hear, "Must have a word with you over coffee." The fat man put down his spaghetti-laden fork to raise a podgy fist in a thumbs-up.

"So!" said the editor, triumph in his voice, "What are we eating?"

From the moment I saw Dalgety, I was like a man hypnotised. Today, my memory of the meal is like that of some vanishing nightmare recalled in the first few seconds of waking up, just as the details evaporate, leaving only a disturbing shadow of fear. I have no memory of what I ate, but I vividly recall that Dalgety had spaghetti in some sort of rich creamy sauce and a plain ice cream onto which he tipped a cup of espresso coffee, and then slurped the melting mess down with a teaspoon. All the time his bulging baby-blue eyes never seemed to leave me. Whenever I turned to look at him, he caught my glance and grinned back, or winked or raised his glass in my direction. I swear he once did all three at the same time. Harry and the editor's conversation flittered around me like a cloud of fruit flies, mildly annoying but of little consequence. When either of them spoke to me I found myself stuttering out disjointed and rambling utterances that can hardly have made any sense at all. I remember they were surprised that I didn't know that Argo had an important collection of paintings that he had left to the National Galleries of Scotland. I know there was talk of eco-terrorism and how *The Herald* should cover it, and of the future of the Argo Corporation now that its founder was dead, but I can't have contributed anything useful or even lucid. Sometime during the main course they stopped talking to me altogether. My eyes were constantly drawn to the fat man lunching not more than ten yards away. Somehow I managed to mechanically chomp my way through two courses and drink every drop of wine that was poured for me, which was quite a lot. After all, we were celebrating and having what the editor called "an old-fashioned newspaper lunch". Once I'd have taken it in my stride, but in my fragile state I suppose I got pretty drunk, pretty quickly.

We were looking at the dessert menu when I felt the light touch of a hand on my shoulder, and found Dalgety looming over me. He'd finished his meal and had come over to greet the editor. They exchanged pleasantries, his enormous hand still resting on me. The editor introduced Dalgety to Harry and then waved his hand towards me. "So Bill, it seems you already know Jon Armour. You're not going to tell me that one of my best writers is your main suspect are you?"

Dalgety gazed down at me. His stomach bulged inches from my face. Yes, he was fat, but tall and imposing too, physically threatening. "On the contrary, Mr Armour is ... a valued witness." He turned towards the editor and lowered his voice. "As for suspects ... well, who says we suspect anybody? However, we do have some ... interesting leads."

"Oh come on, Bill! How interesting? What mutter from the gutter are you picking up? Remember, you're among friends here."

"Let's just say that there's someone ... we're still very keen to speak to ... and it's not Mr Armour here."

Dalgety squeezed my shoulder. The editor's hand made an involuntary gesture towards the inside pocket of his jacket. Unconsciously his fingers, journalistic to their tips, were itching for a pen.

"It's great to see you, Bill. I've been meaning to call you about the Free Radicals business, but now you're here, why don't you join us? I thought I might order another bottle of this Barolo, it's excellent."

The fat man released my shoulder and clapped his fleshy hands together. "That would be ... splendid."

At that instant I knew for certain that I was going to be violently sick. My stomach heaved.

"Excuse me ..." I stood up immediately, already retching and gagging, and only half-caught the erupting mess of masticated food, wine and digestive acids in my feebly cupped hands as it was propelled from my stomach with such force that it splattered onto the table and my two seated colleagues. There was a collective gasp of horror from the diners and waiters, and a muted "For fuck's sake, Armour" from the editor. I was aware that the overweight detective had taken a surprisingly nimble step back an instant before I vomited.

"I'm sorry, Jonno's not been well. I'm terribly sorry," I heard Harry shout as I staggered to the toilet.

My throat burned and I was covered in clammy sweat. I vomited again until there was nothing left to throw up, and then remained in the Gents for more than half an hour, cleaning myself as best I could and putting off the moment when I would have to walk through the restaurant to reach the door and the stone steps that led up and out into Bath Street. Harry came in to make sure I was OK, and to remove his soiled tie and dab at some sick stains on his jacket with a paper towel. The editor, he said, had gone. I asked him about Dalgety and he looked at me blankly.

"The detective, the fat guy."

"Oh, him. He went off with the boss. The two are as thick as thieves, but I don't think the cop was going to spill the beans until they were alone." Harry chuckled. "Christ it was pandemonium in there when you boked up. The manager was bellowing orders to everybody in Italian and one of the waitresses collided into him and dropped these plates of pasta. One fell on a woman who screamed and knocked a full bottle of wine off her table. If you hadn't completely fucked this silk tie that Anne gave me, it would have been hilarious."

Harry reckoned I was now clean enough to satisfy a Glasgow taxi-driver and escorted me through the restaurant, which smelled of disinfectant, muttering apologies to anyone we passed. The place was half empty now, whether because of my efforts I can't say. I noticed that the elderly couple who had eaten at the table where Grizzel and I sat had gone.

Harry quickly found me a taxi. I clutched my flat keys like a talisman throughout the journey back. I ached to get home, to shut off the world behind me, throw away my loathsome clothes and stand in the shower with the heat on high and the pressure at full force. At that moment I wanted to be in that shower even more than I wanted Grizzel. I fumbled with my keys, the Yale and the heavy mortise, and let myself in. The man I'd bought the place from was a criminologist who had told me that you couldn't be too careful. I peeled off my rancid, stained clothes down to my underpants and then crashed out on my bed.

Dreaming

Jonathon Armour slept deeply, and dreamt the weird and vivid dreams of an invalid.

He was walking down the pier at Vallaig. He could hear wind chimes, borne from far away on a light breeze. Grizzel and Tyler were standing on the deck of the *Ran*. He knew they were waiting for him, but the strap of his shoulder bag was ridiculously long, and he kept getting it entangled in his legs and tripping on it. The *Ran* was about to leave – Tyler was untying the mooring ropes – and he would need to run to catch them, but the bag swung between his feet again and he stumbled and fell. He wanted to throw the bag away, but there was something in it he needed to give to Grizzel. As he struggled to his feet, he saw that they were talking to each other, and laughing, and hadn't seen him. He knew he was very late. He began to run but the bag strap was now wound round his ankles, hobbling him so that he only moved a few inches at every step. The *Ran* was moving now, heading out towards the harbour entrance and the loch. He tried to yell to them, "Grizzel, Grizzel I'm here!" but the noise of the engine thrummed in his ears, drowning out his voice. He staggered to the pier end, waving his arms and shouting, but they neither saw, nor heard him. A "V" formation of geese passed noisily overhead and he knew they brought the winter with them.

On Calltain, for he was there now, he took the *bealach* path over the peninsula's spine to Caleb's cave, but inexplicably found himself on the southern shore track beside the giant warriors. Grizzel was there. He tried to explain to her how terrified he'd been of the sculptures, but she seemed bored or distracted and wandered off to the crumbling cliff edge to look down onto the rocky shore. He kept warning her about falling, but she laughed at him, and as she did she stepped back and plunged over, laughing, all the way down.

He was cold and wet now, and he realised he'd been in the loch. His mouth tasted of salt water. He was lying on the deck of the *Ran*. Where was Grizzel? They had both fallen from the cliff, and Tyler had rescued him in his boat, but Grizzel wasn't on board. Aaronson was with Tyler in the tiny wheelhouse. Didn't they realise that Grizzel was still in the loch? He grasped the gunwale and pulled himself up. He could see Grizzel in the water, floating tragically like Ophelia in a Pre-Raphaelite painting – but he knew that she was alive. Why didn't she wave or shout? The men in the wheelhouse took no notice and the *Ran* was heading away from her at full speed. The little deck was now crowded with people. Everyone was happy and smiling and took no notice of him or the drowning woman. Doug and Ruth were there, and Ruth was talking in sign language to her deaf and dumb sister. A young man with dreadlocks was tuning his guitar while his girlfriend watched and smoked a cigarette, and some children spoke excitedly about a film they had seen. Nobody but he had noticed that Grizzel was being left behind in the loch, getting smaller and smaller as the *Ran* ploughed on. It had begun to rain, and the wind was blowing hard. His hands grasped the side of the *Ran* to stop him from being blown overboard by the storm. He shouted, "Grizzel, Grizzel I'm here."

And then he woke up, and the nightmare began.

The Herald, 18th November 2000

Multi-millionaire death: Police don't rule out murder

A *Herald* exclusive

Detectives investigating the death of businessman Joshua Argo believe that the controversial multi-millionaire may have been murdered.

The Herald has learned that while police publicly maintain that Argo's death on board his yacht was probably the result of an accident, a secret murder investigation is under way by members of Special Branch.

Special Branch is the arm of the police principally responsible for fighting terrorism. Formed in 1883, following a series of bomb attacks on mainland Britain by Irish nationalists, it plays a major role today in the surveillance of subversive organisations. We can reveal that a number of militant environmentalist and anti-capitalist groups are currently being investigated, and that Special Branch officers want to question a number of individuals in connection with the death of Joshua Argo. These individuals are described by our source as "eco-warriors".

Last month, a group calling itself "Free Radicals" contacted *The Herald* claiming responsibility for an attack on a West Highland fish farm. It is not yet known if the cases are connected, but *The Herald* has evidence that a spate of relatively minor attacks on property over the past year – previously written off by police forces throughout Scotland as "unconnected" and "petty vandalism" – are now being treated by the authorities as coordinated attacks by a recently emerged eco-terrorist group or groups. These include arson attacks on earth-moving machinery employed on new motorway projects, the destruction of fish farm cages, and attacks on the private property of several leading industrialists. Joshua Argo's car was fire bombed only days before *Herald* columnist Jonathon Armour found him dead on his yacht.

The Herald showed the file it has collected on possible eco-terrorist attacks to Dr Laurence McHardy, a terrorism expert at Aberdeen University. He said last night: "Special Branch's belief that it might be dealing with a 'newly emerged' terrorist group or groups has important implications for the police and the public.

Most of the attacks on *The Herald* file look pretty amateurish. If in fact they were carried out by a new, untrained and inexperienced group, then the perpetrators are likely to make very simple mistakes and could be apprehended quickly. On the other hand, if many of its members have no criminal records, such 'clean skins' might be very difficult to trace."

The Herald has learned that Special Branch is urgently attempting to trace one individual who they believe may have information about the fire on board Mr Argo's yacht *The Argonaut*.

Dr McHardy warned that even attacks by amateur eco-warriors were a serious danger to public safety. "The actions of such people are often hot-headed rather than cold-blooded. Such individuals are also more likely to panic and bungle operations than experienced hard-core terrorists would be. Any bomb, whether it is Semtex or a home made Molotov cocktail, or any gun, is more dangerous in the hands of an amateur than a professional, so a 'weekend' eco-warrior is a serious threat to ordinary members of the public."

Dr McHardy added that the death of Joshua Argo could have been the result of a botched plan to intimidate the multi-millionaire by threatening him, or by destroying his yacht.

He warns that eco-terrorists may be hard to track down. "What we may be seeing may not be the emergence of an organised eco-terrorist group or groups, but of a movement of very loosely connected individuals who act on their own or in very small numbers. The rise of the Internet allows the creation of what I'd call 'virtual movements' of people with little or no connection to each other except for some vague political or philosophical beliefs. Such groups can share tactical information, such as bomb building, and draw inspiration from each other's actions without ever implicating or endangering other groups. It makes them very difficult to hunt down."

Last night the Northern Constabulary continued to deny that Mr Argo's death was the subject of a murder investigation. A spokesman for the Argo group of companies continued to maintain that its Chief Executive's death was "a terrible, terrible accident".

Tyler

He could smell the cigarette smoke, carried through the large flat on imperceptible currents of centrally heated air. Tyler was waiting in the living room for him. He lounged on the black leather settee with his feet on a low glass table and didn't bother to stand. There were three empty beer bottles in front of him and he flicked the ash from his roll-up into one of them. Armour stood in the doorway, facing him.

"You look shite, Armour. You OK?"

"How the fuck did you get in? Why the hell are you here?" Armour's voice sounded hoarse and hushed in his own ears, he was too worn out for surprise or outrage.

"To see ma old pal, of course. Heard he wasnae too well." Tyler waved his hand around proprietarily. "Anyways, I like it here ... real designer stuff by the way. I've had your keys for months now. Copied them in Calltain when you were hanging around Caleb ... quite a tricky job, it's a fuckin serious lock you've got on that door. You must be fuckin paranoid. Mind you, it's a nice pad, very ... well, designer. I stayed here a couple of nights when you were away shagging Grizzel in America. No hard feelings though ... I watered your plants."

"Grizzel told me about you and her, Tyler. You must have known you were out of your depth."

"And you're no? Grizz is her father's daughter. She's a genius like he is. You're just an old fart who got lucky ... or maybe not.' He looked at Armour steadily. "You think you love her then?"

"Yes, I do."

"Yeah, I reckon you do, you poor fuck."

"Where is she, Tyler? You know, don't you."

Tyler reached for his battered tobacco tin and prised it open. "Yeah, I huv a good idea."

"Tell me where the hell she is or I'll call the police!"

"Don't threaten me, you sad fuck. Do you know you smell of spew? It's boggin. You might have showered before you crashed out. And by the way, even I don't sleep in my drawers, and I'm a clarty cunt."

Armour strode towards the lounging man, trying to be as threatening as he could, but humiliated and ridiculous in his underpants. “You bastard, I know you killed Argo. Tell me where she is, and I won’t tell the police what I know.”

Tyler looked up from his half rolled cigarette and grinned. “You know fuck all, pal. Even the cops know it wasn’t me.”

Armour stood staring down at Tyler in bemused disbelief. The man swung his feet to the floor and sat up, licked the gum edge of his cigarette paper and rolled it between thumbs and fingers before speaking again.

“I was in the jail when the fucker was killed.” He put the thin roll-up between his lips, lit it, inhaled and shook his head in an ironic rueful gesture. “I got totally pissed in Oban that day ... It was a Saturday, right? I’d been drinking from when the boozer opened at eleven, and was steamin’ by three o’clock. Then the barman wouldn’t serve me so I gave him a belt in the mooth. Stupit bastard. Then the polis came and banged me up overnight in the cells.” He grinned. “Best alibi in the world, pal.”

“You’re lying! The police have been looking for you! I know that ... my newspaper talks to Special Branch.”

“Ahh, well that’s the thing. When I got lifted, it seems I didnae exactly gie the cops ma right name. They say I told them ma name was Matthew Taylor. Mebbe they misheard, or I was confused or somethin. Anyways, they couldn’t suss out anything about me or who I was, so they kept me in the cells. Then yesterday they started getting a bit heavy with me and the bastards didn’t feed me all day, so I finally telt them who I was. I can tell you, they were well fucked off ... said I was lucky not to be done for obstructing a police inquiry. Then it turns out there was some cop in Glasgow who wanted to talk to me about the Argo hoo-ha ... I told them that it served the rich bastard right, but that I knew fuck all about it ’cept for what I’d read in some copper’s *Daily Record.* But anyways, they phoned this Glasgow guy. It seems he was very disappointed to hear that I’d been banged up since before Argo snuffed it. The Oban cops bundled me into a car and brought me to Glasgow to see this fat poof Dalgety. Well, he asks me all the same stupit fuckin questions for about six hours then they turf me out ... don’t take me back up north ... just chuck me out in Glasgow at four in the fuckin morning ...

no charges or nothing, an no fare hame. So I'm stuck. Ah've got no money. Ah blew it when ah was oan the piss, so I thought I'd come and tap some off my old mate. So here I am ... I rang the bell, but when nobody answered, I let myself in. There were you zonked out on the bed in your knickers so I just came in here for a beer and a wee kip. By the way, if you want a beer, tough ... ah've finished it."

The smoke from Tyler's cigarette curled up through a shaft of low afternoon light. Armour watched it, mesmerised. Clouds were the souls of elephants, he remembered. He struggled to focus on the here and now. How long had he been asleep? An hour? Two? It was impossible! Dalgety was still hunting Tyler only hours ago, yet here was the man crowing about confusing the police with his alibi. Slowly, realisation seeped into Armour's foggy consciousness.

"What day's this?" He looked at his watch, which he'd failed to remove in his drunken wretchedness.

"It's Friday all day. November eighteen. Aye, and it's still 2000 if you're that dozy."

Twenty past three on Friday afternoon to be precise. He'd been asleep for more than twenty-four hours. In just one circle of the earth round its sun his world had changed utterly.

"So who was it? Who killed Argo? You know who it was, don't you!"

Tyler rose to his feet in one swift movement. "Can you no work it out, Armour? Was it no you that found the body? Aren't you such a clever fuck that you write in the papers and that? Work it out man! Maybe it was Campbell? Maybe it was an eighty-year-old murderer? Or maybe Burgess came out of his cave long enough to do it! What about Doug? Maybe he fuckin forgot he was a hippy pacifist! Me? I only kill angry hostiles for the fuckin Army, no rich bastards on yachts. So who the fuck did it pal? Can you no work it out?"

Armour felt a wave of terror engulf him. His mind was fogged, his breath short and his limbs tingling. He began to shake.

"Where the hell's Grizzel?"

Tyler began to laugh a low bitter laugh. "Where the hell's ... Grizzel! You're a fuckin poet, man!" He lunged towards Armour and grabbed him by the throat, his stubby muscular fingers digging painfully into soft flesh. Armour, too weak to resist him, stood gasping for breath, staring into his attacker's face, which was red and twisted with anger or hatred or despair. The smell of neglected teeth, and of stale beer and tobacco on Tyler's breath, made him nauseous all over again.

"Grizzel was a scientist ... she didn't believe in hell or God or any of that afterlife shite. Well, she'll know the truth now ... she's fuckin deid! She's lying on the sea-bed somewhere. Right now she's probably being eaten by crabs and wee fishes!" He shoved Armour hard, and the man careered backwards against a bookshelf. "So now you know." Tyler stooped to pick up his tobacco tin from the table and strode towards the door.

"I don't believe you!" But at the very instant, Tyler's wild claim clicked into place alongside the stark fact of Grizzel's unaccountable silence. It made terrible sense.

Tyler turned round to stare at him with angry half-shut eyes. When he at last spoke his voice was low. "Well where the fuck else can she be? Nae sign of the boat. Nae wurd frae her. You better believe it pal. Ah'm tellin you the truth."

Despair washed through Armour's veins. The final capitulation of hope. But he had to ask. There was nothing else to say or do.

"How do you know?" His voice rasped like a Dalek.

Tyler made a low wounded sound, and leaned heavily against the doorframe as if suddenly exhausted.

"Tyler ... if you know what's happened to Grizzel, tell me for God's sake!"

The man glanced at Armour, but no longer in anger. His eyes couldn't hold a fixed gaze, but meandered around the room. It was as if he was bewildered, trying to make his mind up where he was, or struggling to remember something long forgotten. At last he spoke, his focus seemingly fixed on some spot on the pine floor.

"She said she just wanted to scare the shit out of him ... to do something ... outrageous." He stopped, made a noise in his throat somewhere between a sigh and a growl, and went on. "War is declared! War to the knife, knife to the hilt! We have to make him think we'll stop at nothing."

"What? Tyler, for God's sake, what are you saying?"

"It's what Grizz said: 'We have to make him think we'll stop at nothing.' That was the idea ... to make Calltain safe ... to make him think we'd do any fuckin thing ... anything."

Armour realised he was no longer afraid of Tyler, now that the man had joined him in the ranks of the sad, confused and fucked-up.

"Tyler, I love her."

Tyler looked up, stared him in the face now, and spoke slowly so that there could be no doubt as to what he meant.

"Well, Grizzel sure as hell didn't love you." He shrugged. "Don't worry pal, you're no alone, she never loved anyone, 'cept maybe Campbell. Don't get me wrong! Grizz loved the world, she loved Calltain ... she loved the whole fuckin universe! She loved it and she was going to save it, all on her own." He screwed his eyes closed, and clutched his temples as if in sudden terrible pain. "It's ma fault. I got her the wee boat ... it came from Ireland, and ah towed it up the loch at night and hid it in a cove. She could handle it no problem ... but the storm ... aaaw fuck." He dropped his hands to his side and glowered at Armour. "Want ma advice? Don't ever think of what might have been. You'd nae chance wi Grizzel. You were just useful. Welcome aboard, pal."

He turned, and lurched into the hall. Armour croaked out a plea for him to wait, but the front door slammed and Tyler was gone. Only then did Armour realise that, although there were questions unanswered, he had no questions to ask.

The Herald, 20th March 2003

Composer dies burning heather

A composer, who became a cult figure in avant-garde music circles before founding the artists' colony on the Calltain peninsula in the West Highlands, has died in a fire. A police spokesman said that the man's clothes may have caught alight while he was burning heather, but friends of the composer are demanding an inquiry into the death.

Campbell Aaronson, 83, had been prominent in the campaign to stop the Calltain peninsula being turned into a giant super-quarry. Highland Council granted outline planning permission for the development of the quarry earlier this week. Ironically, Joshua Argo, the founder of the company behind the super-quarry scheme, died in a fire in his yacht while it was moored off Calltain just over two years ago.

Douglas Fowlie, a close friend of the composer, said that the entire community of Calltain had been "shattered" by the death of Aaronson, and claimed that he may have been driven to his death by the imminent destruction of the peninsula and the artists' colony that he founded there. "Campbell's body was found close to the shore at a place he was planting trees," said Mr Fowlie. "But he doesn't seem to have made any attempt to jump into the water and douse the flames. We believe that he just couldn't face up to the destruction of what he loved. We demand a full inquiry into the circumstances of Campbell's death."

Mr Aaronson was said by a local woman to have been upset by his estrangement from his daughter with whom he had not been in contact for some time.

A report has been sent to the Procurator Fiscal.

Two years ago it was revealed by *The Herald* that Mr Aaronson, the grandson of a wealthy Scottish industrialist and arms manufacturer, had worked on the Manhattan Project to build the atomic bombs that ended World War II.

THE SHAMAN (4)

The old Shaman woke. The dance had reopened the wound, which had bled into the baked earth.

He had known how hazardous it was to kill even one white man. Their power and vengefulness were terrible, and there were more of them than stars in the night. He and his people could not stop them defiling the sacred Black Mountain, home of the Sky God who had danced all things into being. The sun was not hot enough, the desert not vast enough to dry the blood the white men would spill. He had heard of the Jesus that their God had sent to the whites to tell them what was right, and he knew that they had slain him. Now, in their madness, they were killing the bison in numbers they could not eat. The whites killed or enslaved all other creatures. In his mind he saw them driving his tribe from their lands and from the mountain where the spirits of their ancestors lived. The mountain itself was being violated, the soul of the world destroyed. If it died, all creation would perish.

As the certainty of what he must do entered his heart, blood oozed out his body.

He would return to the Black Mountain. On its bare flank he would carve – for all to see – the image of the Sky God who lived there and was the ancestor of all things. The white men did not know how the world was made. They spoke only of their Jesus. They did not know how the Great God of the mountain and the Piping Spirit had created even them. He would carve the God as it had danced to the music of a pipe on the world's first morning. The power and will of the God would be there to see as clearly as the first day of creation was shown on the wall of the cave below the Sheltering Boulder. The God would be embodied in the carving. His immense power would turn back those who would defile the mountain and destroy the world.

He left the Sheltering Rock forever. As he travelled he scanned the ground for sharp flint, jasper and agate and stored the shards in his leather pouch. This time his journey took three suns. He kept well away from where he knew the whites to be. At the foot of a high cliff he found a brackish pool to drink from. He rested a night there and in the morning followed the side of the mountain to the east. The tracks of iron-shod horses and of wheeled wagons showed that this was the way the whites had come. The God had guided him. From where the tracks were, he could see at the foot of the cliff a smooth rock face the height of two men. Even when the surface was in shadow, the whites that travelled this way would see the Dancing God he'd carve there. He scrambled clumsily over jagged scree and placed the palms of both hands and the side of his face on the living flank of the mountain. He felt the presence of the Sky God and strength returning to him. Stepping back he unslung his pouch, emptied the flints, jaspers and agates onto the ground and selected a small sharp one. He turned once to make sure that no whites were approaching along the trail. He needed to cast his mind back through countless generations of Shamans to remember how the Sky God had danced on the new-made earth, but knew he must keep alert for the sound of iron hooves on the track.

He gazed long at the surface of the rock. He struggled to chant a prayer for guidance silently within himself as he dared not drown the sound of approaching whites with his voice. The sun bore down on him. He swayed, hardly knowing if it was from devotion or exhaustion, and chanted and prayed without cease until the sun was high and the God appeared from within the mountain wall. It shimmered before him faintly, as if just under the surface of the rock. He stepped forward and, where the God's head was, scratched the first mark. It took all the power of his mind to keep the God from disappearing back into the mountain. All fear of the white men left him. The music of the Piping Spirit and the rhythmic pounding of the dancing Sky God's feet suffused his being. He held the God in his mind for long enough to complete the thinly scratched image. When the vision vanished he staggered back and collapsed onto the ground. He crawled to his pouch, took the water skin from it and drank the brackish liquid. He lay back and rested, looking up at his work. The scratching was so weak he could scarcely see it. He recalled the ancient carvings in the crevice under the Sheltering Boulder. The creatures there had been etched deep into the stone. He scrabbled among the scree until he found a weathered rock that fitted comfortably into the palm of his hand. Using it as a hammer he began chipping into the rock face where before he had only scratched. The first chisel, a dark agate, shattered after a few blows. The flints worked better, and the image of God grew in strength and power on the mountainside.

In his urgency to carve, he grew careless, mis-striking a jagged flint with the hammer stone so that his hand slipped and his knuckles tore themselves on the abrasive surface of the living rock. With a grunt he dropped the chisel and thrust a bleeding knuckle into his mouth to ease the pain. When he grew sickened by the taste of his blood he spat it out and looked at the back of his hand. A flap of skin hung loose from the joint of the middle finger. He pushed the skin back over the wound, and globules of blood welled from under it and ran down the back of his hand. He bent to retrieve the chisel. Striking again, slowly and carefully, he pecked grain by grain into the dark weathered surface of the cliff, exposing the lighter rock beneath. He only stopped to drink again when he had completed the downward pointing triangle of the body. The blood on his hand had dried into a dark crust in the heat.

As he worked that long afternoon, discarding chisel after chisel as they shattered or became blunt, the Dancing God began to grow strong. Its arms stretched out in ecstatic dance, the fingers splayed in vital gesture. He threw aside a blunted shard of jasper and chose a flint to carve the God's antlers. His knife hung sheathed at his side. He and his people possessed plenty of iron, some of it wrenched from the hands of dying Conquistadors many generations ago, but since time began none of the magical signs in the desert had been inscribed with the metal of the white men.

He stopped carving and gazed a long time at his work. The sun rested momentarily on the horizon, illuminating the Dancing Sky God in brilliant light. He was no longer aware that blood once again seeped out from the wound in his side. He no longer felt pain, no longer feared the whites camped nearby. When it grew dark he returned to the shallow pool and washed his face and hands and sat on the warm earth to watch the sky. The last light faded in the west and the stars grew brighter. It was as if he was travelling towards them, faster and faster until he was plunging towards a star that filled his vision with clear white light. It did not blind him or sear his eyes, but filled him with delight. The whiteness shattered into a maelstrom of glistening particles of colour, shapeless and shimmering – blues of the sky, reds of blood and the earth, greens of the valley where the river ran. All was silent. He knew this place. It was what existed before the God had danced, and would exist again, beyond the world of chaos.

gabonds Other Vagabonds Other Vagabo

www.vagabondvoices.co.uk

Allan Cameron's ***In Praise of the Garrulous***

About the book

This first work of non-fiction by the author of *The Golden Menagerie* and *The Berlusconi Bonus*, has an accessible and conversational tone, which perhaps disguises its enormous ambition. The writer examines the history of language and how it has been affected by technology, primarily writing and printing. This leads to some important questions concerning the "ecology" of language, and how any degradation it suffers might affect "not only our competence in organising ourselves socially and politically, but also our inner selves."

Comments

"A deeply reflective, extraordinarily wide-ranging meditation on the nature of language, infused in its every phrase by a passionate humanism" – Terry Eagleton

"This is a brilliant tour de force, in space and in time, into the origins of language, speech and the word. From the past to the present you are left with strong doubts about the idea of Progress and the superiority as a modern, indeed at times post-modern, society over the previous generations. Such a journey into the world of the word needs an articulate and eloquent guide: Allan Cameron is both and much more than that." – Ilan Pappé

I like *In Praise of the Garrulous* very much indeed, not only because it says a good many interesting and true things, but because of its *tone* and style. Its combination of personal passion, observation, stories, poetic bits and serious expert argument, expressed as it is in the prose of an intelligent conversation: all this is ideal for holding and persuading intelligent but non-expert readers. In my opinion he has done nothing better." – Eric Hobsbawm.

Price: £8.00 ISBN: 978-0-9560560-0-9 pp. 184

www.vagabondvoices.co.uk

Luciano Mecacci's ***Freudian Slips***

About the book

This historical and scientific study of psychoanalysis and its founding group brings together Luciano Mecacci's own work and existing material, and presents the reading public with a story that is not only fascinating and terrible but also essential and thought-provoking, given the enormous influence of Freud's ideas on Europe's art, writing and wider culture throughout most of the twentieth century (perhaps coinciding almost exactly with what has been defined as the Short Century: 1914-1991).

It is important to distinguish between Freud the scientist and Freud the creative thinker. The former was something of a charlatan, precisely because of his scientific pretensions which were understandable in a man whose training was in medicine and whose formative years were influenced by positivism. The latter was brilliant, innovative and prolific, but the material he produced was untested, as Mecacci demonstrates quite convincingly, and therefore not suitable for clinical application. Freud's psychoanalytical therapy established a movement and set in train a series of often tragic events, which were almost always ignored or glossed over at the time of their occurrence. Mecacci argues that there was nothing casual about these, and their roots are to be found in the manner of the psychoanalytical movement's birth and its historical context – dark times of war, economic crisis and xenophobia that affected both analysts and their patients.

The obsessions of psychoanalysis were also the obsessions of the short century, and now they have worked their way through, they can appear old-fashioned, but their residue persists in our thinking, and we would do well to re-examine what was useful and what was dangerous in this remarkable history. The belated publication of *Freudian Slips*, the English translation of *Marilyn M. e altri disastri della psicoanalisi* (Rome, 2000) will allow professionals, students and general readers to do just that.

Price: £10.00   ISBN: 978-0-9560560-1-6   pp. 224

d Two Vagabond Two Vagabond Tw

www.vagabondvoices.co.uk

Allan Massie's ***Surviving***

About the book

Surviving is set in contemporary Rome. The main characters, Belinda, Kate (an author who specialises in studies of the criminal mind, and Tom Durward (a scriptwriter), attend an English-speaking group of Alcoholics Anonymous. All have pasts to cause embarrassment or shame. Tom sees no future for himself and still gets nervous "come Martini time". Belinda embarks on a love-affair that cannot last. Kate ventures onto more dangerous ground by inviting her latest case-study, a young Londoner acquitted of a racist murder, to stay with her.

Allan Massie dissects this group of ex-pats in order to say something about our inability to know, still less to understand, the actions of our fellow human beings, even when relationships are so intense. It is also, therefore, impossible or at least difficult to make informed moral judgements of others. This is an intelligent book that examines human nature with a deft and light touch.

Comments

"Massie is one of the best Scottish writers of his generation. *Surviving* – sympathetic, unsentimental, atmospheric – is an overdue reminder of how good he is." – Alan Taylor, *The Herald*

"... an impressive novel which poses moral and philosophical questions but works equally well as a compelling thriller." – Joe Farrell, *TLS*

"... an excellent little novel." – Ben Jeffery, *The Guardian*

"The dark brilliance of Massie's style ... *Surviving* may be an instant classic in the alcoholic literary canon." – Patrick Skene Catling, *The Spectator*

Price: £10.00   ISBN: 978-0-9560560-2-3   pp. 224

www.vagabondvoices.co.uk

Allan Cameron's ***Presbyopia***

About the book

Cameron's collection of bilingual poetry is introduced by an essay on the distinction between myopic and presbyopic poetry: the former focuses on the self, its emotions and its immediate vicinity, while the latter focuses on what is distant in space and time. Poetic myopia is not as negative as the name might imply, nor presbyopia the only desirable form of poetry, but now that two centuries have passed since Wordsworth, whom Heaney has described as the "an indispensable figure in the evolution of modern writing, a finder and keeper of the self-as-subject", the time has perhaps come to put aside our prejudices against the presbyopic. In reality, all poetry reflects a mixture of the two, and Cameron's poetry is no exception. He writes on politics and philosophy, but always with the passion that comes from a humanist sensitivity.

Comment

"Cameron confesses to a weariness with poetry's old forms and old concerns, particularly the perennial Romantic subjects of love and exploration of the self. As a corrective he steers clear of personal topics, turning his presbyopic gaze outward in a sequence of poems that takes in eco-vandalism, press barons, George W. Bush and death. One admires this determination to reject ... pretension and obscurantism ..." *The Sunday Herald*

Price: £10.00 ISBN: 978-0-9560560-3-0 pp. 112

www.vagabondvoices.co.uk

Allan Massie's ***Klaus and Other Stories***

About the book

Allan Massie, the prolific novelist and non-fiction writer, is here revealed as a consummate master of the short story. This should not surprise, given his dense and highly effective style. Some of the short stories come from his early career, and some are the product of a recent return to the genre.

Klaus, the novella that opens and, to some extent, dominates this collection, tells the story of Klaus Mann, son of Thomas, and in spite of the long shadow of so famous a father, an important novelist and political activist in his own right. His struggle against Nazism gave him a focus, but its demise and what he perceived as Germany's inability to change led to depression and an early death.

Massie succeeds in evoking that period of courage and hypocrisy, intellectual fidelity and clever changeability, sacrifice and impunity, personified by the tragic Klaus and the mercurial and indestructible Gustaf Gründgens, his former brother-in-law and ex-lover. Between these two lie not only those broken relationships but also a novel – Klaus's novel Mephisto, a thinly disguised attack on Gründgens that for many years could not be published in West Germany. Massie's subtle prose merely suggests some intriguing aspects of this network of relationships and the self-destructive nature of literary inspiration.

Comments

"Allan Massie is a master storyteller, with a particular gift for evoking the vanishing world of the European man of letters. His poignant novella about Klaus Mann bears comparison with his subject's best work." Daniel Johnson, editor of Standpoint

"The tale of Klaus Mann's final days is, however, tremendously interesting, a warning and an example. Aspiring authors should read it. They'd do worse than study Massie's craftsmanship." – Colin Waters, *Scottish Review of Books*

Price: £10.00 ISBN: 978-0-9560560-6-1 pp. 208

www.vagabondvoices.co.uk

Allan Cameron's ***Berlusconi Bonus***

About the book

"Allan Cameron's intriguing novel is set in a near future where the predictions of the US theorist Francis Fukuyama have been taken to their logial conclusions. Fukuyama declared that, with the collapse of the USSR and the hegemony of neoliberal capitalism, history has come to an end. In Cameron's book, history has indeed been halted by decree and the citizens live in a permanent present of spurious consumer choice and endless material consumption, their bovine lives ruled by the embedding of Rational Consumer Implant Cards in their brains. A cardless underclass exists in the Fukuyama Theme Parks, vast squallid concentration camps on the outskirts of cities. At the pinnacle of this society sit those lucky individuals who, because of their dedicated pursuit of stupendous wealth, are awarded the Plutocratic Social Gratitude Award, popularly nicknamed the Berlusconi Bonus as it effectively puts the recipient beyond the law.

"The book take the form of a confession by Adolphus Hibbert, a recent recipient of the Berlusconi Bonus, who is recruited by the sinister police officer Captain Younce to spy on dissident elements. Adolphus embarks on a dizzying journey among the clandestine opposition, in which he finds love, betrayal and violence; discovering terrifying truths about himself and his society." – *New Internationalist*

Comments

"… a profound, intelligent novel that asks serious, adult questions about what it means to be alive." – *The Herald*

"The *Berlusconi Bonus* is an adroit and satisfying satire on the iniquities of present-day life from insane consumerism to political mendacity, globalisation to the War on Terror. It is both very funny and an extremely astute analysis of the evil results of a philosophy that which sings the victory song of extreme free-market economics." – *New Internationalist*

"It makes you think." – *The New Humanist*

Price: £10.00 ISBN: 978-0-9560560-9-2 pp. 208

Vagabond Six

www.vagabondvoices.co.uk

Alessandro Barbero's ***The Anonymous Novel***

About the book

Set in Gorbachev's Russia, this complex but highly readable novel not only provides a portrait of a society in transition, but also fascinating studies of various themes including the nature of history and the Russian novel itself. Barbero uses his skills as a historian to study the reality of Russian society through its newspapers and journals, and his skills as a novelist to weave a complex plot – a tale of two cities: Moscow and Baku. And throughout, the narrative voice – perhaps the greatest protagonist of them all – represents not the author's views but those of the Russian public as they emerged from one dismal reality and hurtled unknowingly towards another.

Comments

"In the depiction of these changing times, Barbero's political intelligence is apparent. So, however, is his skill as a novelist, for he contrives to integrate the socio-political analysis in his story of imagined characters. It never obtrudes itself; yet you can't ignore or forget it... If you have any feeling for Russia or the art of the novel, read this one. You will find it an enriching experience." – *The Scotsman*

"He writes in a bright and breezy, satirical style ... which leads the reader to believe that some Russian master has been leaning over his shoulder, guiding his hand... It is a deeply rewarding pleasure to be lost in this novel." – *The Herald*

"Barbero uses the diabolic skills of an erudite and professional narrator to seek out massacres of the distant and recent past. *The Anonymous Novel* concerns the past-that-never-passes (whether Tsarist or Stalinist) and the future that in 1988 was impending and has now arrived." – *Il Giornale*

Price: £14.50 ISBN: 978-0-9560560-4-7 pp. 464